CORDUBA: A COLLISION OF EMPIRES

CORDUBA: A COLLISION OF EMPIRES

Book V in the Middle Empire Series

CONN HALLINAN

Ballingarry Press

To my extraordinarily wonderful grandchildren
Tyler, Vance, Mia and Milo

Contents

Characters in Corduba

Aelia Dasumi. A wealthy merchant, companion of
    Marcus Favonius.
Annius Fabius. Tribune VI Legion from Gaul.
Antonius Crispus. Centurion Third Century, Tenth Cohort,
    VII Legion Hispania in Tarraco.
Coventina. Celtic woman, companion to Demaratus.
Cassius Cornelius. Commander Ala II Flavia Hispanorum
    Romanorum.
Demaratus. Signifer, VII Legion Hispania.
Flavius Priscus. Optio, VII Legion Hispania.
Gallienus Publius Licinius Egnatius. Emperor of Rome.
Gaius Porcius. Head Duoviri in Tarraco.
Julius Dasumi. Wealthy merchant, brother of Aelia.
Julia Aquillius. Marcus's sister, mother of Sabina.
Lucius Thorius. Second Duoviri in Tarraco.
Lucius Aquillius. Sabina's father.
Macro Lucilius. Former tesserarius of the III Legion Augusta.
Maximus Clodius. Legate, VI Legion, Gaul.
Marcus Favonius. Legate, VII Legion Hispania.
Postumus Marcus Cassianius Latinius. Emperor of the
    Gallic Empire.
Publius Felix. Tribune, VII Legion.
Quintus Junius. Tribune of the VII Legion Hispania at Legio.
Quintus Titius. Former optio of the III Legion Augusta.

Rachel Levi. Former slave, adopted sister of Aelia.

Sabina Aquillius. Marcus's niece.

Tiberius Favonis. Marcus's brother.

Tacitus Agrippa. Tribune VI Legion, Gaul.

Timotheus. Greek doctor for the VII Legion.

Vipsania. Leader of the women's Legion of Tarraco.

Map showing Corduba and surrounding regions

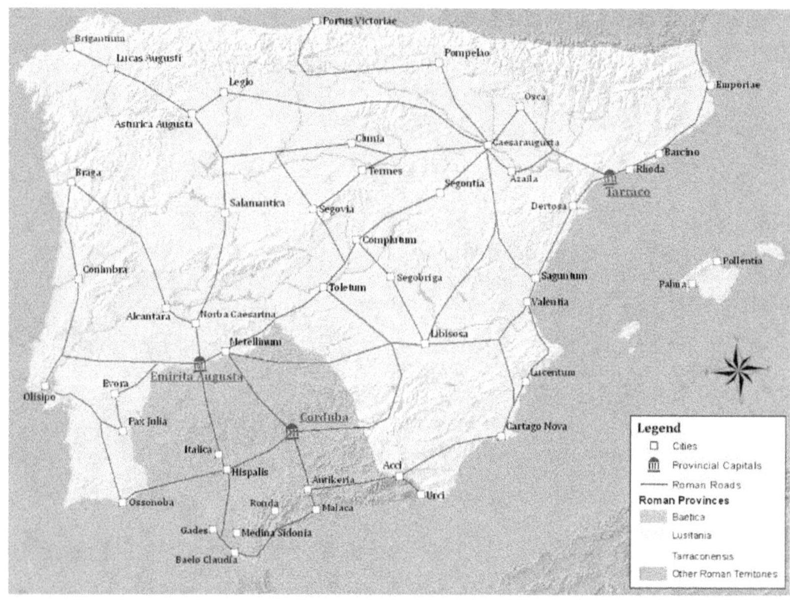

I

Sextus Aelius, tesserarius, Second Century, First Cohort of the VII Legion Hispania Gemina Pia was bored.

His state of mind was hardly surprising. For the past several months, the VII Legion had been the toast of Hispania. It had defeated a larger Frankish army in the field and re-taken the city of Tarraco from the invaders. Sextus couldn't remember when he had paid for a drink at the city's taverns. His uniform meant everything was on the house. And the girls! By the gods, Tarraco girls were spectacular, or at least spectacular to a rural boy from Emerita Augusta in Hispania's western hinterlands. Priscilla! The woman made his head spin.

Returning to the Legion's headquarters in Legio was a shock. It was cold, wet, and drab, with men outnumbering women three to one. Army food, sour wine, endless drills, and now here he was on an extended patrol to Lucus Augusti with three contuberni. As third-in-command of a century, he could order the men around, but an officer who did that while sitting on his bottom would not be popular.

So, each night he joined the 24 men as they dug a ditch, put up posts and laid out a marching camp, even though there wasn't an enemy for hundreds of miles. The Lusitanians were quiet, the Celts were peaceful, and the Franks had all gone off to Mauretania. So, what was the point?

Because the army said so.

What Sextus wanted was a bath and some decent food. He really couldn't complain about the march so far. The weather had been mild with just a nip at night. It was not yet fully fall. There was no rain—a definite anomaly in these northern mountains— and the expedition had gone, so far, without a hitch. Lucas Augusti was a decent-sized city with two good public baths, and Sextus had had quite enough of washing off in cold creeks.

And now the road into the small town up ahead was jammed with carts. Sextus told his men to take a break while he found out what was up. "Nerva and Antonius, you're with me," he said, indicating two of the newer legionnaires, who dutifully dropped their belongings and unshipped their scutum shields, shouldered their pila, and fell in behind him.

Sextus threaded his way through the jam until he reached a crowd of merchants and drivers milling around a mid-size cart pulled by two patient-looking oxen. "What's the problem?" he asked a man in the crowd.

"Axle broke," replied the man.

"Well, move the cart," Sextus said, with a hint of exasperation.

"Owner won't let us," said the man. "Says he wants to do it himself."

"Oh, he does, does he?" said Sextus, slipping by the man and moving up to the cart. "Whose cart is this?" he asked.

A burly-looking man turned and gave the tesserarius a startled look, which Sextus found odd. Why would someone be surprised by an army officer so close to Legio?

"This your cart?" asked Sextus.

The man hesitated, finally answering in the affirmative.

"Well, move it," said Sextus impatiently.

"I am waiting for some men from the town, sir," said the man, who was looking decidedly nervous. Sextus was not normally a suspicious person, but something about the man's demeanor seemed off.

"Men," said Sextus turning to his two soldiers, "lend a hand. And a few of you lot, too," he said to the crowd.

"No, that won't be necessary," said the burly man. "My men will be here shortly."

"I'll decide what's necessary," said Sextus, putting an officer's growl in his voice. The man backed away.

The two soldiers unhitched the oxen and with two other men grabbed the cart and heaved. The cart went exactly nowhere. "It's heavy, sir," said Nerva.

"What's in the cart?" asked Sextus, turning to the owner.

"Just wheat, sir, and a few boxes," said the man, who suddenly looked pale.

"Unload the cart," ordered Sextus, and his two soldiers began grabbing the sacks of wheat and tossing them to the side of the road. After three layers of sacks had been removed, a stout wooden box came into view. "Toss that as well," ordered Sextus.

Nerva grabbed the box, picked it up and then quickly dropped it. "It's real heavy, sir," he said.

This was all rather a puzzle. "Get the sacks off, and let's see what we have," said Sextus. Between the soldiers and the civilians the cart was cleared in a few minutes, leaving 10 wooden boxes in the bottom. "What is in those?" asked the tesserarius, turning to the owner, who had suddenly disappeared. Sextus searched the crowd, then shrugged. If the man chose this moment to be absent, that was his business.

"Antonius," said Sextus, "fetch me a dolabra," referring to the Roman Army's ubiquitous all-purpose tool for everything from digging ditches to constructing latrines. While he waited, he continued to search the crowd for the owner, but the man seemed to have vanished. Eventually, the legionnaire arrived with the dolabra.

Sextus nodded at Antonius. "Open one up," he directed.

The man inserted the tip of the dolabra into the top of a box and pried. The wood came up with a screech of nails to reveal something wrapped in linen. Sextus drew his pugio and cut into the fabric.

A sheen of gold glittered under the knife's blade.

"That's gold, sir," said Antonius, with a touch of awe.

"I can see that, soldier. Pull out another of those boxes and open it up," said Sextus. "And someone locate the cart's owner."

Another box was pried open to reveal more gold.

"Nerva, bring the men forward," said Sextus quietly. Those two boxes probably represented a quarter's pay or more for the entire VII Legion. He needed to secure it. "All right, now back off," he roared to the crowd, which paid him no attention, instead jamming in closer to look at the gold. He drew his gladius out and indicated that Antonius should do the same. Between them they finally got the crowd to back off. Within minutes the rest of his men had arrived, and he established a civilian-free ring around the cart. He had several soldiers unload the eight other boxes, but decided not to open them.

No one in the crowd seemed to know who the cart's owner was or to where he had disappeared. There was nothing in the cart that indicated where the gold had come from, nor any indication where it was going. Given the road, the likely destination was the port of Brigantium. But where was it bound from there?

He commandeered a wagon from a loudly protesting merchant, hitched the oxen to it, and had the men onload the boxes. Throwing out a screen of soldiers front and back, the legionnaires headed back in the direction of Legio. This was a matter for the Legion's legate, not a lowly tesserarius.

* * *

Marcus Favonius, the newly appointed legate of the VII Legion, and Optio Flavius Pricus contemplated the stack of boxes in the legion's headquarters. They had had the crates moved to the cellar of the principia, where the legion's treasure was kept. The legate was dressed casually in a simple uniform. He was a plain-looking man—brown eyes, brown hair—and slightly heavy around the waist. A month of food in Roma had added some unwanted pounds to his frame. The optio was stocky, scarred, with a prominent broken nose.

"Did you notify the tribune?" Marcus asked.

"Yes, sir," answered Flavius. "But Tribune Quintus Junius is indisposed."

"Indisposed?" asked Marcus.

Flavius shrugged. "Too much wine will do that, sir."

Marcus liked the old tribune, who had befriended him early on and had been indispensable in helping to organize the auxiliaries in the fight against the Franks. On the other hand, the man drank too much and was long past time to retire. However, Marcus did not have the heart to push him out and with the other tribune, Publius Felix, in Tarraco, he needed Quintus to help him ease into his new role as legate. The old tribune had been with the VII Legion for almost half a century. In any case, he did not trust Publius, and he was in no rush to have him back in Legio.

"That's a lot of money, sir," said Flavius, breaking into his commander's thoughts.

Marcus nodded. "Enough to pay this legion's wages for a year and leave some over for new equipment," he said.

"On an oxcart, with no guards, in the middle of nowhere," observed the optio.

"With no owner to claim it," added Marcus.

"No one walks away from that kind of wealth," said Flavius.

"Unless it was ill-gotten or headed some place it wasn't supposed to go," said Marcus crossing his arms and nudging one of the boxes with his boot.

"And where might that be?" asked the optio.

Marcus said nothing for a moment. "Sextus did a good job on this, optio," he said finally.

"Well, we knew he was a good officer. He showed that in the fight with the Mauri and the Franks," said Flavius.

"See to it that he gets an extra stipendium," said Marcus, "and have the Second Century take over guarding all this. Excuse the men from drills."

"That will go over well, sir," said Flavius. "Easy guard duty always does."

"Let's hope it's easy, optio," said Marcus. "Where is our signifer?" he asked. As legion treasurer, Demaratus would be responsible for cataloguing the gold, and possibly figuring out where it had come from.

"We let him go to meet Coventina's people, sir," replied Flavius. "He won't be back for two weeks." The signifer was on leave to introduce himself to the family and village of his soon-to-be wife, a Cantabrian Celt from Hispania's northern mountains. In the huge backlog of official business waiting for him on his return from Roma, Marcus had forgotten that he had approved the leave.

Marcus shook his head, "It slipped my mind. Well, get a clerk to do an inventory, and we will wait until our Greek friend gets back."

"Hopefully in one piece," said Flavius. "Those Celts are a rough lot. I am not sure how a pretty boy from Athens will do up there."

Marcus grinned. "He will do just fine, optio. As I recall, our 'pretty boy' can take care of himself. And he is with Coventina, who we know can handle anything from Franks to Roman assassins." Coventina had been part of a resistance movement during the Frankish occupation of Tarraco and had killed two of the invaders. She had also killed an assassin who had tried to kill Marcus's companion in Roma.

"Who are you going to alert about all this?" asked Flavius, indicating the cases of gold.

"Once I get a catalogue of what is here, I will send a note to Carthago Nova informing our superiors of the situation and asking for instructions," answered Marcus. "Until then, we guard this."

II

Postumus Marcus Cassianius Latinius, governor and imperial legate of Germania Superior and Inferior, was concerned. Not alarmed—yet, but uneasy. It was not the troublesome Alamanni and Franks plaguing the northern border of Gaul. Those he could deal with. In fact, he had already begun deploying his legions and auxiliaries to confront them. What worried him was gold.

He wasn't getting it.

He required that gold. It would pay for the legions he needed for his planned endeavor. When he thought about that project, it sometimes took his breath away. He was determined to build his own empire. But the time was ripe. Roma was distracted. The Goths were pressing in from the north, the Parthians from the east, and one never knew how long an emperor would last. He could count off eight—10 if you included those who tried to seize the throne and failed—in his time alone. Anarchy and civil war had become the norm. A Gallic Empire in the north—Gaul, Germania, Britannia and Hispania—would be welcomed. An oasis of calm, a threat to none, a boon for all. Well, Roma would not look at it that way, but with enough gold and 10 or 11 legions, it would not matter what Roma thought?

There was a knock on his door, and his adjutant, Rufus Servius, put his head into the office. "Prefectus Castroum Atticus Aemilius is here, sir. Shall I send him in?"

"Yes, yes," said Postumus distractedly. He was looking over a map of Gaul without really focusing on it. He couldn't stop thinking about gold.

"Ave, sir," said Atticus, a short, stocky man with a receding hairline and a well-trimmed beard rimming his face. He was in uniform, with only a signet ring and a gold band around his right wrist as adornment. The band was an Armilla, won for conspicuous gallantry in a battle with the Franks when the prefect had been a junior officer in the I Minerva Legion.

"Come look, Atticus," said Postumus, refocusing on the map. The prefect was exactly the man he wanted to see. Atticus was third-in-command of the VI Legion Victrix in Norba, and Postumus had summoned him to this northernmost city in the Empire. Atticus was a fighting man, unlike his two tribunes, who owed their posts to favors called in. Postumus was glad to have someone who would engage in argument, not a tribune who would dutifully tell him what he thought the governor wanted to hear.

The prefect joined the governor at the table and scanned the map. "You are beset with two invasions, sir," Atticus said. "Here near the coast and here," he said, pointing to a spot not far from the headquarters at Colonia Ara Agrippinesium.

Postumus was silent for several moments. He was a large man, handsome, with a full beard and a certain quality that took over a room even when he was not saying anything. "It is not clear that they are invasions, Atticus," he said at last. "A few border forts overrun and some villas sacked feels more like a raid than an invasion."

"I have ordered the XXX Legion Ulpia Victrix based in Limonum to move north. Your old legion, the I Minerva, is already deployed, and the VIII Augusta and XXII Primigenia at Lugdunum are on the move. There are, as well, two auxiliary legions gathering near Lutetia. Within a week, we will have 20,000 legionaries in place, with another 10,000 auxiliaries to back them up. That is more than enough to stop both invasions, if that is what they are," said Postumus, tracing the roads that would move the legions to the frontier.

"Will you cross the Rhenus, sir?" asked Atticus.

The governor shuddered. Every Roman flinched when the subject of crossing the great river that divided the Roman Empire from the tribes to the north came up. It was more than 200 years since Publius Quinctilius Varus had taken three legions and auxiliaries—more than 20,000 men—to subdue the hostile tribes that inhabited the vast region north of the Rhenus. Those legions had been ambushed in the Teutoburg Forest and destroyed. An expedition to find them a few years later found nothing but mounds of bones, and skulls nailed to the trees. No sensible Roman since had made an effort to conquer the north.

"No," said Postumus. "But this invasion may work to our benefit, prefect."

"How so, sir?" asked Atticus.

"There was a time when the most powerful legions of Rome were in Gaul," explained the governor. "Caesar built an army that made us the envy of the world. Now we have the weakest legions in the Empire. The armies in Pannonia and Dacia vastly outnumber us, as do those in Palmyra and the east. We are ignored. If I ask for reinforcements, I'm told to recruit auxiliaries. If I ask for gold to pay our troops, I'm given silver so polluted with bronze or lead as to be virtually worthless. Our taxes flow to Roma, but we get nothing in return."

Postumus had begun pacing back and forth during this tirade. "If we kept those taxes and put them to use here in Gaul, Britannia, and Hispania, our citizens would be more secure. We are like the boy who has grown into a man. It is time we left home and made our way in the world."

"It is a good argument, sir, but I imagine our parents would disagree," said Atticus. "And those more powerful legions would be turned against our weaker forces."

The governor paused, went over to a sideboard, and poured two cups of wine from a pitcher. He handed one to the prefect and signaled for him to take a seat. Atticus took the wine and seated himself on a stool. Postumus ran his hands through his hair, took a sip of wine, and remained standing. "We are no threat to the Empire, Atticus. We are not marching on Rome. We will cross no Rubicons. We will ensure that the Empire does not need to worry about an invasion on the northern tribes. Indeed, we are allies, a brother empire."

The prefect arched an eyebrow. "And you think that argument will win over the Senate and the Emperor?"

The governor paused, took a seat, and turned the cup in his hand. "The Empire is beset with two major enemies. The Goths threaten Pannonia and Moesia, and the Persians threaten the east. A two-front war is difficult. To attack us would be to start yet another war, and in my judgment, Roma will not follow that path. We do not threaten the Empire. The Goths and the Persians do."

Atticus shook his head. "I do not dispute your argument, sir, and I support your endeavor. I just want to be realistic. Suppose Rome decides we are more of a threat than the Goths and the Persians? And remember, we have our own troubles with the Franks and the Alamanni. Wouldn't that put us into a two-front war?"

"You see only the dangers, prefect, not the opportunities," answered Postumus. "Every undertaking involves risk, but the question is, are the risks worth the game? I think they are."

"You are ever the optimist, sir. And this is a discussion we have had before. I do not think that is why you summoned me," said Atticus, taking a pull on his cup of wine.

"No, I know this is old ground, comrade. But a new matter has come up, and I need your thoughts on it," said Postumus. "As you know, we have been receiving shipments of gold from Hispania's mines. That gold is essential to our plan. But it appears that our latest shipment has been intercepted."

"By whom?" asked Atticus.

"By the VII Legion," replied the governor.

"A troublesome legion, that one," said the prefect. "Not the first time we have encountered them."

"No, not the first time," said Postumus, rising and beginning to pace again.

"And not so weak," said Atticus quietly.

"No. Indeed, were they not so troublesome they would be a valuable ally in our plan," said Postumus.

"I thought you were working on that, sir," said the prefect.

"I am, but it is complex. We have one of the VII Legion's tribunes in our camp, as well as the commander of an auxiliary legion, but the new legate of the VII is the man who defeated the Frankish army and lifted the occupation of Tarraco. I am told he is popular with the legionaries and a hero to the civilians, and I do not count him among our friends," said Postumus.

"And now this legion has seized your gold," said Atticus. "Yes, that is complex indeed. Do you know how it happened and if it can be traced to us?"

"Apparently a patrol of the VII intercepted our shipment before it could get to Brigantium," said the governor. "It was supposed to have arrived at Itius Portus, but the captain said the shipment never appeared. Instead, the patrol took it back to Legio, and it's ensconced in the legion's headquarters."

"Does the legion's legate know where it was bound?" asked Atticus.

"I think not. The man transporting the shipment evaded the patrol and made it to Brigantium. It was he who brought us the news of the seizure," said the governor.

"However, the VII Legion is now alerted," mused the prefect. "And they will be asking questions about the mining operations. Those will not be comfortable questions to answer."

"You think I don't know that?" said Postumus, an irritated edge to his voice.

"Sorry, sir. Just thinking out loud. Will they have an answer?" asked Atticus.

Postumus poured himself more wine and refilled the prefect's cup. "We have been careful. There is nothing in writing that will indicate where the gold was bound or how it got into that cart."

"Will that 'careful' stand up to torture?" asked Atticus.

The governor was silent for a long moment. "I don't know," he finally admitted. "But all they will learn is that the gold was diverted in what looks like a plot to steal it. No one at the mining operation knows what the final destination was to be or what it would be used for."

"Sir, the commander of the VII Legion is not stupid. He knows the Gaul legions and the legion in Norba let that Frankish army pass without challenge and was likely to conclude that someone was out to do them a considerable amount of harm. He will ask why. And it doesn't take a lot of brains to answer that question, sir," said Atticus.

"I know," said Postumus, going back to the map. "But there is nothing I can do about that now. We will have to make another arrangement with the mining operation. On its own, the VII Legion can't do much to us, and remember, we have allies in Roma as well. I hope this will blow over, but if it doesn't, I will have to take some action aimed at neutralizing the VII Legion.

"And that would be?" asked Rufus.

"Getting rid of a certain legate, for starters," replied Postumus. "Your legion, the VI Victrix in Narbo, may have to intervene. We must continue to press our allies in Hispania to step up their activities on our behalf."

Atticus said nothing, taking a long pull on his wine.

III

Decurions Tiberius Porcius and Arrius Granius of Norba Caesarina sat facing one another over a small, marble table in Arrius's villa. The couches were carved from exotic wood, inlaid with ivory, and furnished with embroidered pillows. By the standards of Lusitania in Hispania's west, it was sumptuous. A pitcher of wine sat between them. There were no slaves present.

The topic was far too dangerous for that.

Tiberius, heavy and florid, nervously spun a ring on his finger. "People are asking questions, Arrius, and they make me uncomfortable."

"People?" said Arrius, a man almost Tiberius's opposite—tall, rail thin, gray.

"Well, that bastard, Fabricius Tuscus. And he has put a bug in the ears of others," replied Tiberius. "There are a lot of army veterans in Norba, Arrius, and they want to know how that debacle with the Franks happened."

"What's to know?" said Arrius. "The Franks slipped by the legions in Gaul. How is that our problem?"

"Slipped by?" said Tiberius. "How do tens of thousands of people 'slip by' our legions? Where was the VI Legion Victrix in Norba? Those are questions that are pretty hard to answer."

"Why do we need to answer them, Tiberius? We are in Norba. These are questions for the VII Legion in Legio and the authorities in Roma. Listen, you need to relax," said Arrius, taking a sip of wine. "This will blow over. There are people far more powerful than you and I who will make sure an investigation never goes anywhere. What we need to do is bide our time and raise doubts about the willingness of the Emperor to defend our province."

"I am not sure that is a good idea," said Tiberius. "People will think that's not patriotic."

"You need to raise doubts, Tiberius," said Arrius, "We don't attack the Emperor, we talk about the need to defend our province. Aren't the Goths threatening Moesia? Haven't the German tribes grown bolder? Maybe we should think about defending ourselves. Put some doubt in their minds about what we can expect from Roma. That thought gets people thinking the way we want them to think, that Hispania could do better on its own."

Tiberius flinched and looked around nervously.

"There is no one here but us, Tiberius. I am a careful man," said Arrius. "The men Governor Postumus sent to contact us were discreet. They are careful who they talk to and to whom they hand out gold."

Tiberius took a deep drink from his wine. "Do you know what the penalty for treason is?" he asked quietly.

"I do and I do not intend to suffer it," Arrius replied. "Remember what the rewards of this endeavor will be, sir. Riches and power like we have never experienced. And we will finally deal with those upstart Lusitanians."

"What about the VII Legion and that bastard Favonius?" asked Tiberius.

The Lusitanians had overrun a century of the VII Legion. Marcus, who commanded another of its centuries, had successfully fought off an attack by the same Lusitanians. He had also used his influence—and oratory skills, defeating Arrius in debate—to convince the council at Norba Caesarina not to wage a war of revenge. As a result, a plot by Tiberius and Arrius to confiscate Lusitanian land through warfare had been thwarted.

"Yes, Marcus Favonius," said Arrius thinly. "We have a score to settle with that one. As for the legion, all we need to do to neutralize the VII Hispania is divide its loyalty. We have people in the heart of that legion."

* * *

Lucius Thorius, junior duoviri of the city of Tarraco, paced about the atrium of Decimus Domitius's domus. The day was warm, and the duoviri, who was seriously overweight, was sweating. "There is going to be an investigation of the market, Domitius," he said. "And Julius Dasumi is off in Roma. It is all going to come down on us." He was a suave-looking man with a neatly trimmed beard.

Lucius was referring to a market that several wealthy families, led by Julius Dasumi, had set up during the Frankish occupation of Tarraco. The market had charged usurious prices for its goods, which eventually sparked a riot.

"What will come down on us? That we set up a market in order to feed the people of Tarraco? How is that a problem?" asked Domitius.

"The prices were high, mostly because Dasumi pushed us to raise them. People are angry, and they are looking for someone to blame. Julius left us holding the bag," said Lucius.

"He did do that," said Decimus, "but we will argue that food was scarce and, therefore, expensive. We will say we did our best. You worry too much, Lucius."

"And you don't worry enough," hissed Lucius. "People will say what we did was treason."

"Let them," replied Decimus. "Our story is simple. Food was expensive for buyers and sellers alike, and people needed food. The town might not like it, but that doesn't make it treason. And since no one in Roma seems interested in investigating the matter, why should we be nervous? Act insulted that anyone would question what we did."

"Easy for you to say," grumbled Lucius. "You don't have to work with that gimpy little bastard, Gaius Porcius. Since he ended up figuring a way to end the occupation peacefully, he has been impossible. And he is asking questions."

Decimus sighed. He didn't like Lucius Thorius, whom he thought was a coward. That flaw was dangerous. To save his own skin, the man would throw his own mother to the lions in the arena. But as a duoviri. he could be useful. Decimus was reluctant to include Lucius in the plot to establish a breakaway empire, but the men Governor Postumus sent had insisted Lucius be involved.

"Stick to the story and raise questions about Roma's

incompetence. Get people to start doubting that the Empire gives a pinch of owl shit about Hispania," said Decimus.

"I am already working on that, Decimus," assured Lucius.

"Good. Now what about our leading families. Yes, Julius abandoned us to pursue his mission to overthrow his father's will, but remember, he is one of the wealthiest men in Hispania. We need him."

"I suppose," grumbled Lucius.

"The Aemilii and Ulpii?" queried Decimus.

"The Ulpii have always been about the Empire. A family that produces an emperor like Trajan is not likely to join any breakaway from the center. If the Ulpii remain loyal, so does Baetia and southern Hispania. As for the Aemilii," said Lucius, "they will always wait and see who is going to win before making a decision about whom to support."

"But Dasumi's base is Corduba in the south, which means the province may be divided," said Decimus.

"If Julius wins his case, then Corduba may, indeed, be our friend. But his sister is the consort of the current commander of the VII Legion, so I wouldn't put Corduba in our pocket just yet," said Lucius.

"Interesting," said Decimus. "So many pieces moving in multiple ways, Lucius.

"This is not a board game," said the duoviri. "We are gambling with our lives here."

"Yes," said Decimus, taking a sip of wine and reaching for a fig. "That makes it all the more fascinating."

* * *

Centurion Lucillius Oppius and Optio Cnacus Pontius of the VI Legion Victrix sat on a pair of camp stools watching the sun begin to set over the mountains to the west. The legion's camp outside of the city of Narbo Martius was one of the most extensive in southern Gaul. The two men looked cut from the same cloth—stocky, clean-shaven, and rough-featured. The centurion's dark hair was laced with gray

"We have a problem," said the centurion.

"Which one would that be? asked his second-in-command.

"Our comrades in Hispania are going to ask questions," Lucillius said.

"Yes, I suspect they will. And I am not quite sure how to answer them," said Cnacus. "But then, that won't be our problem, will it, sir? The tribunes and the legate will handle that."

The centurion said nothing for a long moment. "Do you know anyone in our century who isn't asking why we let an army of Franks march past us to take two of Hispania's biggest cities without doing anything about it?"

"No. But so what? Our century knows we didn't make that decision. Why should they worry about it?" said Cnacus.

"Because something big is afoot," said Lucillus. "I am not exactly sure what it is, but I think someone wanted to get rid of the VII Legion. And why would they do that? Because the VII Legion might get in the way of what they want to do."

"And that would be?" prompted Cnacus.

The centurion shook his head. "I don't know. But whatever it was, it didn't work."

"It sure didn't," said Cnacus. "The Hispania boys kicked those Franks' asses."

"Right. So, if the Franks didn't take care of the VII Legion, who will? Might that be us, optio?"

Cnacus frowned. "Us? Why us?"

"Because we are closer than anyone else, optio," answered Lucillius. "And you notice we were not called on to march up north and deal with the barbarians crossing the border."

"Fight a brother legion?" said Cnacus. "I know our guys wouldn't be happy about that, nor am I sure they would like to tangle with the likes of the Hispania legion."

The centurion poked the ground with his vitis. "The question is, would they obey orders to fight them?" he asked.

"Let's hope it doesn't come to that, sir," said Cnacus.

IV

The cart track wound down to a meadow surrounded by dense forest. A small stream ran through the woods, pooling at one point to form a pond. The mountains of northern Hispania loomed to the west, the trees on their slopes spotted with orange and gold, the first inklings of fall. Coventina, mounted on a stout gray gelding, picked her way across the meadow and toward the pond. Demaratus, on his narrow-faced Arabian, followed, leading a pack pony.

"This will do," she said. Demaratus nodded. "A good spot," he agreed. They were an interesting contrast. The tall, rangy Celtic woman with shoulder-length red hair; the Greek, smaller, slim, and handsome, with large gray eyes. Coventina slid off her horse and led it to the pond, where it began to drink. Demaratus followed with his horse and the pack pony, and they both quietly watched the animals drink their fill. The day had been warm, but there was a hint of chill in the shadows. They would need a good-sized fire tonight.

When the horses finished, Demaratus unloaded the pony,

while Coventina began setting up camp and gathering rocks for a hearth. He led the three animals to the center of the meadow, where he slipped hobbles over their hooves and tied the Arabian to a stake. The horses were unlikely to wander, but keeping one staked would guarantee that they would stay in the meadow. He took three feed bags from his packs and filled them with several handfuls of oats, slipping them over the horses' ears. They would feed on the oats for a while, then he would let them graze. The grass was long and untouched, so he had no worries about them getting enough to eat.

Coventina had chosen a roundabout way, little traveled this time of year, to her home village. That meant their campsites were pristine and well-endowed with rich graze. It was also a pleasure to be alone after the hectic weeks in Roma, not to mention to be free of the close quarters they had all endured at sea during the passage to and from Italia.

It had been a tense time. His commander, Marcus Favonius, now legate of the VII Hispania Gemina Pia Legion, had escorted his companion, Aelia Dasumi, to the Empire's capital to help her defend her inheritance from her brother. Demaratus, the Legion's signifer and third-in-command, along with Marcus's optio, or second-in-command, Flavius Priscus, had accompanied the party that also included Coventina and Aelia's adopted sister, Rachel Levi. The trip had been successful, in that Aelia managed to keep her part of the inheritance, but it had included two assassination attempts. A few weeks in the backwoods of Hispania were exactly what he needed.

The animals finished with the oats, and Demaratus slipped off the bags and let them graze. Having seen several rabbits when they first entered the meadow, he decided that fresh roasted meat would put a nice finish to the day. Slipping a sling out of his bag, he loaded it with a lead projectile and began moving slowly toward the tree line. The rabbits would be in that part of the meadow, feeding on clover and other plants, but ready to bolt for cover in the surrounding forest.

Within a few minutes, he spotted one munching away on a small bush. Sensing movement, the animal froze, only its nose wrinkling, testing the air for potential enemies. Demaratus whirled the sling over his head and sent the projectile at the rabbit. If the animal was concerned, it gave no indication. The missile missed it by several feet and struck noiselessly into the grass.

"You are out of practice, Demaratus," he said to himself and slipped another missile into the sling. This one terrorized a nearby lily but did not discomfort the rabbit, which had gone back to nibbling on the bush.

Cursing under his breath, Demaratus spun the sling again and launched a third missile. This attempt was successful, but not due to accuracy. The rabbit must have noticed him and taken a hop in the direction of the trees. Had it remained in its original position, the missile would have missed it. The animal essentially had put himself in harm's way. The rabbit thrashed about, and the signifer dashed forward, seized the animal by its ears, and quickly broke the creature's neck.

It was a fine, fat rabbit. Coventina would be pleased. And while it was hardly a big game animal, still he'd had a successful hunt (and he wouldn't mention the misses). Slipping the sling back in his bag and checking to see that the horses were grazing, he headed back to their camp.

As he approached, he saw Coventina talking with what he took to be a very large man. As he got closer, he could see the "man" was a bear, the biggest bear Demaratus had ever seen. It was on its hind legs—which is why he had initially thought it was a person—standing at least eight feet tall. Coventina was speaking—no, not speaking, chanting—in a soft voice in the language of her own people. Demaratus had heard Celtic before, in Britannia, in Gaul, and even in northern Greece. But he had no understanding of the language, which, by reputation, was difficult to master.

He pulled the sling from his bag but thought better of trying to use it. A sling projectile striking a bear that large would do little more than annoy it, and while Demaratus was no expert on bears, that seemed a bad idea. So, he stood and watched. The bear seemed to sway a little as it stared intensely at Coventina. The animal was no more than 15 feet away from the woman. She continued to chant, all the while holding on to an amulet around her neck. Demaratus knew that the amulet was a bear, and that Coventina had said that the bear was her protector and totem. She credited the bear god for preserving her during the Frankish occupation of Tarraco and for bringing Demaratus to her aid when she was arrested by the Franks.

For several minutes the bear and the woman faced one another, then the animal turned and looked at him. Demaratus felt the hair on his neck rise. The animal was staring directly into his eyes. He had never felt this way with an animal, not even his horse, Aura. There was a considered intelligence in the look the bear gave him, as if the creature were seeing inside of him. When Coventina had told him the bear came to her rescue he did not challenge her, but he regarded it as superstitious nonsense, something the barbarians—which the Greeks classified as anyone other than Greeks, and not even all of those—believed in. Macedonians were at least half barbarian. The signifer was not sure the gods even existed, although in times of stress he was willing to entertain that point of view.

But he had the distinct feeling that this bear was not just a very large, shaggy, and potentially dangerous animal, but a sentient being that was examining him. Finally, the animal dropped to all fours, turned and shuffled off towards the tree line. Just before it disappeared, however, it turned back and looked at him, as if to say, "I am watching you." He stood stock-still for several moments trying to sort through his feelings. Finally, Coventina stopped her chant and turned, beckoning to him. He noticed that he had dropped the rabbit, so he picked it up and strode into their camp.

"She spoke to you, my love," said Coventina.

Demaratus shook his head to clear it. "I don't know what that bear wanted or what it said, but I did feel it was not just an animal."

"That was the great mother of these mountains, Demaratus. She is my heart. She came all the way to Tarraco to save me from the Franks. She carried the soul of my uncle into the west. She brought you to my side in my time of need. There are none more powerful than she," she said in a voice that had taken on some of timbre of her chant.

"What did she want?" asked Demaratus.

"She wanted nothing. She was weighing you."

"Weighing me? To see if I am worthy of you?" asked the signifer.

"Yes," said Coventina, "I am her daughter."

Demaratus was not sure how to respond to that statement, but he sensed this was a powerful moment for Coventina. "Do you think she approved?" he finally asked.

"If she hadn't, you might have joined that rabbit," she said.

Demaratus laughed. "Please, Coventina, I am not laughing at that bear, or whatever it was, I am just relieved it is gone. I don't know what it was saying, but I felt something."

She nodded. "I have only encountered her once before. When I was a young girl my father found me speaking to a bear. My mother had died several weeks before. I was very sad and was wandering in the forest looking for mushrooms. I remember feeling that something was examining me, and when I turned, she was there. She stood like she did today, and I was not afraid. She came very close and I felt my sadness lift."

Coventina stopped and sat, or collapsed rather, as if drained. "When my father discovered me, the bear left, but he said I had been speaking with her. I don't remember that, but I knew she was telling me that I had to become like my mother and raise my brothers and sisters. My father was suffering from a war injury and could not farm or care for the animals. I knew then that it was my job to do that, and I did." She sighed. "The mother of the mountains is not an easy taskmaster, but if you please her, she will protect you. She has always done so for me."

"You have carried a heavy burden, my love," he said softly.

She nodded. "But I have no regrets, Demaratus. I am pleased

with my life." Then she smiled. "And I have this handsome Greek to take into my bed. Now go fetch me some firewood while I clean our supper," she said. Coventina's moods shifted swiftly, sometimes so quickly that Demaratus strained to keep up. She drew a knife from her bag, carried the rabbit to the forest's edge, and quickly gutted the animal, stripping it of its fur. Demaratus gathered wood near the pond where the stream had deposited it.

The two sat quietly while the rabbit roasted on a spit. Coventina sprinkled some herbs she had gathered, adding salt, and pulled bread and wine out of one of the bags carried by the pony.

"Tell me a little of your family," said Demaratus. "Do you think they will approve of me?"

"Hmm," said Coventina. "They will first see you as a Greek, and your people are not overly popular with mine. We fought you when you first came into this land. True, it was a long time ago, but my people have long memories."

"Did my people mistreat you?" asked Demaratus. Immediately, he regretted asking what he realized was a dumb question.

"All conquerors mistreat the conquered, but you were not successful. We defeated you and also the Carthaginians, who were the worst of those who wanted our land," she told him. "But we could not defeat the Romans."

"Neither could we," admitted Demaratus with a sigh. "I am not sure anyone can."

"Oh, their day will come, my love," said Coventina, turning the rabbit to roast another side. "Someday their statues will be dust. Someday their great buildings will be ruins. Empires do not last forever, only people."

It was times like these that made Demaratus understand why he was so taken with this sometimes-difficult woman, whose sharp tongue could be a trial. But she was probably the most thoughtful and observant person he had ever met, and never boring. "But you digress. Do you think they will approve of me?" he persisted.

"If they don't, I will give them a good thrashing," she said with a smile. She reached across and touched his cheek. "Are you worried?"

"Yes," he said. "In a few days I will be in the middle of a town where I know no one but you, a foreigner in all ways, surrounded by a large family that will be judging me. That would worry anyone."

She shrugged. "They are different. Brennus is the oldest and thinks he is head of the family. As the eldest male that would normally be true, but not in our household. I raised him. But he is our warrior and has demonstrated his courage in fights with the Autrigones, our traditional enemies. He will be standoffish and a little full of himself.

"Colin is in charge of our animals, and he is good with them. He practically talks to horses. He will love your Aura, so you two will get along fine. Balor is a farmer and quiet. He is married and has a daughter and a son. Amatista assumed my duties when I left to care for my aunt in Tarraco. She is much like me. She will like you.

"Brigida is," here Coventina paused, "difficult," she finally said. "She is headstrong and opinionated, but in a family of seven children that is how she survived. I don't know how she will react. Riona has become a healer and a priestess. She is the youngest."

Demaratus was silent for a long moment. "So, your answer is that they will approve if I give them reason to?"

"Yes," she said, slipping the roasted rabbit off the fire and cutting it up on a cedar plate. "But you have charm enough for all of them, my love. You will do fine."

Demaratus was not so sure, but that was the end of the conversation. So, they ate, drank wine, and snuggled by the fire as the fall chill crept out of the forest and spread across the meadow.

V

Sabina Aquillius was terrified, although she did her best to conceal it. She sat on her bed and hugged one of her dolls. She had given up dolls a long time ago, but now she felt like a little girl instead of a 13-year-old, and this doll had been her favorite.

Her terror had begun a month before when her uncle, Tiberius, arrived at her family's domus with a senator in tow. Her mother, Julia, and her father, Lucius, had been deeply impressed with the visitor and how Tiberius was now rubbing elbows with some of the most powerful men in Roma. Her mother was a Favonius, and the family had chosen wisely in the civil war between Emperor Philip and the usurper, Decius. Decius had killed Philip in a battle near Verona and the Favonius family's fortunes had gone up in the world. Tiberius had been appointed a quaestor, and her Uncle Marcus was now a legate, commanding the VII Legion Hispania.

A few weeks before Tiberius had brought the senator to their house, he had mentioned that Sabina needed to be married, but Sabina had not paid it much mind because her mother had told him she was too young. The two had argued a little, with her uncle claiming 12 was the ideal age for marriage, and that since Sabina was 13 going on 14, it was time for her to marry. Her mother had disagreed.

But Tiberius had not given up, especially since a union between his niece and a powerful and wealthy senator would open up more opportunities for his own advancement. So, she suddenly had found herself being examined as if she was a side of beef in the Forum Boarium. And it was an old man doing the examining!

She was speechless, a rare condition for Sabina. Her mother had looked distressed but said nothing. Her father had nodded in agreement with Tiberius when he'd proposed the match with —what was his name—Quintus Aemilius, who was too old to be her father, more like her grandfather! Nothing had been finalized that evening, but after the senator and Tiberius left, her father patted her on the head and said, "Well, Sabina, you are about to be a bride."

She wanted to vomit.

Sabina looked down at her body. She was tall for her age, with long legs and delicate features, much like her mother's. Her eyes were gray and her breasts were starting to swell. She had always thought of her body as a friend, but now it was betraying her. She wanted to cover up her breasts and make herself ugly, but she did not know how. So, she hugged her doll and wept.

Nothing much had happened since that night, because the plague had arrived. Roma was in turmoil. The streets were filled with carts carrying the dead, and rumor had it that the Emperor's youngest son, Hostilian, had taken ill. Julia had arranged for herself and her three children—Sabina and her brothers, Julius and Sergius—to leave the city to decamp at a cousin's villa in Carsulae, a provincial town north of Roma on the Via Flaminia. But that would not save Sabina. As soon as the plague passed, they would all move back to Roma and Sabina would be married off to an old man. She would kill herself. No, she knew she would not. Life was too interesting, and she was not sure if there was anything on the other side.

There was a knock on her door and her mother peeked in. "Are you ready, my love?" she asked. "Love?" Sabina thought. If her mother loved her, she would never have let this happen, but she had remained quiet, not arguing with her husband. By the gods, she hated them both! She did not answer her mother, but picked up a bag of clothes and followed her mother into the atrium.

Her brothers had left several days before, so it was just Julia and Sabina. She did not say a word to her mother or even look at her. If she was going to be miserable, she had every intention of making anyone around her equally miserable.

The streets were sobering. Sabina had stayed at home for most of the past month, and in that time the plague had spread to virtually every part of the city. She passed several carts with bodies wrapped in linen. Many of them small. Plagues took the young first. She was glad she could not see their faces. She covered her mouth and nose with a cloth mask and tried not to breathe deeply. The authorities were overwhelmed with the number of dead, and from the odor it appeared that they had left some of the bodies to ripen. Sabina gagged several times and fought the urge to retch.

They followed the cart loaded with their luggage down the Quirinal Hill to the Porticus Aemila, where the men pulling it loaded their things onto a barge. Sabina kept her distance from her mother, only nodding in reply to questions or comments directed at her. There was a small awning set up with a few chairs and a table in the ship's bow, but Sabina stood by herself at the boat's side and refused to look at her mother or sit under the awning.

The crew loosened the lines that tied the ship to the wharf and stowed pieces of gear and luggage in the craft's stern. The captain pulled on the steering oar and the boat moved out, heading downstream. This puzzled Sabina. Carsulae was north of Roma, upstream, not downstream. She wanted to ask her mother why the boat was going in the wrong direction, but she was not going to give her mother the satisfaction of hearing her speak. So, she stood with her back to her mother and sulked.

Eventually Julia tapped her on the shoulder. Sabina tried to ignore her, crossing her arms and deepening her glower. Julia finally grabbed her by the sleeve, pulling Sabina in the direction of the awning. The girl initially resisted, but she didn't want to make a scene in front of a bunch of strangers. She wasn't going to talk or even sit, so she just crossed her arms again and looked down at the deck.

"Oh, you silly goose," her mother said. "Sit and listen, because I am going to ask you to grow up."

Sabina flared at her. "Grow up by marrying a man who is older than my father? I would rather die!"

Julia sat in one of the chairs and composed herself. "I have no intention of letting you marry that dried-up old prune, Sabina. Now sit down and listen."

"What?" said Sabina. "But you never said a word when uncle Tiberius was there, nor since that awful old creature came to our domus."

"One does not argue with Tiberius, Sabina, one outmaneuvers him. And I did not want anyone to know what I was planning," she said. "Now sit. And close your mouth, it's bad manners."

Sabina did sit and did close her mouth. "Mother, I don't understand."

There was a long pause and Julia looked off into the distance. She sighed. "Sabina, when I was your age, I was married. It was the only way I could get out of my house. My two oldest brothers, Tiberius and Mamercus, were either fighting one another or bullying me and Marcus. My father not only did nothing to stop it, he encouraged it. And my mother," she stopped for a moment. "Well, my mother could not stand up to my father. None of us could. So, I left and married a man I did not love."

When Sabina looked shocked. Her mother patted her knee. "I have come to be quite fond of Lucius, Sabina. He gave me three wonderful children, he never raises a hand to me, he is kind, and he is a good provider. I have no regrets, especially because I have my children. But I do not want that for you, Sabina, and this marriage that Tiberius would force you into would make you deeply unhappy. I won't allow it," she said with a set to her jaw.

"But how will you stop it, mother? Father has approved it," asked Sabina.

"Oh, I will handle your father." She shrugged. "As for Tiberius, what can he do about it?"

"But won't he force me?" asked Sabina.

"He would if he could get at you, but he won't be able to do that, my love."

"I don't understand how you will stop him, mother," said Sabina.

"No one can force you to do something if you aren't there," she said, sitting back in her chair.

"Where will I be?" asked Sabina.

"Hispania, or Corduba, to be precise. I am told it is quite lovely," said her mother.

"What!"

"I have been quite busy for the last month, Sabina. The day after that horrid old senator left with Tiberius, I wrote a letter to Marcus's consort, Aelia. We had discussed you going to Hispania before she left Roma, and I told her you were on your way," said Julia.

"I am?"

"This is the part that will be difficult for you, Sabina. Normally I would go with you, or send a servant to accompany you, but I cannot do that. We only have two servants, and one went with the boys. Lucretia cannot go because she has children of her own and a grandchild on the way. I simply could not afford to buy you a slave, and even if I could, it would raise suspicions," said Julia.

"This had to remain a secret. I made arrangements in Ostia for you to take a ship west to Tarraco, but you will be on your own, and you are only 13 years old," she said, suddenly tearing up. "If you do not want to go, I understand. I will try something else, but this seemed to be the best way to ensure you do not have to marry someone you don't want to."

"But couldn't uncle Tiberius tell them to send me home?" asked Sabina.

"He could, but it is your Uncle Marcus who commands a legion, and I have a letter here giving him guardian status," she said.

"Father signed such a letter?" asked Sabina.

"Well, not exactly. The letter bears his seal. I know because I was the one who put it on there," said Julia. "In any case, once you are in Hispania and under my dear brother's wing, there is nothing that Tiberius can do about it." She paused in thought for a moment. "Actually, that will be a delicious moment. Not only will he not be able to steal my daughter, but the younger brother whom he bullied all those years will have more power than he does."

Sabina's mind raced with a thousand thoughts and emotions. Relief, joy, uncertainty, and fear waged equal battles. How would she contact Marcus when he was almost certainly a long way from Tarraco? How would she get to Corduba? She felt like a little girl again.

Julia watched the torrent of emotions wash over her daughter. She put her arms around Sabina and pulled her daughter to her. "This will not be easy, Sabina. You will have to be an adult and you are still a child. But you can do this, I know. Your name will open doors in Hispania. Who would not want to help the niece of the man who liberated slaves in Mauretania and who defeated the Franks? But to do this, my love, you must act like an adult. And that is a heavy burden. Is it too heavy?"

Sabina pulled back from her mother. "No," she said. "Yes, I am frightened, mother, but I can do this. I am, after all, your daughter."

Julia smiled. A tear rolled down her cheek. "I thought you hated me?"

"Aren't children allowed to make mistakes, mother?" said Sabina with a smile.

The two hugged, then Julia pulled back and said, "To practical matters." Pulling a leather folder from her bag, she systematically went through a series of documents. "This is your letter of guardianship. This is a letter to the commander of the Tarraco garrison. This is a letter to Aelia and Rachel. And in this small bag is money." She poured out the bag and counted a considerable number of silver denarii and some sestertii. "This will pay your way to Corduba, although I suspect that the VII Legion will help you out. It will also give you spending money and enough to buy clothes if you need them."

Sabina did much of the food shopping for the household, so she was familiar with money and knew what it would buy. She was a little nervous about carrying that many valuable coins, but Julia pointed out that she would never be alone. "The captain of the ship is in the navy, and he knows all about Marcus. He will see you to Tarraco and arrange for you to make contact with the VII Legion."

Sabina relaxed. Her mother had planned out all the details. She realized that she hadn't really known her mother. She loved her, but frankly had thought she was a bit shallow. She had been wrong. What she had taken for timidity was rather Julia quietly maneuvering to get her way. In fact, she was much like Marcus, who had none of the bombast of his brothers, but was quietly formidable.

The two talked and planned for several hours until the boat pulled into the Harbor of Claudius, and Sabina's luggage was transferred to a trim liburna tied to the wharf. The captain welcomed them aboard, and Julia huddled with him for a few minutes. Sabina saw her mother pass a small bag to the captain, who slipped it into his pouch.

Julia came back and hugged Sabina until the captain told them he needed to get underway, there was a tide to catch. Julia kissed her daughter. "Be strong, Sabina. Have a good life." Then, with a sob, she turned and fled down the gangplank to the wharf, waving as she ran. Dockside slaves unhitched the ropes tying the ship to the dock, and crew members manning several long sweeps began rowing the ship to the harbor entrance. Midway there, several crew members raised the sail, and the ship leaned away from the wind. Sabina watched her mother waving from the dock and waved back. She watched until the liburna cleared the entrance and caught the land breeze, leaping forward into the sea.

Sabina felt a wave of uncertainty pass over her. She was bound for terra incognita.

VI

⸎

The village was clustered at the bottom of a small valley flanked by mountains, the upper peaks laced with streaks of snow. The houses were stone with thatched roofs, except for one large building set off from the road. The houses were scattered, most with small pens holding sheep, pigs or horses, many of the former two, fewer of the latter. There were no stores that Demaratus could see, except for a blacksmith shop, where the sound of iron striking iron echoed up to the hill where he and Coventina had stopped. Coventina pointed out her family's house and the large building.

"It is our meeting place, Demaratus. We also hold weddings and feasts there," she said. The building reminded Demaratus of some of Greece's older cities, Mycenae for one. The walls were constructed of large, unpolished stones, as if giants had gathered them from the surrounding hills. The Greeks, too, built with large stones, unlike the Romans, who preferred brick covered with marble sheets. The roof was timber, with carvings at the corners and open spaces below the roof line. There were no windows, but those open spaces would allow air to enter and smoke to exit. It was quite impressive, but out of place with the surrounding houses.

"The village is small," said Coventina, as if reading his thoughts, "but that is because there are many houses scattered throughout the valley. We do not pack ourselves into cities like you Romans and Greeks, but our clan holdings embrace most of the land you see. An important meeting or a wedding might draw 3,000 people."

She pointed to the eastern part of the valley. "Most of our fields are over there, and our grazing meadows are there and there," she said, pointing to the north and west.

"Does your family own meadows and fields?" asked the signifer.

"We don't own things in the way your people do, Demaratus. My brother who farms uses several fields to grow barley, wheat, and oats, and Colin grazes our sheep in meadows alongside other shepherds. Our clan owns the lands, not my family. We own our house, our garden, and our animals. Because we use the common lands, we give meat, milk, cheese, and grains to the clan for festivals and gatherings," she told him. "No one is either rich or poor in our village, although some have more than others. We were poor, but no more. Colin has increased the size of our herd, and Balor can grow food from rocks."

"You have horses?" asked Demaratus.

Coventina nodded. "The last I heard we had eight, plus two mules for the plowing. Colin rents out some of our horses because we do not need them all. He will be interested in your fancy little mare."

"She is fancy, but most of all, she is fast," said Demaratus. The Greek was inordinately proud of his Arabian.

Coventina pulled her horse back onto the cart track and started down toward the village. "We don't have a lot of use for speed, my love. We like a good, strong horse that can carry a load and walk all day. And when we fight the Autrigones, we want a stout one."

As they drew closer to the village they began to encounter people, with whom Coventina stopped and talked in her people's language. A small crowd of children had gathered to watch them, and chickens ranged about, scratching and pecking. A few dogs joined the children, but kept back from the horses. Demaratus realized that Coventina was introducing him to people when his name came up amid a whirl of indecipherable language. He nodded and smiled and tried not to look lost, but lost was how he felt.

"So, you're the Greek," one older woman said to him in Latin.

"I am," he said in response, but could think of nothing else. The woman said something in Celtic and several other people laughed. When Demaratus looked blank, she switched back to Latin. "I was just commenting on how cute you are."

Demaratus was not sure how he felt about that, but given that he was now surrounded by Cantabrians, he smiled gamely and said nothing. Coventina led the way toward a house with a small garden of flowers in the front, trailed by several neighbors who bantered back and forth to her and to one another. As they drew up in front of the house and dismounted, a younger woman came out of the door and flung her arms around Coventina. The two embraced for a long time, until Coventina pushed her away and held her at arm's length.

By this time Demaratus had figured out that the woman was Amatista, in many ways a younger version of Coventina—tall, rangy, with a long cascade of red hair bound up with an elaborate hair broach. Coventina stepped back and looked her up and down. "My sister, I am going to speak in Roman because my love does not know our language. I cannot tell you how I much I have missed you. No matter where I am, my heart is here." Turning to Demaratus, she introduced him and he gave a little bow.

"Oh, my, he bows!" teased the woman who had described him as cute. "You are too rich for our blood, Greek."

"Watch your tongue, Perla," said Coventina. "This is a man who faced down Lusitanians, Mauri slave traders, Franks, and Roman assassins. And he is my love. Annoy him and I will toss you into our pigpen." Her tone was good-natured, but Coventina towered over the woman and looked like she could carry out the threat.

"Oh, men as handsome as that ought to be teased, Coventina," said Perla with a grin. "And when was the last time a man bowed to one of us?" She looked closely at Demaratus and said, "I rather like him for that, and you can't deny he is cute." That last remark set off a round of comments from the others, but the signifer could follow none of it.

"Shall I take the animals around to the back?" he asked, wanting to get out of the throng of neighbors. Coventina nodded, and he led the two horses and the pack pony to a fenced enclosure that held a water trough. A covered shed was packed with straw, and after unloading the animals, he rubbed them down with the straw and piled it up for the animals to eat. He would feed them oats later. Coventina and Amatista joined him, and together they hauled their bags into the house.

The cottage consisted of a large, central room, with a deep fireplace and several kettles hanging over a banked fire. There was a distinct odor of onions and meat. A large table dominated the room and two large chests with drawers filled one wall. A door led off to inner rooms. The beams that held up the roof were hung with hams and cheeses, and a basket of apples and pears provided the table's centerpiece.

Amatista placed a pitcher and three cups on the table and laid out a board with thick black bread and cheese. Demaratus gratefully poured the wine, downing a cup in a single gulp and pouring out another.

"Our people will drive anyone to drink," said Amatista with a smile. "Sit and eat something."

Demaratus laughed. He already liked this woman who looked so much like Coventina.

"Perla means no harm," she said. "She just can't keep that mouth of hers quiet."

Within minutes the house began to fill, mostly with relatives and mainly women. A torrent of unfamiliar names assailed him —Aine, Una, Digna, Silvana, Fearghat, Magocunos and more. Demaratus figured out that most were cousins, plus two aunts and at least one uncle. Coventina asked people to speak Latin, but some of the visitors either couldn't or wouldn't, and within a short time the signifer was lost again in a sea of incomprehensible language, so he sat off to one side sipping wine.

A little girl—not more than five or six—dragged a chair in

front of him, sat herself upon it and stared at him. She was cute, round-faced and dead serious. He attempted to talk with her only to be met with silence and that intent stare. Two other children joined her, and the three conversed, obviously talking about him.

Enough, he decided, and told Coventina that he had to see to the horses and the pony. She waved at him distractedly and he slipped out the back to the fenced enclosure. Aura gave him a whinny of recognition, and he rubbed her ears. He fed the animals oats and sat on the trough, his back against a post.

Well, he had agreed to take this trip, so he was going to have to make the best of it, he told himself.

VII

The VII Legion had gathered on Legio's Field of Mars and was breaking up into its 10 cohorts. Officers were debriefing their cohorts, century by century. Almost the entire VII was on the field, some 5,000 men, all in full battle gear. For the past two days the Legion had been on maneuvers, breaking camp, forming into fighting lines, practicing the testudo—the centuries gathering like tortoises, their walls of shields protecting them from arrows and sling missiles.

Maneuvering and flexibility on the battlefield were the essence of the Roman Army. Camps were built with four gates so that a legion could quickly exit and form up. Each cohort was divided into six centuries, thus building in a flexibility of movement that made a legion almost impossible to outflank and enhancing the legion's ability to envelop an opponent. The centurions would later meet and analyze their units, mapping out what needed to be worked on. The goal was to build a fast moving, fighting army that functioned like a well-oiled machine.

All in all, the exercise had been a success. The VII was coming off a successful fight with a larger Frankish army and feeling pretty good about itself. High morale and self-confidence had helped turn it into a formidable fighting force.

Marcus and Flavius moved from gathering to gathering, listening to the officers and getting questions from the legionnaires. He had instructed officers to ignore his presence because he wanted to hear the back-and-forth, so he stood quietly at the edge of the gatherings being as unobtrusive as he could. He liked what he heard. Junior officers felt free to talk up, and even rank and file soldiers were willing to comment on the exercises.

Eventually the legion broke up, and the men headed for their barracks, the baths, and supper, while the centurions held their first round of meetings. They would meet on and off for the whole week, delineating where the men needed more training. Marcus, Flavius, and the tribune, Quintus Junius, gathered in the principia, and an aide poured out cups of wine and set out bread, olive oil, cheese, and dates. The old tribune gratefully collapsed in a chair and took off his helmet and breastplate. "I am getting too old for this, sir," he said to Marcus and took a long pull on his cup of wine, refilling it from a pitcher.

They were soon joined by Cassius Cornelius, the cavalry commander.

"Comrades," said Marcus, "I think the VII Legion has not lost a step. Do you agree?" The old tribune nodded. "Agreed," he said, but he looked exhausted and ready for a nap, and was starting on his third cup of wine.

"We need to coordinate with the infantry better," said Cassius. "I was generally pleased, but there is too much time between when orders are issued by the infantry and when the cavalry receives them. Swiftness is our major asset and we are not taking advantage of it."

"Do you have a suggestion for how to improve that?" asked Marcus.

"I do, sir," said Cassius, "but I want to think about it a little more. I will have a report for you by tomorrow."

"There is no great rush, commander," said Marcus. "Sometime in the next week will do."

Marcus looked around the room and indicated that Flavius should close the door of the office. "And tell my aide we are not to be disturbed." When Flavius returned from the outer office, Marcus indicated that Cassius and his optio should take seats in a circle.

"There is an important matter we need to discuss, comrades," he said. Even Quintus put down his wine, but not before he had refreshed it.

"You all know about the gold we intercepted?" Marcus asked, and the others nodded. "It is my analysis that the gold was bound for Gaul and was meant to purchase the loyalty of the Gaul legions."

Cassius frowned. "For what purpose, sir? Loyalty to whom?"

"I do not know for whom, commander, but I suspect for what," he answered. "I believe there is a plot to break Gaul away from Roma and create an independent empire in the north that might include Britannia and Hispania."

"What evidence do you have for this, Marcus?" asked Quintus.

"Very little, and much of that is circumstantial," he admitted. "The Gaul legions allowed a Frankish army to pass from the border of Germania to Tarraco without confronting it. Not only did they not challenge a major invasion, they did nothing to warn Hispania that it was coming. I can only conclude that whoever was behind this hoped that the Franks would either defeat or neutralize the VII Legion. The only reason for doing so would be that they were convinced that the Legion would remain loyal to the Empire. It is, after all, part of our name—Pia."

"That is a tenuous conspiracy you have woven, sir," said Quintus. "I am not saying it is not so, but convincing people with so little evidence may be difficult."

Marcus passed his hands through his hair. "I realize the case is thin, but does anyone else have an explanation for the intercepted gold and for the failure of the Gaul legions to intervene with the Franks?" asked Marcus.

The group was silent.

"I hope I am proven wrong, but let's for a moment accept my analysis, because if it is true, we must be prepared," Marcus said.

"What do you have in mind, sir?" asked Cassius.

"Let me start with a question. Is there anyone here who would support such a movement? And I want people to be honest. Regardless of how you answer, it will be kept within this room," said Marcus, looking around the circle. When no one said anything, he continued. "Can we say that for everyone in the VII Legion?"

Again, he was greeted with silence.

"Publius," said Quintus softly.

Marcus nodded. "Tribune Felix comes to mind," he said. "Might there be others?"

"Aren't we moving a little fast here, sir?" asked Cassius.

"Tribune Publius Felix is not my favorite person, but do we have any evidence that he would engage in treason?"

"We do not, Cassius, and I am not accusing him of it. I am asking a question—are we certain that the VII Legion is 'pia'?" the legate persisted.

"Yes," answered Flavius. "The legion is loyal to you, sir, and you are loyal to the Empire. You brought the Second Century through the fight with the Lusitanians, you defeated the Mauri, and you compelled the Frankish army to surrender. The VII Legion has known nothing but success with you in command, sir. They would storm the gates of Hades for you."

"I agree with Flavius," said Cassius. "I think I can vouch for the cavalry as well. The Ala II Flavia Hispanorum Romanorum is loyal, sir, but I can see complications."

"Explain," said Marcus.

"I have no doubt about my ala, sir, or the VII Legion, but Hispania is a complex place, legate. For instance, what might my people, the Lusitanians, do? What about the Celtic tribes in the northern mountains? Or, for that matter, what about those decurions we tangled with in Capera?" he said. "Some of them are certain to bear the VII Legion a grudge for not helping them steal Lusitanian lands."

Marcus nodded, "Good points all, Cassius. I don't have an answer to those questions, but what I need from you all at this point is an opinion about whether what I am suggesting might be true."

Quintus shrugged. "I don't think we have a choice, Marcus. If it is not true, then we will look silly, but if there is even a remote chance it is so, then we need to be prepared. I think we should proceed as if there is a conspiracy and hope we are wrong."

"Does anyone disagree with that statement?" asked Marcus. When no one said anything, he continued, "Fine, then we will keep our ears open and watch. Cassius, I want you to send a rider to fetch our signifer. We need to start by trying to sort out this matter of the gold, and I don't know anyone better for the job."

"Yes, sir," said Cassius, "Do you know where he is?"

"Find the middle of nowhere, get lost, and you will probably find him," said Flavius, drawing a round of chuckles.

"I do not, commander, but Coventina is a Cantabrian, so that should help you narrow the search," Marcus suggested.

"I will take care of it immediately, sir," said Cassius.

"Good," said Marcus, rising and indicating the meeting was over. The others also rose, but Marcus signaled to Cassius and Flavius to stay. After the old tribune had left for his quarters, Marcus turned to Cassius. "Cassius, I want you to do something that will temporarily take you out of your command. Is that possible?"

The cavalry commander frowned. "Yes, sir," he said. "I am always at your command."

"That is not what I mean," said Marcus. "I am sending you on a delicate mission, but I need to know if you have a competent second-in-command who can step in. If not, I will not ask you to undertake this matter."

"Yes, sir. My second-in-command is more than competent to run the ala in my absence," Cassius answered, "but what is it you want me to do?"

Marcus went to a side cabinet and took out several letters.

"These are addressed to Aelia Dasumi, Cassius. It is essential that she receive them. I cannot trust them to the cursus publicus. I want them delivered by hand. And for you to brief her on what we have talked about today."

When Cassius looked questioningly, Marcus continued. "If what I suspect is true, civilians are certainly involved. Aelia is in the best position to learn the sentiments of the powerful local families. We need that information. And there is another matter."

"Yes?" inquired Cassius.

"I want you to come back to Legio through Lusitania and talk with the leaders of your people. Find out if they know anything about this and maybe what their attitude toward it would be," said Marcus. "Can you do that?"

Cassius hesitated. "I am not sure I am welcome among my people, but I will try to find out what you need. I do need to travel through Tarraco on the way to Corduba, however. I am picking up a contingent of new ala recruits. Will that be a problem?"

"Not at all, commander," answered Marcus.

Cassius saluted. "Then I will be going, sir. It is a long way from here to Corduba. I will start tomorrow morning."

"Excellent, Cassius. Have a good and safe trip," said Marcus, returning the salute.

After he left, Flavius said, "He made some good points about his people and the Celts."

Marcus nodded, "We always knew he was smart, optio. And we will have to work on the complexity he raised. Demaratus might have some interesting things to say about the Cantabrians."

VIII

Sabina watched the wharf draw nearer. The liburna had dropped its sail and the crew was manning the sweeps, edging the ship toward dockside. She was wrestling with a torrent of emotions, wishing that the liburna would take a long time to dock. It had taken them only a little more than three days to make the voyage. The weather had been clear and the ship had had a steady wind from the east. She was elated about dodging a marriage with an old man, but frightened about what lay before her. She was arriving at a city she had never seen and where she knew no one. She had done a good job of masking those feelings up until now, but that had been easier when they were at sea. Approaching Tarraco brought them to the fore. She was more alone than ever before.

"Almost there, Lady Sabina," said the captain, who had moved from the stern to where she was standing at the starboard side.

"Yes," she said flatly, clutching the ship's side.

"I will have some crewmembers escort you to the VII Legion's headquarters," he said. "There it is," he said, pointing at a large temple near the top of the city. "They will set you up until you can leave for Corduba."

"Is Corduba far?" she asked, doing her best to keep her voice steady.

"I have never made the journey by land, Lady Sabina. But I think it's probably a week away. About a week by sea as well. It's upstream on the Baetis River. If you go by land, there is a good road that will hug the coast all the way to Valentia. From there you can get the road that takes you over the mountains and into the Baetis Valley and Corduba. It is quite lovely. I have been to the port of Gades, which is not far from Corduba, and visited the city several years ago."

"Wouldn't it have been better for me to go there directly, instead of through Tarraco?" asked Sabina.

"It would have, but we are not bound there," he replied. "But your mother was in a rush to get you to Hispania, and we were the only ship headed that way. We go from here to Barcino in the north, then Emporiae and Massilia, then back to Ostia."

Sabina nodded mutely, tightening her grip on the rail. The captain and crew had been most solicitous for the entire journey, voicing concerns that she might get seasick—she didn't, that she might get cold—the weather was mild and warm, and that she might not sleep. She hadn't, but not because of the ship. Her bed was a stuffed pallet with a partial awning near the stern. Throughout the voyage she alternated between relief and anxiety, and the crew had picked up on the latter. They had brought her food, pointed out flying fish and dolphins, and once altered the ship's course so she could see a whale.

"Well, Sabina, your mother has saved your life and put you

on fortune's path," she said to herself. "It is time to grow up." She reminded herself that she was the niece of the commander of the VII Legion, a hero to the people of Tarraco. The captain had mentioned that on several occasions, which had made her feel better. Still and all, her stomach swarmed with butterflies.

Eventually the ship slid alongside the wharf. Several slaves grabbed the hawsers thrown their way and secured the ship. Sabina went aft only to find that her belongings had already been gathered up, and two crewmembers were carrying them toward the gangway.

"These men will accompany you, Lady Sabina. I will arrange for a litter," said the captain, patting her on the shoulder.

"That won't be necessary, Captain. After all that time at sea I would rather walk, and it will give me an opportunity to see the city," she replied.

He looked doubtful. "The VII's headquarters is at the top of the city, Lady Sabina. It is not a stroll."

"Still, I would rather stretch my legs," she said. "You and the crew have been wonderful, captain, and my mother asked me to give you this." She handed him a small leather pouch.

He put his hands behind him. "No need for that, Lady Sabina. We were honored to be of service. Your uncle is a hero here in Tarraco. Take out a few denarii for the men who carry your luggage, but they may not take it either. Do you have someone waiting for you?"

"No," she said, trying to keep the apprehension out of her voice.

"Well, you can expect a welcome from the men of the VII Legion, Lady Sabina," he said, again patting her shoulder. His easy reassurance did nothing to dispel her qualms, but she controlled the urge to cry.

With the ship firmly docked she gathered her cloak and descended to the wharf, where two men, one quite young, the other older, awaited. When she told them she did not need the litter and that she would rather walk, they shrugged and picked up her bags.

The captain watched her depart the ship, then called one of his men over. "Sestus, go find the head duoviri and let him know that Marcus Favonius's niece is in town and is alone. He will know what to do." The man saluted and set off into the city.

The docks had few ships and many of the warehouses looked empty. There were people in the streets, but for a girl from Roma, the city seemed almost deserted. The area around the docks appeared somewhat run-down, as if the port had seen better days. But the quality of the houses improved the further into the city she went.

Walking improved her mood, and by the time they reached the plaza at the top of the city she was feeling much better. The headquarters was a small building next to a very large—well, large for a provincial city—temple. She stopped for a moment outside the entrance—there was no sentry—and pulled out her letter of introduction. She also took the opportunity to take out two silver coins and handed them to the two men. But they, too, refused to take them. "It was a pleasure serving you, Lady Sabina," the older one said.

She thanked them, then turned, took a deep breath, and stepped through the door. A young man in uniform was standing in front of a desk, where a clerk was writing something down on a wax tablet. The clerk looked up, and said, "Yes? Can I help you?"

She handed him the letter, which he put to one side. "I am busy right now, girl, so please wait until I finish," he said impatiently. It was not exactly the greeting she was hoping for.

The young man in uniform looked at her curiously. He smiled and said, "I am Tiberius Cicero, tesserarius, Third Century, Tenth Cohort. That probably doesn't mean anything to...."

"I know what a tesserarius is," she said quietly. "You are in charge of setting the sentries and you are third-in-command."

He looked a little taken aback. "Quite right. How does a pretty little thing like you know that?" he asked with a smile.

"A pretty little thing like me is the niece of Marcus Favonius, and my uncle writes to me about the VII Legion," she answered without smiling. "My name is Sabina Aquillius. I am not a 'little thing.'"

Tiberius blanched and stumbled for words. The clerk looked like he wanted to disappear under the desk. "Oh, I am sorry. Please accept my apologies," he said. "I had no idea."

"It is generally a good idea to ask a person what they want before making assumptions about who they are," she said with more than a hint of steel in her voice.

The tesserarius made a little bow. "You are right, Lady Aquillius, I stand corrected. I will not make that mistake again."

The apology felt sincere to Sabina and she gave him a little smile. "I did not feel it was proper to just announce who I was," she said. "I was happy to wait."

"Again, you have my apologies, and I am sure Gaius here feels the same." The clerk looked distressed. She suddenly realized that both of them were afraid, and it shamed her a little. She didn't intend to threaten or humiliate them. Even her anger, she recognized, was more the result of feeling out of control and insecure, rather than genuinely insulted.

"Please, think nothing of it. A misunderstanding and partly my fault," she said, adding, "but I am not that little."

Tiberius laughed. "No, you are not." He picked up the letter from the table, opened it, and quickly read it. "We will arrange for your lodging, Lady Aquillius, and I will show you where the baths are and where you can procure food. You will be the only woman here, so we need to make some adjustments."

"That will be fine, but call me Sabina. Lady Aquillius makes me sound like a matron, or my mother, neither of which I want to be at this time in my life."

"And please call me Tiberius," he said. "Let me show you your accommodations. There are not many people here, so you have your pick of them, though all are a bit, well, Spartan."

"A safe assumption in the headquarters of a legion, Tiberius. Please lead on," said Sabina.

The tesserarius gave her a broad smile and indicated a long hallway. "Hmm," said Sabina to herself, "Is he flirting with me?" The thought immediately put her into a better mood.

The accommodations were, indeed, Spartan, but there was one room that wasn't bad. It was sparsely furnished, with just a small desk, a chest for clothes, and a bed with rope springs and a straw mattress. Well, she wasn't going to live here. It would do.

Another clerk brought in her baggage—she suspected the clerk at the desk was too frightened to show his face—and she unpacked and put her clothes away. Just as she finished there was a knock on her door. She opened it to find Tiberius. "I thought I would show you the facilities here, Sabina, if this is a good time."

She indicated it was, and Tiberius squired her around to the deserted mess hall. "You might want to get food at a thermopolium near the plaza," he said. "And while we do have baths here, there is a public bath not far away that is much more comfortable and has a library attached to it. Actually, quite a good one."

He took her out to the plaza and showed her the thermopolium and pointed at a side street leading down to the city center. "The baths are a short distance down that street, Sabina. If you need company, please let one of the clerks know and we will find you an escort. Or if I am available, I would be happy to do so."

She gave him a warm smile and he actually blushed. "My," she thought, "this is fun." She thanked him and told him she was tired and needed to rest.

"Of course. And if you need anything, please don't hesitate to ask for help. I will also make some enquiries concerning your journey to Corduba," he said, giving her a little bow.

Sabina decided that being Marcus's niece had all sorts of advantages that she had never considered. She went back to her room feeling considerably better than she had upon disembarking from the liburna.

* * *

She actually did go to sleep, only to be awakened by a knock at her door. The shadows were gathering in the plaza, so it must be late afternoon. She had slept for at least two hours. She was a little annoyed at the knock. What now? She opened the door to confront two women, one short and stout, the other clearly in charge.

"Oh, you poor chick," said the women, looking her over. "They put you up in a barracks! This will not do! I am Vipsania and this is Pacia, and we have come to fetch you and bring you to a place that is proper for a young lady."

"What?" asked Sabina, still a little groggy from her nap.

"I am Vipsania and this is Pacia. We are from the Women's Legion of Tarraco that helped chase those hairy barbarians out of our fine city. We greatly admire your wonderful uncle, and we will simply not allow these men to keep you in this awful place. Well, not awful, but not suitable. So, we have come to take you to my domus where you can have a proper bed and good food."

Sabina's mind went blank. The voyage, the uncertainty, the new faces, and now these strange women telling her what was going to happen to her. It all boiled over and she burst into tears.

"There, there," said Vipsania. "No need for tears. Pacia and I will take care of you. We can't wait to introduce you to the rest of our league." These words added yet another ingredient to Sabina's emotional cauldron. "Pacia," Vipsania said, "Go fetch that officious little clerk and tell him to pack up and move this young lady's belongings."

Sabina made a major effort to collect her feelings. She wiped her eyes and took a deep breath. "Please," she said, "I need to understand what is going on."

Vipsania was not particularly good at tuning in on other

people's states of mind, but she recognized that Sabina was upset and stepped back. "You must forgive me, Sabina. I have a tendency to run over people. The First Duoviri —a lovely man— contacted me when he heard that you had arrived in Tarraco and asked me to come and fetch you. Both of us felt that the barracks of a legion is not a fitting place for a young woman, or any woman, for that matter. I live alone, so I have plenty of room in my domus, and it is certainly more comfortable than this place. It is also more centrally located, so you would be near shops and markets," she said, adding, "Of course, the decision is yours."

Sabina felt torn. On one hand she was feeling that the barracks was a safe harbor, especially as Tiberius had been so helpful and friendly. On the other, it was a military establishment with no other women and not very well located for bathing and shopping. She also began to reconstruct some of what Marcus had written about the Women's Legion, in which Coventina had played a major role. Sabina had developed an affection for the Celtish woman when Coventina had been in Roma with Marcus and his companions, Flavius and Demaratus.

"You know Coventina?" Sabina asked them.

"She was the reason we formed the Women's Legion, my pet. She brought down two of the barbarians on her own, and she and that handsome Greek seized the ships in the harbor, forcing the Franks to surrender," said Vipsania. "Well, that and the fact that your uncle defeated their army."

Sabina found herself relaxing, embarrassed now by her tears. She viewed herself as someone in control, and hysterics were not part of that self-image. "Please forgive my outburst, Vipsania, I was just waking from a nap and there was just too much for me to deal with."

"Oh, pet, I do that to people all the time. The fault lies with me. But what do you say to my proposal?" asked Vipsania.

"It seems like the reasonable thing to do," said Sabina, "but I will do my own packing."

"Of course. Of course. We don't want men pawing through our things. Why don't you start and I will see what Pacia has arranged," said Vipsania.

Sabina nodded and began moving her clothes and jewelry to the bed to fold and pack in her bags. "One adventure after another," she thought.

IX

Julius Dasumi surveyed the anchorage at Barcino and liked what he saw. The harbor was jammed with ships, loading and unloading. Gangs of slaves carried amphorae of wine and olive oil onto the wharf, while others loaded sacks and amphorae of garum fish sauce onto vessels tied up to the wharves. Warehouses jammed with goods provided a stream of everything from grains to carvings boxed in pine to be added to the piles waiting to be loaded aboard ships ranging from small coastal freighters to oceangoing ships.

There was the smell of money about the city, a sharp contrast to Tarraco, which was becoming more and more like the old Greek port of Emporiae, its time of glory long past. Julius was not ready to return to Tarraco just yet. He had worn out his welcome in that city by organizing a market during the Frankish occupation, and he knew it. Yes, the prices were inflated, but any good businessman took advantage of supply and demand. And if he made money due to scarcity, well that was just a tribute to his business sense. But the fools who ran the city did not see it that way, so relocating to Barcino had seemed a good idea.

But if his plans came to fruition, he would be back in Tarraco. Oh, yes, he would return and there were those who would come to regret that. For today, he had to locate the domus he had rented and begin a round of meetings that would repay the insults his enemies had inflicted upon him. In particular, Aelia, his whore of a sister and her lover, Marcus Favonius. But there were others who would pay as well. He had a long list and an excellent memory.

The ship docked and he headed for the gangway. The captain strolled over to him. Julius had not bothered to commit his name to memory, as this was a task his nomenclature had always performed for him. But he was reduced to only a few slaves, and one whose job it was to know everyone's name was not a priority for him right now. The man started to say something, but Julius cut him off by tossing a small bag at his feet and ignoring him. He didn't bother to see if the man picked up the purse.

His three slaves followed him carrying some of his luggage. He would need a change of clothes once he had a bath. The rest of his things would come later after the ship was unloaded. He signaled to a nearby porter and showed a piece of papyrus on which the address was written. "Do you know where this is?" he asked the man.

The man looked at the address and nodded.

"Is it far?"

"No, sir, but would you like me to provide a litter?" asked the porter.

"No, I will walk. I want to see some of the city," he said.

"Your first visit, sir?" asked the man.

Julius nodded in assent, but silenced the man with a wave of his hand. "Just show us."

The porter led them from the docks and warehouses to a large central street that led straight into the town. The street was lined with thermopolia, small shops and open-air stalls. The street was packed with people haggling over prices, carrying bags, or just hurrying about their business. It felt like Roma, but fresher, newer, and more vibrant. After what turned out to be a very short walk, they reached the domus and Julius rapped at the gate. A servant quickly appeared and ushered Julius and the three slaves into a large atrium, an extensive peristyle garden off to one side. What he needed was a bath.

"Where is the nearest bath?" he asked the servant.

"Not far, sir. Do you wish to walk or take a litter?"

Julius decided he had walked enough that day. "Get me a litter." He turned to his slaves and instructed them to make up a bundle of fresh clothes. He glanced at the colina and inspected the rooms of the domus. They would be adequate, he decided. The garden, too, was acceptable.

By the time the slaves had readied a fresh change of clothes for him, a servant had arranged for a litter. Julius climbed on, and four young slaves lifted the litter and headed for the baths.

* * *

A slave appeared at his elbow. "There is a visitor for you, master. Tribune Publius Felix."

Julius had been in Barcino for three days and was finally

beginning to feel human. Regular baths, good food, and a quiet garden will do that. He had sent a note to the tribune on the day of his arrival and had received a reply that the man would be available this afternoon. He had met the tribune once before but didn't really know him. He was carrying a letter of introduction.

Publius Felix was a handsome man who had not given over to the softness of middle age. He was of medium height, but gave the impression of being taller by standing straight as a pilum. His uniform was richly appointed, and he carried a command rod carved of ivory.

"Tribune, so good to see you," said Julius, rising from his chair. "And thank you for coming."

"I am always ready to meet with our leading citizens, sir," replied Felix, although he looked watchful.

"Please sit, tribune, and may I offer you some wine?" said Julius, signaling to a slave.

"No, that will not be necessary, sir," he replied. "Can I ask the nature of your concerns?"

Julius handed him a scroll and waved off the slave attempting to refill his wine glass. The tribune unrolled it and read it through, then read it again. When he finished, he rolled it up and slipped it into his belt. "I would rather keep this between the two of us, Dasumi," he said.

"Of course, sir. And please call me Julius."

The tribune nodded but said nothing.

"It is possible I have a piece of news you may not be aware of, sir," said Julius.

The tribune cocked an eyebrow and waited.

"Emperor Decius's youngest son, Hostilian, has just died of

the plague in Roma. There is no news of the Emperor or his son, Herennius, both on the Moesian front. Trebonianus Gallus is acting emperor in Roma, but the political situation is very uncertain," said Julius.

"I see," said the tribune.

"Let me be blunt, sir," said Julius. "It is time for Hispania and Gaul to see to their own destinies. Roma is mired in corruption and its legions can no longer hold off the barbarians in the east. We must look after ourselves, and the time to make that break is rapidly approaching. I am in contact with some of the leading families here in Hispania, and they must know that the legions in Gaul and Hispania stand with them."

The tribune looked uncomfortable. "I, too, share your concerns, Dasumi, but to act precipitously is to hazard treason. The price for that is high."

"I know that as well as you, tribune. But I am in contact with powerful and wealthy families here in Barcino and Tarraco, and in Hispania's west. Those families will not move unless they have assurances that they will be supported. Surely you can see that," said Julius.

"I am also in contact with important forces, Dasumi, but they are not ready to act. We can depend on one auxiliary legion based in Valentia, but not on the auxiliary legion in Caesaraugusta. And it is my opinion that the VII Legion will not join such a break from the Empire. The new legate is popular and the legion will do what he wishes," said Felix.

Julius masked his impatience with the tribune's caution. "Consider this, tribune. The VII Legion is based in Hispania's northwest. If a legion from Norba were to march on Barcino and Tarraco, both cities would join such an endeavor, although in the case of Tarraco it might require some strategic assassinations. That means the east is already lost to Roma. A march south would take Corduba. That would mean that virtually all of Hispania would fall under the new empire, which I believe is going to called 'Gallic.'"

"Do you think we haven't worked all of that out, Dasumi? I suggest you stick to recruiting those important families and leave the military matters to us," said the tribune sharply.

Julius put up both hands. "I was not attempting to tell you your job, tribune. But I am concerned that we might let this opportunity pass us by."

"We cannot move without Gaul, and so far, I have heard nothing from Gaul except complaints about their gold supply drying up," said Felix.

"What is that about?" asked Julius.

"A unit of the VII Legion intercepted a gold shipment, and we have been forced to temporarily back off our shipments to Gaul," answered the tribune.

"Will that be a problem?" asked Julius.

"We are working on it," said the tribune, cutting off further discussion.

"Then I will continue to talk with my allies, tribune, as you should continue in your work," said Julius, rising from his chair.

"Your information on Hostilian is of interest, Dasumi. I will pass it on. If I hear anything about Moesia, I will let you know. I assume you intend to remain in Barcino?"

"I do, tribune. Please feel free to call on me at your pleasure."

The tribune nodded and a slave showed him out.

Military men could be difficult, thought Julius. They are over-cautious and have little in the way of imagination. But we need them, so I will curb my tongue. In the meantime, there is work to be done.

X

It had been a long week, much of it pleasant, some of it difficult. Demaratus liked Coventina's family, although a few of them taxed even the Greek's deep well of charm.

Amatista was much like Coventina, largely immune to fancy language but engaged by straight talk and common sense. Brennus was a bit full of himself and played the role of the "warrior," but he was fascinated by the signifer's description of the battle with the Mauri in Mauretania, which engaged Demaratus. He talked horses with Colin, who rode Aura several times and came away deeply impressed with her speed. "No wonder you named her after a wind," he commented.

Balor was silent most of the time, but Demaratus drew him out with his knowledge of knots, a skill that also impressed Brennus and Colin. Hours were spent demonstrating bowline, reef knots, carrick bends, rolling hitches and monkey fists.

Demaratus was less successful with the other sisters. Brigida was as Coventina described her, "difficult." She argued, alternating between being aggressive and friendly, and it was almost impossible to predict which mood would seize her. Riona was, to the signifer's way of thinking, the most different from the rest. She was a tiny, birdlike creature, with huge, luminous eyes, who always seemed to be someplace else. She spent hours with Coventina, comparing herbs and healing strategies, essentially ignoring the Greek.

But in general, Demaratus felt welcomed, or at least tolerated, which was fine with him. He was full of stories and the Cantabrians loved stories, "sagas" as Brennus called them. He told them the one about his horse's name, how the Greek admiral Themistocles tricked the Persians into dividing their fleet at the battle of Salamis and then using a wind, the aura, to crush the smaller enemy ships. He strung the tale out—the desperate and doomed battle by the Spartans at Thermopylae, the fall of Athens, and the final destruction of the Persians at Salamis. It was in the classical Greek story mold, going from darkness through blood to light.

The stories had become a nightly event, and Demaratus held forth on the Peloponnesian War, the conquests of Alexander the Great, and the VII's Legion's fight with the Lusitanians, the Mauri and the Franks. The signifer knew how to downplay the military details and emphasize the human elements. The young Cassius, bleeding from his wounds, saving them from the Lusitanians at the meadow. The double-dealing governor of Mauretania plotting to destroy Marcus and his century. The costume ruse that tricked the Franks at the battle of the river, allowing the VII Legion to outflank the enemy and leading to the surrender of the invaders.

Not everyone was engaged. Brigida asked questions, sometimes it seemed just to just break up Demaratus's narrative. But the others shushed her, so she generally remained quiet. Riona looked bored and sometimes excused herself, claiming she had to see a patient.

That night the discussion had been lively and family-focused, so Demaratus edged himself away from the table to watch and listen. In the middle of a rather heated argument between Brennus and Colin—with Brigida chiming in to support whomever she thought was losing—there was a rap at the door. Amatista went to answer it, then turned to Demaratus. "There is a man here for you," she said.

The signifer rose and the discussion went silent. He made his way out the door to confront a young cavalryman, who saluted him and said, "Sir, a letter from Legate Marcus Favonius."

Demaratus took the letter, broke the wax seal and unfolded the papyrus. It was just a few lines that essentially said he was needed as quickly as possible. "Do you know the reason for this?" the signifer asked the courier.

"Not really sir, although I think it has to do with the gold thing," the young man replied.

"Gold thing?"

"Yes, sir. The VII Legion intercepted a shipment of gold, sir, and no one has claimed it. That's about all I know, but the legate was quite concerned about it, sir. I know that because our commander, Cassius Cornelius, told me himself that this message was important, and I was not to return without giving it to you." The man looked exhausted and Demaratus suspected he had been in the saddle for most of the past 24 hours.

"Your name?" asked Demaratus.

"Vettius Junius, sir."

"Take your horse around back, Vettius. You will find food and water for it. Then come in," Demaratus told him.

"Sir," the man saluted, then led his horse around to the stable.

Coventina had come outside. "News?" she asked.

"Orders," he answered. "Marcus wants me back. Apparently, something to do with a gold shipment gone astray. I will have to go back early, my love."

"So, you will rush back and then wait, right? Isn't that what you say always happens in the army?" she said with a smile.

"Probably," he said with a wry grin, "but orders are orders."

"Well, you can get a start early in the morning, I will stay another two weeks and then join you in Legio," she said.

"I'm sorry, love," said Demaratus.

Coventina shrugged. "I signed on to this when I took up with you, although I seem to recall that there were going to be exotic places to visit and long afternoons in the warm sun. Not that I believed any of that," she added, "but it was a nice illusion."

"We will visit interesting places, Coventina, and there will be long afternoons, I promise," he said.

"I am just teasing, signifer. I am not much for illusions," she said.

"But I am," he declared, "so it will happen at some point."

"Hmm," she mused. "Well, in the meantime we should feed this young man, let Brigida flirt with him, and pack you up for the morning."

* * *

The dawn was sharply cold. Fall had come to the mountains, and the horses stamped their feet and blew clouds of steam. Demaratus, as always, traveled light. Coventina would come later with the pack pony. The young cavalryman was bleary-eyed. Brennus and Colin had fed him strong drink, and Brigida had indeed flirted with him. Demaratus suspected that the encounter involved more than flirting and that the man had had very little, if any, sleep.

Coventina emerged with a bundle that she tied to Aura. "There is plenty of food for both of you, Demaratus. Do you plan more than two nights?"

"I was hoping for one," he replied. "We will push hard today and see how far we get."

Amatista had arisen with them and made their breakfast. She joined them in the front yard. "There is a feel of rain, maybe late tonight. You will need shelter," she said.

A few high clouds, painted pink by the growing light of dawn, clung to the mountains to the north. It didn't have the look of rain to Demaratus, but Coventina's family knew these mountains and their ways, so he did not disagree. "We have a tent," he said.

Amatista scanned the sky. "It may not be enough. I would advise you to find a house to shelter in."

"We will look for one," said Demaratus, although he was not convinced there was any call for concern. The weather looked fine to him. He and Coventina embraced. "I will see you in Legio," he said, mounting Aura. The cavalryman mounted as well, and the party left at a brisk trot, Demaratus looking back and waving.

But Amatista was right and he was wrong. By late afternoon clouds began crowding the sky, and a cold, damp wind blew in from the north. They had passed several houses where they could have found shelter, but Demaratus had been sure that Coventina's sister was mistaken. By the time it was obvious that they were in for a wet night, they were in a part of the mountains that was devoid of people and houses. They camped in a dense thicket where they set up a tent, but the night was cold, wet, and uncomfortable. The only upside to the storm was that their misery gave them an early start and drove them to accelerate their push for Legio.

XI

Cassius looked over his uniform and tugged his sagum slightly to set it at just the right angle. He was a handsome young man, with dark, curly hair, and a thin white scar running down his left cheek. His phalarae, one of them brand new, were attached to his chain mail, and he wore a pugio blade on his right side. He had left his long spatha sword in his quarters. This was a social visit, not a raid. He tucked his helmet under his arm and rapped sharply on the door. Within a few minutes it opened to a middle-aged woman dressed in a workaday stolla.

"Cassius!" she said, throwing open her arms and flinging them around him. "How wonderful! We have not seen you since those awful Franks left for wherever they were going. Please, come in and meet your glorious commander's lovely niece."

The young cavalryman embraced her in return. "And how fares the mighty Legion of Women?" he said with a grin.

"Oh, well, well indeed. Come and say hello," she said, grabbing his arm and pulling him into the atrium. Several other women were seated around a table filled with honey cakes and wine. He recognized all of them, but could only come up with two names, that of the older sedate one, Cornelia, and the young talkative one, Poppaca. The names of the three others eluded him. There was an attractive young woman, tall, slim, with high cheekbones and large gray eyes, seated amidst the women. He assumed she was Marcus's niece.

"Look what I found at my door," said Vipsania. "The commander of our wonderful cavalry that freed our city from the invaders."

"Well, Vipsania, I had a little help," said Cassius. "Some of it right here in this domus."

Vipsania beamed.

"Cassius Cornelius, you are most welcome," said Cornelia rather formally.

He gave a short bow. "It is good to see the league has not disbanded. The Goths are troubling our Moesian frontier, and we thought we might send you to straighten matters out," he said, drawing a round of laughter and offers of wine.

"And this is Sabina Aquillius, our wonderful VII Legion commander's niece," said Vipsania. Sabina smiled shyly, nodding in greeting.

"Lady Aquillius," he said to her. "I have been asked by the authorities here in Tarraco to look in on you and discuss your forthcoming trip to Corduba."

"Will you be taking her?" asked Vipsania. "We were, this very minute, discussing what she should do."

Cassius put his helmet down and accepted a cup of wine. "That depends on what Lady Aquillius decides, Vipsania. There are at least two options to consider," he said.

"What would those be, commander?" asked Sabina.

"One way, Lady Aquillius, would be to take a ship south to Valentia," he said. "There is a road from there that takes you through the mountains to the Baetica Valley. Corduba is on the Baetis River. That would take a week by land, depending on how you traveled. Or you could do the trip by sea through the Pillars of Hercules to Gades on the Oceanus Atlanticus. From there you could take a boat that would carry you up the Baetis to Corduba. I confess I do not know how long that might take, but I suspect several days," he said. "I can find out that information for you."

"Will you travel with her?" asked a short, stout woman whom he now remembered was called Pacia.

"I am afraid I cannot," he said. "I am taking several recruits to Corduba, but we are going by land because I have purchased a small herd of horses. If Lady Aquillius chooses to go by land from Valentia, I can meet her and escort her from there."

"How long will it take you to get your horses to Valentia?" asked a thin woman who vaguely resembled a stork. Valeria? Cassius was not sure, so he did not address her directly. "It will take me three days to reach Valentia."

Vipsania wrinkled her nose. "Valentia smells like a big, dead fish," she said.

Cassius smiled. "They make garum there, Lady Aquillius. It does have a strong odor, but the city is quite attractive."

"If you hold your nose," threw in Pacia. "Is there not another way? Going by ship seems the easiest, but she would be by herself and have to make all those arrangements without any help."

"What is the trip by land like?" asked a plain-looking woman whom he overheard being called Annia.

"Quite nice," answered Cassius. "The road hugs the coast all the way to Valentia, then turns in and goes over the mountains. It is rich country, some of it not overpopulated."

"Where does one stay?" asked Pacia.

"That would depend," said Cassius. "There are comfortable inns in the towns and cities along the way, and citizens are required to offer the army lodging, although that is freely given these days."

"I should hope so," said Vipsania. "You saved us all from those awful barbarians."

"If Sabina were to accompany Cassius, she would be a lone woman among many men," put in Cornelia.

"Sounds delicious," put in Poppaca, biting into a honey cake. Cassius was not sure if the "delicious" referred to the cake or the men.

"Really, Poppaca," said Cornelia. "A young woman alone among all those men? That is just not proper."

"Oh, pish," said Poppaca, eyeing another honey cake. "Cassius is about as honorable a man as you can find, and he could show Sabina all sorts of interesting things. It would help to give her an understanding of our wonderful Hispania. And I don't see anything wrong with being a woman surrounded by all those men. I would do it in a moment."

Cornelia shook her head but said nothing.

Cassius looked at Sabina. "I think we should hear from Lady Aquillius," he said. "We have thrown a great many things at her without giving her much time to think about them."

But Sabina wanted nothing to do with "choices." She was feeling vulnerable, even in the midst of women who were caring for her. She did not want to make any more decisions or to make the arrangements that traveling by sea and riverboats would entail, and she suspected that Vipsania and the VII Legion could be relied on to make a lot of those things happen. But in the end, she would be alone. And even though she had just met him, Cassius seemed familiar, a direct link to her uncle.

"Will you teach me to ride?" she blurted out.

Cassius appeared taken aback. "Of course, Lady Aquillius," he replied.

Her question and Cassius's answer stirred up a storm of remarks. "How exciting!" "Improper!" "Dangerous!" and "An adventure!"

"Please, please," said Vipsania, waving her hands, "We need to have a calm discussion, and we need to hear from Sabina. Calm down everyone." When the room quieted, she asked, "Who would like to speak? I think it would be best to first hear what people want to say, then to call on Sabina after she has heard us out." She looked questioningly at the young woman, who nodded mutely.

Cornelia spoke first. "I think it is unseemly for a young woman to travel unchaperoned with a herd of males. It might raise a scandal, given that Sabina is the niece of our VII Legion's commander. I strongly oppose such a course." Cornelia had a quiet dignity about her, and Valeria and Vipsania looked approving.

"It is no scandal for a woman to travel under the protection of the VII Legion and officers of that legion, of which Cassius is one and an honored one at that," countered Poppaca. "We put our lives in their hands and they delivered us from bondage. This man," she said, indicating Cassius, "not only fought the Franks, but helped free our citizens from the clutches of the Mauri slave raiders. If there is a scandal here, it is in the minds of those who denigrate our fighting men. I, for one, am not among them." The speech left Pacia nodding in agreement.

There was a short silence, then Annia spoke. "One of the greatest things that ever happened to us was fighting back against the Franks. We live lives largely dictated by others, mainly men. They tell us what is proper, what is honor, what to wear, even what to think. But the League of Women was ours. And it was a great adventure, one that we will be able to tell our children and our grandchildren. It was an adventure in a life in which women are not allowed to have adventures. I do not know what Sabina wants to do, but if she chooses to ride all the way to Corduba amid a company of men, then I think we should celebrate her. It will be her adventure."

When she stopped there was dead silence. Finally, Sabina stood and looked around the room. "I cannot tell you how important it has been for me to be taken under your wing. I have not told you all of my story. I am not just visiting my uncle. I am also fleeing from an arranged marriage that would have been the death of me. Hispania is not a vacation, it is my refuge," she said, her eyes glistening. "I know you call me a woman, but it was not so long ago that I was just a child, playing with dolls." She stopped for a moment, wiping her eyes. "Well, I did give up dolls a long time ago, and instead fell in love with politics. But I do not want to be a mother, working at a loom, and keeping house. I am a terrible cook, and I have no patience with weaving. I would much rather read. Maybe I will do all of those things at some point in my life, but not now. I don't know what is the right thing to do, but for now I want to be only part grown-up. I want to make my own decisions, but I want someone to look after me. Does that make sense?"

She paused and looked around at everyone. "And if this band of men are even half as cute as their commander, I think it will be a pleasant adventure."

That comment set off a round of deep laughter. Even Vipsania, Valeria and Cornelia joined in. Cassius blushed but couldn't stop himself from laughing as well. "This is very much Marcus's niece," he thought to himself.

When the laughter died down, Cassius spoke up. "I can guarantee your safe passage, Lady Aquillius. My men and I will be your personal guards. We would be honored by your presence."

"Very gallant," interposed Vipsania. "When would this happen?"

"I am at your disposal, Lady Aquillius. I take it you have no familiarity with horses?" Cassius asked.

"None," she replied. "I have never sat on one. Is it hard?"

"It will be hard on your rear end," quipped Poppaca, which drew another round of laughter.

"No, it is not hard, and I will arrange for a special padded saddle, Lady Aquillius. Let's plan on a week of instruction before we start south," Cassius offered. "Is that acceptable?"

"Yes," agreed Sabina, "but Commander, you will have to stop calling me 'Lady Aquillius,' Just Sabina please. 'Lady' makes me feel like I was not successful in avoiding that arranged marriage."

He bowed. "So be it."

XII

❧

"It is a well laid-scheme, sir," said Demaratus. The signifer sat on a campstool in front of a long table piled with scrolls.

"How so?" asked Marcus.

"They recorded a drop-off in the ore content, so that they could say they were producing less gold than they had before. They added more slaves to the workforce, supposedly to produce more ore to make up for the reduced gold content, then skimmed off the extra gold and never recorded it," said Demaratus. "The scheme would have gone unnoticed if Sextus had not intercepted that shipment."

"If there are no records, how do we prove it?" asked Marcus.

"Well, Flavius took care of that, sir," assured Demaratus.

"How?" asked Marcus.

"He arrested one of the mine foremen, sat him near a brazier, glowing white-hot and filled with several hooks and blades, and explained what would happen to the man if he didn't tell Flavius what he wanted to know," said Demaratus. "A bit crude, but quite effective."

"Did he put those things to use?" asked Marcus. Torture—while a normal part of Roman life—always made him uncomfortable.

"Didn't need to, sir. Flavius can be most persuasive. The foreman laid out the whole scheme, which apparently has been going on for almost two years. There was a shipment of gold every two months," said Demaratus.

"Why wasn't the drop-off in gold production brought to our attention?" asked Marcus.

"There was very little actual drop-off, sir. The production by the extra slaves made up for the gold that was skimmed off for Gaul. That was the clever part. Rome was satisfied with the gold it was getting, so no one really looked very closely at the operation."

Marcus did some calculations in his head. "If we assume that the shipment that we intercepted was typical of the amount shipped out every two months, that means there were close to 12 of those shipments before we got wind of the scheme."

"Yes, sir. That's a lot of gold," said the signifer.

"Enough to pay for several legions," said Marcus.

"Certainly enough to get them to ignore an army of Franks marching on Tarraco," added Demaratus. "And given that the Frankish army tried to kill us, I take this all rather personally."

"This will put a spike into that scheme," said Marcus.

"Maybe," said Demaratus.

"What are you thinking, signifer?" asked Marcus.

"I doubt the enterprise we think is afoot here, sir, is totally reliant on Hispania gold. If you are right about Britannia being involved, then they must have another major source of gold. I am not saying that cutting off their supply from Hispania's mines won't have an impact on their plans, but it seems to me that the scheme is much larger than that," said Demaratus. "And if it has been going on for the last two years, it is probably much further along than we thought."

Marcus's clerk knocked to announce Flavius. The optio entered and looked around the room. "Been busy, have we?" he said to Demaratus.

"No more than you, optio," replied Demaratus. "Your persuasive skills are what made my analysis of their records possible."

"Aye, nothing like a hot poker to jar a man's memory," said Flavius, removing his helmet and unhitching his sagum.

Marcus and Demaratus filled him in on the number of shipments involved and how long they had been going on. Flavius whistled. "Whoever they are, sir," he said, addressing Marcus. "They are further along than we thought."

The legate nodded. "It presents us with a problem," he said.

"Which is, sir?" asked Demaratus.

"The VII Legion's present position," he answered.

Flavius frowned. "I'm not sure I follow your, sir."

Marcus pushed the scrolls to one side and laid out a blank piece of papyrus. "Think about the province, Flavius." He drew a rough sketch of Hispania as a triangle, the widest part in the north, narrowing to the south. He added a mark on the northwest portion of the triangle. "This is Legio. We are stationed here for two major reasons—the restive Lusitanians and the formerly troublesome Celts. Yet the more compelling interests are gold and the nearby port of Brigantium. While Hispania's population centers are to the south and the east.

He drew dots in the eastern part of the triangle. "Here are Barcino, Emporiae and Tarraco, the major ports on the Mare Internum." He then moved to the bottom of the triangle and drew a line from Olisipo, near the Oceanus Atlanticus, to Corduba at the eastern edge of the edge of the Baetis Valley, then south to Gades and the Pillars of Hercules. "And this is the richest part of the province, where most of our food and silver come from."

Flavius and Demaratus looked over the sketch. "All right, I follow that," said Flavius, "but why are we out of place?"

"If I wanted to take this province, optio, I would march a legion from Norba in Gaul straight down the east coast to Valentia," he said, making a mark near the middle part of the triangle, "then march inland to the Baetis River and take Corduba. That would put the major ports in the east and the agricultural center of the province in their hands. The VII Legion would be isolated in Legio. We would control the gold, but we can safely assume Hispania is not its sole source for those behind this scheme, whoever they are. The VII Legion would hold a region with minimal resources and a small population." He stopped and stared at the triangle. "We would be rich and quite irrelevant," he said softly.

No one said anything for quite some time, trying to absorb Marcus's scenario and link it to the crude map. Finally, Flavius spoke up.

"What do we do?" he asked. "Is there any way to stop it?"

"Not from Legio, Flavius," Marcus answered. "So, the answer is that the VII Legion has to relocate."

"Would Roma let us do that?" asked Flavius. "You may convince the signifer and me, sir, but I am not so sure that's how our superiors will see it in Carthago Nova, let alone Roma. And where would we go?"

Marcus tapped the map at the head of the Baetica Valley. "Corduba," he said.

Flavius looked doubtful. "They might send more than one legion, sir. The VII Legion is a good one, but I am not sure we could defeat more than one legion."

"Look at the map again, optio," said Marcus. "There is a line you can draw from Valentia in the east to Olisipo in the west. There are only a few roads leading into that area, and the main one is the Via Augusta that runs from the border of Gaul, through Valentia, to Carthago Nova. There is also a road that runs inland from Valentia and branches off to Corduba. The main road goes through Emerita Augusta and on to Olisipo."

"All right," said Flavius, looking at the map. "So what?"

"Valentia sits on the Via Augusta. Whoever holds the city controls the road," said Marcus.

"Could Valentia withstand a siege?" asked Demaratus.

"Could a legion, or even two legions, take Valentia?" asked Marcus. "I think not. The city is a port, and any successful siege would need to blockade it by sea. But Roma controls the navy. I know our signifer doesn't think much of the Roman navy, but I suspect it has far greater resources than any navy Gaul could put together. If the city can't be starved out, the legions would have to take it by storm, and we can feed in reinforcements any time we like. I think that Demaratus would agree that controlling the seas gives us a decided advantage."

Demaratus nodded. "It would. But whose side is Valentia on?"

"Good question, signifer. We don't know that, but we have

worked before with the auxiliary legion that Valentia and Carthargo Nova sent us to fight the Franks," Marcus said.

"As I recall, their commander, whose name I forget, wasn't exactly friendly," said Flavius. "And how do we know where Valentia and Carthago Nova stand on this matter?"

"Publius Marius," answered Marcus, supplying the forgotten name. "He wasn't friendly, but Septimius Granius, who commanded the auxiliary legion from Caeseraugusta, was. We do not know where those cities stand. There may be people on both sides. But that also defines what we need to do, which is to line up our allies and isolate our opponents. That starts by moving the VII Legion."

"There are a lot of moving parts here, sir," said Flavius.

"I know, optio, I know. And we might fail. But if we can get Valentia to resist any efforts to move it out from under Roma, then we will have an ally sitting on the main supply line of any legion moving south. Even if they don't put the city under siege, they will have to keep a substantial force on watch. It will dissipate their forces."

"There are a lot of ifs in this plan, sir, but I can't see an alternative," said Demaratus.

Studying the triangular map, Flavius nodded. "I agree, but those 'ifs' are not minor. Have you thought about how to begin, sir?"

"I have, optio. Aelia is currently trying to find out where the most powerful and wealthy families stand. That will be crucial. It's not only soldiers that we need to recruit, comrades. We must rally the support of the civilian population."

Demaratus put his finger on the western edge of the triangle.

"What about the Lusitanians? Might they throw in their lot with a breakaway empire? They certainly bear Roma no love."

"We will need Cassius in this," said Marcus. "If we can convince the Lusitanians to remain neutral, that might be enough. But you raise a good point, signifer. What will be the reactions of people like the Lusitanians and the Celts? I don't know, but we need to find out. Cassius can do that for his people."

"And Coventina could sound out the Cantabrians," said Demaratus. "But they are just one of several tribes in the north, and they, too, bear the Empire no great love."

"Our task is daunting, I agree," said Marcus. "Which means we must begin to find out who are our allies and who are our opponents."

"Demaratus," said Marcus, "I suggest you take a few days to return to Coventina's village to let her know what we are thinking. If she is willing, she could sound out her people's thinking, and maybe even that of some of the other tribes."

"They all seem to be fighting one another, sir, so that may not be easy, but I will ask Coventina's advice," said Demaratus.

"Flavius," said Marcus, "I need you to begin thinking about how to move the VII Legion south. I will inform our superiors in Carthago Nova."

"What will you tell them?" asked Flavius.

"I will tell them straightaway what we are doing and why," he answered.

"Do you think that is wise, sir?" asked Flavius. "We don't even know if we can trust them."

"If we can't, optio, then we have already lost."

XIII

Marcus Postumus surveyed the battlefield from horseback. The governor and imperial legate was no stranger to war and its consequences, but even he was sobered by the slaughter. The invaders lay in piles, thousands and thousands of them, almost beyond counting. His men were moving through the carnage, killing those who were still alive and systematically stripping the dead of torcs, bracelets and rings. He had two cohorts guarding the enormous train of loot that the Juthungian had managed to keep after their defeat by Emperor Gallienus at Mediolanum.

That had been their downfall, of course. Publius Gallienus had bested them, but the Germanic tribe had retreated in good order, and the Romans—licking their wounds from the battle—had not pursued. Postumus had caught them laden with loot and slaves, their warriors strung out for several miles. It was not much of a fight, more of an execution. The governor had fallen on them with three legions—the I Minerva, XXX Ulpia Victrix and VII Augusta, plus cavalry—and the fight was over in a few hours.

His adjutant Rufus Servius appeared, his horse picking its way through the debris of battle. "Sir, the commanders of the cohorts would like to know what you intend to do with the seized baggage."

Postumus was silent for a moment, thinking. "Move it north."

"North, sir?" asked Rufus. "Shouldn't we hold it here until Gallienus makes contact with us?"

"Publius Gallienus lost this loot, and my legions won it back. It seems only fair that they should share it among themselves," said Postumus. "Where are Tribune Annius Fabius and Prefect Atticus Aemilius?"

"I will fetch them, sir," said Rufus, turning his horse and trotting back toward where the loot was being collected.

Postumus sat quietly on his horse. He had not intended to break from Rome so soon, but circumstances had ambushed him. Two days ago, he had found out that Emperor Decius and his eldest son, Herennius, had been killed by Goths in some swamp he could not name, and that Decius's younger son had died of the plague currently stalking Roma. Trebonianus Gallus was emperor, but in name only. In essence, there was no one in charge. It was the perfect time to move. And the loot the Juthungian had dropped into his hands would help secure the allegiance of his legions.

The governor watched a legionnaire dispatch a wounded tribe member, who pleaded for his life. "Well, if you had stayed home, you wouldn't have died on some nameless meadow in southern Gaul," he thought.

He was turning back toward his command tent when the tribune and prefect rode up.

"Congratulations, sir," said the tribune, saluting him.

"More like butchering sheep than a battle, Annius, but it is a gift we cannot pass up," Postumus demurred.

"Sir?" asked the tribune.

Postumus continued walking his horse, with the prefect and tribune flanking him. "It is time to move, gentlemen. The emperor is dead and has no heirs. A man known to few sits in the Roma palace. The Empire will be looking to the east and the Danubian frontier where the Goths now threaten Moesia, not to Gaul. And we have suddenly acquired a great deal of wealth that we can use to cement the loyalty of our legions."

"Have you decided to declare the Gallic Empire?" asked the prefect.

"Not yet, Atticus. First, we move the recovered wealth north to Colonia Claudia Ara Agrippinesium. I don't want to distract Roma from their focus on Dacia. After all, the invaders have been defeated in our province. But we must accelerate our plans in Hispania and Britannia and be prepared to move," said Postumus. "Second, I want to meet with the legate of the VI Legion Victrix from Norba. That troublesome VII Legion Hispania Gemina in Legio has cut off our gold supply from the province. If it doesn't join our cause, it must be dealt with."

"Our cause?" ventured the tribune.

Postumus halted his horse and turned in his saddle. "The Gallic Empire will ensure the northern borders against any and all invaders. We have no designs on Roma. Indeed, we see ourselves as allies. Roma need never fear the Goths, the Franks, or the Alamanni while we guard the frontier, and we will not impede trade across our borders," he said. "That, gentlemen, is our cause."

Reaching his tent, Postumus dismounted while a slave held the horse's reins. A cloud of aides and officers surrounded him, some offering congratulations, others asking for orders. The governor disappeared into his tent.

The prefect looked at the tribune. "I am not sure Roma will see it that way."

Annius shook his head. "They will not, and this will eventually come down to a test of arms. I hope we are ready."

XIV

Sabina stared at the horse. And the horse stared back in the expressionless way of her species.

"What do I do?" she asked Cassius.

"Pet its nose," said Cassius.

They were standing in a fenced corral. Sabina was dressed in pants and a wool shirt belted at the waist. Tentatively, she reached out her hand. The horse sneezed, and she quickly withdrew it. "Did I do something wrong?" she asked.

"No. Horses sneeze, just like people. Put your hand on her nose," he repeated.

She slowly extended her hand until it touched the horse's nose, which was surprisingly soft. She patted it, but the horse did not appear to pay any attention. Glancing at Cassius, she asked, "What now?"

"You are both getting to know each other, Sabina. Horses are used to having someone in charge. When they are in the wild that is normally a stallion, but a strong mare can also lead. So, stroke the horse's forehead and then scratch behind her ears. Show her you are friendly," directed Cassius.

Sabina stroked the horse's forehead and reached up to scratch behind an ear. The horse tossed her head and Sabina quickly withdrew her hand. "Did I anger it?"

"No. Horses toss their heads, it is what they do. Now come around and stroke her neck and put your hand on her back," said Cassius.

"It's a her?" she asked.

"Yes, a mare. She is quite gentle and I think you will become good friends. You just have to show her the way," he said.

Sabina had seen horses, but not up so close. They were big, very big, and she wasn't sure why a big animal like this would pay any heed to what she thought or did. But Cassius said horses like to have someone in charge, and he clearly knew a lot about horses. So, she took a deep breath and began stroking the horse, which continued to stand quietly. When she reached the rear end, she stopped. "Would she kick me?" she asked.

"Not unless she was surprised or angry. Stroking the horse prevents her from being surprised," said Cassius.

"How do I know if she is angry?" she inquired.

Cassius thought, "Well, if she kicks you, you can be pretty sure she's angry," but he kept that to himself, resisting the urge to tease her. Pointing at the horse's head, he said, "Look at her ears. What are they doing?"

Sabina looked at the ears, which were standing straight up and turning back and forth, as if the horse were listening. "I'm not sure. How would I know she is angry?"

"If a horse is angry or frightened, she flattens her ears. If she flattens her ears, talk to her in a calm voice and stroke her until the ears stand straight up again. And don't stand behind her while they are flat," explained Cassius.

As Sabina continued to stroke the horse, which turned her head and looked at her. "Is that good, Cassius?" she asked.

"Very. She is looking to see who you are. She is curious about you. She is used to people riding her, but she doesn't know your scent and she doesn't recognize you. She is watching you. So, act confident and kind. That always works with horses," said Cassius.

While Sabina stroked the horse, Cassius went to fetch a saddle and a blanket, which he put on the horse and cinched them. He slipped a bridle over the horse's head and a bit into her mouth. Pulling over a stool to the horse's side, he said, "Now let's take a ride."

Sabina flinched a little. "I have never been on a horse before."

"And your horse has never carried you, so you start even," he said. He helped her onto the stool, then onto the horse's back. She panicked for a moment, fearful that she might fall off. But the Roman saddle had two horns at the rear and two adjustable ones in front, securing the rider like four small arms, which made that unlikely. Holding the reins, Cassius walked the horse and Sabina around the ring.

At first, she gasped and clung onto the two horns in the front, but she relaxed after several circles, even as she noted that the ground looked a long way off. The gait was pleasant and she began to feel more secure, leaning forward and stroking the horse's neck.

After a few turns, Cassius handed her the reins. Her apprehension came back. "What do I do?" she asked.

"If you pull back on the reins, the horse will stop. If you pull them to one side, the horse will go in that direction. If you loosen the reins and give the horse a gentle kick with your heels, she will walk. Always pull the reins gently. If you pull hard, it will hurt her and she won't respond. Try that," he said.

She loosened the reins and bumped her heels on the horse's flank, and the mare started walking. Startled, Sabina pulled back on the reins and the horse stopped.

"See?" said Cassius. "Now try that again, but this time don't pull back on the reins. Just pull them to one side."

She tapped her heels once again on the horse's flank, and the mare began to walk. Gently she pulled the reins to one side and the horse turned. It was a little scary, but also exhilarating. To make a huge animal like this do what you want? She walked the horse around the ring, turning her in circles and finally stopped.

"Oh, Cassius, that was fun!" she said.

He smiled. "Yes, it is, and a very useful skill. Now let me help you off," he said, but she slid off the saddle herself. "Well done," he said. "You are a natural."

"What now?" asked Sabina, flushed-faced with a huge grin on her face.

"We are going to get back on the horse and practice some more. And tomorrow you and I are going riding, and I will teach you gaits," he said.

"Gaits?" she queried.

"You have been walking the horse, but horses have lots of other gaits. Like a trot, and a lope, and finally a gallop. We are going to learn those things. But before you get back on, give her this," he said, handing her a large slice of a pear.

She took the pear and put it near the horse's nose. The mare promptly clamped down on her fingers. She gave a small cry and dropped the pear. "She bit me, Cassius. She must be angry."

He laughed. "No, she didn't bite you. If she had, you would know. She was just trying to get the pear and your fingers were in the way. This is my fault. I should have told you to place the pear on your open hand and feed her that way. Try it."

Carefully, she picked up the piece of pear, brushed it off, and laid it flat on her palm. The horse sniffed it, then took the pear without touching her fingers. "Oh, it worked," she said.

"Yes, my fault for not warning you. And you have made a good start to a friendship. She is now going to associate you with slices of pear," said Cassius.

"Oh," she said, stroking the mare's cheek. "What's her name?"

"She doesn't have one, Sabina. That is up to you," he said.

She looked the horse over critically. "Well, she is red, so I will call her Rosa. Is that all right?" she asked.

"Rosa it is. So, let's get Sabina and Rosa to know one another a little better."

For the next week, Sabina and Rosa got to know each other. Sabina always fed her pears or apples, and Cassius thought they made a good pair. Sabina was fine with the trot, but slightly more anxious with the lope. But while initially frightened of the gallop, she found it exhilarating.

After one quarter-mile gallop, they pulled up, both horses blowing and pacing. "Sabina," said Cassius, "you really are a natural. In a week you have become quite a good rider."

She grinned. "It's because I have the best horse in Hispania."

He grinned back. "That is where good horsemanship begins."

"But I'm not a man. I'm a girl," she said, driving her heels into Rosa and loping off toward the stables.

Cassius shook his head. "That is one surprising young woman," he thought.

* * *

Sabina's rear end hurt, though less than it had at the beginning of the trip, because Cassius had added padding to her saddle after the first day. She was gradually adjusting to long hours on horseback and was quite taken with the rolling countryside south of Tarraco. She had spent almost her whole life either in her family's domus or jostling through the crowded streets of Roma. The feel of open space was new, and she was growing attached to the sense of freedom it gave her.

Her pants scandalized several members of the Women's League, but it was clearly the right choice of garment. Plus, she found that she rather enjoyed scandalizing people. It made her feel very grown-up. The weather had been warm, with just a suggestion of chill in the late afternoon. In any case, she spent her nights at either an inn or one of the many villas that lined the road.

Only once had the party spent the night in the open. A midafternoon storm had blown up, and Cassius was not sure they could make it to the next small town. So, they pulled off the road, picketed the horses, and set out tents. In the end, the storm resolved into a few sprinkles, which they waited out, sheltering under an enormous oak. They had cooked over open fires and, after eating, Sabina wandered off into a meadow, sat on a tree stump, and watched the stars appear as the light faded. At one point Cassius came to check on her. She assured him she was fine, telling him she rarely saw the stars in Roma because the air there was thick with smoke. Here, they glittered like fine jewels spread on a brocade of black silk.

She watched Cassius return to the camp. She liked him. She had initially thought him a little stiff, but soon decided that he was just being careful. It must not be easy to be in charge of his commander's niece, and he was leaning over backwards to be 'proper.' On the third day, Sabina turned to him and said, "Cassius, have I done something to offend you?"

"No, of course not, Sabina," he said, looking flustered. "Why would you think that?"

She smiled at him. "Because you rarely say anything unless I ask you something, and because you look as if you would rather be somewhere else."

Cassius sighed. Turning to his men, he told them to dismount and take their horses to a nearby meadow. When the men had dispersed, he slipped off his helmet and said, "I am sorry, Sabina. No, I do not wish to be someplace else, and you have done nothing to annoy me. Indeed, I am deeply impressed with how you're weathering this journey. You never complain, and you have become a very competent rider." He paused for a moment. "If I have behaved in any way that is lacking in respect, then I apologize."

"I am not looking for respect, Cassius, I am looking for

companionship. I am alone in this land. The few people I know are a long way from here, so silence is not my friend," she said.

"Of course, of course," he said. "It is just, ah, well it is kind of complex, and..."

"Complex because I am the niece of your commander, and I am a girl surrounded by 31 men?" she asked. "That seems simple to me," she said with a grin.

Cassius laughed. "Yes. I just am not sure how to act."

"Well, act like we are friends. Tell me about the trees and the rocks, what those mountains off to our right are called, why people seem more friendly here than in Italia, and how you became a cavalryman," she said. "If this is going to be an adventure, then let's make it one."

Cassius nodded. "Consider me your friend, Sabina. I will tell you about the trees and mountains. People are friendly because you are the niece of a hero," he said, adding, "and also maybe because Hispania is a province and people here are not quite as busy as they are in Italia, so they have more time for guests."

"You said you were a commander, Cassius. Is this an ala?" she asked.

"No, Sabina, you are riding with a turmae. That means 30 men. An ala is made up of 16 turmae, or around 480 men. I actually command two ala."

"So, you are sort of like a legate," she said.

"Not really. A legate like your uncle commands 5,400 men. An ala is more like a cohort, which has about the same number of men."

"Oh, and one more thing," Sabina said. "Why don't your men look at me?"

"Uh, well, because I told them that if they made you uncomfortable their lives would get really difficult," he said sheepishly.

Sabina chuckled. "All these men and no one looks at me. What's a girl to think?"

Cassius shook his head. "You are much like your uncle, Sabina," he said with a smile.

After their talk, the mood improved. Cassius opened up and the men went from silence to the kind of banter one would expect from a group of young men. Some even acknowledged—respectfully—Sabina, bringing her water or offering to rub down her horse after a long day. In turn, Sabina asked about their lives, where they came from, and why they joined the cavalry. At first the men were a bit stiff—obviously remembering their commander's admonition—but Sabina was friendly and obviously interested, not at all what they expected. It didn't hurt that she was also very attractive.

The towns and cities rolled by until they came to Valentia, where Sabina spent an entire day at the public baths. After a night of good food and a soft bed, she met up with Cassius in the city's forum.

"You are well?" he asked.

She sighed. "I love our journey, Cassius, but a real bath, good food, and linen sheets are a gift from the gods."

He chuckled. "I doubt you would get a contrary opinion from any of us, Sabina." He then asked, "Are you ready to continue?"

"I am, but come and sit and tell me what's ahead," she said, indicating a low wall fronting the street.

"We are on the last leg of the trip, Sabina. Just south of here we'll take a road that branches off to the west. It goes over the mountains and then turns south to the headwaters of the Baetis River," he said. "We will follow the river west until it reaches Corduba. I think it'll be three or four days, depending on weather."

"What is the country like?" she asked.

"It is a part of the province that still has the feel of Hispania before the Greeks, Carthaginians and Romans arrived. There are not a lot of people and few inns until we reach the upper Baetis River. We will have to camp in the open for several nights," he said.

"Lovely," she said. "I really enjoyed that night we camped in the meadow. I don't think I have ever been as aware of the stars as that night."

"Well, I can promise you lots of stars, Sabina," said Cassius.

* * *

The first day out of Valentia was much like the country they had already traversed, but on the morning of the next day the road began to climb and travelers thinned out. There were a few inns, but they were uninviting ones, small, dark, and offering little more than a straw pallet or a rope-spring bed. Cassius and Sabina agreed that camping was a better idea.

Cassius had brought two campstools along. After a day in the saddle, Sabina had grown to appreciate this, and the two of them sat companionably by a small fire.

"Cassius," said Sabina, "You are a Lusitanian, and I am not sure what that is."

"I am a Lusitanian," he answered. "We are horse people in the province's west."

"Did you come from someplace before?" she asked.

He shook his head. "No, we have always been in this land. We were here when the Greeks came, followed by the Carthaginians, and then the Romans."

"What do you mean about being 'horse people'?" asked Sabina.

"We were not farmers or traders, although we sold horses," he said. "We did not have cities, just villages. And we moved around a good deal, because horses constantly need new pastures. We also raised sheep, but not many because they are not easy on the land. If you graze horses, a pasture returns in a few months. With sheep it may be a year or more before you can use it again."

"Did you grow up traveling around like we are doing?" she asked.

"No, I grew up in a village, although my family raised and traded horses," he answered. He poured two cups of wine, but Sabina wrinkled her nose at hers.

"Sour stuff," she said, handing it back.

Cassius laughed. "Acetum is indeed sour, Sabina. It is said that they feed it to us solders to ensure that we will not over-indulge," he said. "It doesn't work. Men will hold their noses and drink it by the amphora."

"If you raised horses, why did your family live in a village?" she asked, bringing the topic back to Cassius.

He was silent for a time. "Because they took most of our land," he finally answered.

"The Greeks and Carthaginians and Romans?" she asked.

"The Greeks were not interested in our land. They were

tradesmen, so they stayed close to ports and rivers, but they did buy our horses. Once they tried to tax us, but that didn't work out," he said.

"Why?"

"It is hard to tax people who don't stay in one place," he answered. "And when they tried to use force, it failed."

"Tell me more, Cassius," she said.

"Do you know about military matters, Sabina?" he asked.

"Probably more than you think," she answered, "and they don't bore me."

"The Greeks invented a military formation called a phalanx, Sabina," he explained. "It is a bloc of soldiers with closely locking shields and long spears. It is powerful and difficult to defeat, but it is slow. My people could not defeat it, but the Greeks could never catch us, and if they broke the phalanx, they were vulnerable to our cavalry. We had several battles. but very few people got hurt on either side, and the Greeks finally gave up in frustration. And their cavalry stinks," he added.

Sabina laughed. "It is a wonderful image, Cassius. A big mass of slow-moving soldiers flailing about trying to catch the wind."

He grinned. "Something like that."

"Is that what happened with the Carthaginians?" she asked.

"No," he said. "Carthaginian cavalry is very good, as the Romans discovered. We fought them. Sometimes we won, sometimes they won. But they soon focused on the Romans and lost interest in our lands. When Rome destroyed Carthage, my people rejoiced. They were a hard enemy."

"And then the Romans came?" she said.

Cassius nodded. "Yes. And we could not defeat them."

"Why? Did they have good cavalry?" she asked.

"No, Romans are not much for cavalry, although that is beginning to change. The Romans do not fight in big, slow-moving blocs of soldiers. A legionnaire is not as agile as a horse, but almost. And the Romans were not distracted. Behind those legions came roads and cities. They were relentless. And they tricked us."

"How?" she asked.

"The Roman general, Sulpicius Galba, tried to conquer us, but we fought him to a standstill. He sent emissaries offering us peace and land, and invited our people to a great banquet. When everyone was drunk, the Romans fell upon us. Those they did not massacre, they sold into slavery. Our people were defeated by treachery, and we have never forgiven them," he said.

"And then they took your lands," she said.

He nodded. "They said no one owned the lands, because among my people the land was owned by everyone. So, they took it, and we did not have enough land to graze our herds. We had to move to villages, and some of us took up farming instead."

"Was that such a bad thing?" she asked.

"It was not our choice, Sabina. We were forced to become farmers, and we were not very skilled at it. And good pasture land is not necessarily good farming land. We are not comfortable in villages," he said. He paused for a long moment. "We miss the stars."

"I am sorry, Cassius," she said, placing her hand on his arm. "I must seem an ignorant young woman to you."

"No, not at all, Sabina. First, you are one of the few Romans who has ever shown any interest in our history. And, second, this happened hundreds of years ago, hardly something you bear any responsibility for."

"Why do you fight for us, Cassius?" she asked.

"You do not ask easy questions, Sabina Aquillius," he said quietly.

"I am sorry if I offended you," she said, drawing back.

"You did not," he said, "but it is a question I don't have an easy answer for." He took a drink from his cup and looked at the fire. Sabina remained silent. Finally, he looked up.

"I joined the cavalry partly because it was a way to help out my family," he said. "There was not enough land, and competition for grazing was intense. Only a few could make a living at it. So, I joined because it meant a regular wage for something I loved, riding and taking care of horses."

He looked off toward where the men were camped out. "But then my people went to war to protect the little land that was left to them. And I was on the side that was fighting against them," he said. "I don't even know if I can go home, or what my reception would be among my family. Would I be the fourth son, the boy that could talk to horses and ride anything on four legs, or just another Roman oppressor?"

He threw another small log on the fire and spun the cup in his hand. "In many ways, Sabina, I am a man without a people. I am a citizen of the Empire, but a Lusitanian, a member of a tribe that destroyed a century of the VII Legion. My home is no longer in the meadows of the land where I grew up, but in the army, which doesn't much care who you are or where you came from, just whether you can follow orders and wield a sword."

Sabina put her hand to her throat. "I cannot imagine how

difficult that must be, Cassius. My silly worries seem so trivial next to yours."

"It is not a small thing to go out into the world alone, Sabina. At your age, I was still a child surrounded by family. You have chosen to resist tradition, which is hardly trivial. And you are a Roman woman, not exactly a status with much power or authority. I think what you are doing takes great courage."

She leaned across the fire and touched his cheek. "Thank you," she said softly. "But will you go home?"

"I don't know," he said. "When I leave Corduba I will go to Capera, where I have a cousin I am close to. I will consult with him. But my people don't have kings or emperors. There is no one leader. Finding out what they all think will not be simple."

"Why are you interested in what they think, Cassius?" she asked.

"I want to find out what they would do if there was a civil war," he said.

"What?" she said, sitting up.

"Your uncle has not spoken with you about this matter?" he asked.

She shook her head.

"I may have misspoken, Sabina," he said, looking suddenly uncomfortable.

She smiled. "Well, if I may use a metaphor consistent with our journey, Cassius, since the horse is now out of the corral, you might as well tell me about it. I also know how to keep secrets," she assured him.

He smiled. "Not a metaphor that would have come to mind a few weeks ago."

"No," she acknowledged. "Please go on."

Cassius outlined what Marcus had told him about the possibility of a civil war when the legate had first returned from Roma. It is why he had been ordered to sound out the Lusitanians. When he finished, Sabina nodded. "That explains some things," she said.

"Like what?" he asked.

"Like how that Frankish army got to Hispania," she told him.

Cassius looked startled. "You knew about that?"

"It was the talk of the Senate for a while," she said.

"You know what the Roman Senate talks about?" he marveled.

"Yes. It is my favorite thing. I sit in the forum and listen to people talk. Senators are free with their opinions and don't pay any attention to a little girl standing close by and admiring cloaks or necklaces," she said. She frowned. "And it also makes sense why Uncle Marcus got appointed legate."

Cassius looked at the sea. "It does? Wasn't he appointed because he was the best man for the job?"

"Oh, being good at something doesn't have a whole lot to do with being appointed to an office, Cassius. It is all about whether or not you will be useful to the people appointing you," she said distractedly, still thinking about the implications of what Cassius had just told her. "Of course, Uncle Marcus is the best person for the job, but they appointed him because he is loyal. They know this because that Frankish army was supposed to destroy the VII Legion, and that's the legion he commands. Why would someone try to destroy the VII Legion? Only because it is loyal to the Empire, as is he. So, ipso facto, the Empire appoints him legate because he will keep the VII Legion loyal." She looked up and smiled. "It is all so simple."

Cassius shook his head. "Those senators had no idea, did they?"

"No. You know, Cassius, one of the most dangerous things in the world is a woman who pays attention," she said.

XV

Tribune Publius Felix of the VII Legion Hispania paced back and forth under a large oak tree just off the Via Augusta. His aide, Servius Salonius, held their horses off to one side. The tribune had been in contact with the VI Legion Victrix in Norba for the past year, and he hoped this meeting would finalize the plot to break Gaul, Germania, Hispania, and Britannia away from Roma. Publius had been promised a high office—exactly what was not yet determined—in the new Gallic Empire, plus a considerable quantity of gold.

"They are late," he complained, to which Servius didn't respond, since there was nothing he could do about it. The two had been waiting for over two hours, and there was no sign of the men they would be meeting.

Finally, the aide ventured that it was hard to be exact when people were coming all the way from Norba.

"When I want your opinion, I will ask for it," snapped the tribune. But almost as soon as he finished his remark, Servius pointed at the road. "That could be them, sir," he said. Two distant figures had topped a small hill, but they were too far off to identify.

Publius stopped pacing, but he was tense as the riders approached. "No uniforms," observed Servius.

"I have eyes," said the tribune. "The men we are meeting would not be in uniform. That would raise too many questions, like what are members of the VI Legion Victrix doing in Hispania?"

Eventually the two men arrived. Neither party initially said anything, then one of the arrivals turned and looked around him.

"We came alone," said Publius.

"One can't be too careful these days," said the man who'd been surveying the landscape. Turning back to Publius, he said, "I am Tacitus Agrippa, Tribune of the VI Victrix, and this is Prefect Atticus Aemilius."

"Publius Felix, Tribune of the VII Hispania Gemina," he replied, not bothering to introduce his aide.

Both riders slid off their horses. Atticus groaned and stretched his back. "I am not used to three long days on horseback," he said.

"It's good for you," said Tacitus. "Everyone is going to have to toughen up in the months ahead." Turning to Publius, he asked the tribune, "What is the status of the VII Legion?"

"It is in Legio," said Publius.

"All of it?" asked Tacitus.

"There is a century each in Barcino and Tarraco, but otherwise the legion is at its homebase."

"Auxiliaries?"

"There is a legion at Caesaraugusta and Valentia, but they are small and mostly they repair roads and irrigation systems," he answered. "And one of the legion's commanders is an ally."

"I heard they fought those Franks," said Tacitus. "Seems like they can do more than fix roads."

"The VII did most of the fighting," said Publius impatiently.

"And I take it the VII Legion is not of your mind," said Atticus.

Publius hesitated. "No. But I don't see how that is a problem. The VII is off in the west guarding mountains. A legion could cross the border and march all the way to Corduba before the VII could try and stop them."

"Emporiae, Barcino, and Tarraco are reliable?" asked Atticus.

"Emporiae and Barcino will join us with great enthusiasm. Tarraco is a little more complex," the tribune replied.

"Explain complex," demanded Tacitus.

"Tarraco is much in debt to the VII Legion, and our legate is a local hero. Most of the population feels much the same way, including some of the leading political figures in the city. But several wealthy merchant families are supportive, and I have made arrangements to remove anyone who is not with us," explained Publius. "In the end, Tarraco will join us."

Tacitus nodded. "You see, tribune, I have a problem. If we march south to take Corduba, the VII Legion can march east and cut to the Via Augusta. We would be left in the south with no line of supplies. That concerns me a lot."

"The VII will have its own supply problems, Tacitus," said Publius. "Our eastern cities will be barred to them, and if they choose to lay siege on one of them, it will take time, enough time for another legion to march to our aid. Then the VII will be caught between two forces. They can either retreat or be destroyed."

"There are a lot of 'ifs' there, tribune. What 'other legion' do you refer to? This legate of the VII is a clever fellow. He out-smarted the Franks, didn't he? So, we are a little less confident about this than you are," said Tacitus.

"Tribune," said Publius, "if you march on Emporiae, the VII will have to commit itself. If it moves east to confront you, then you can destroy them. If it stays in Legio, it will be out of the fight and by the time it moves, all the major cities in the northeast will be yours. In any case, I don't think the VII will stay in Legio permanently. I think it may move south to defend Corduba, where we have less support," he said, adding, "I don't think this will be a problem. We will watch what the VII Legion does and inform you immediately."

"It sounds risky," said Atticus.

"Of course it is risky," said Publius. "Everything worth doing is a risk. Roman Emperor Gallienus could march north from Italia and defeat Postumus. Postumus might die of the plague that has already claimed the late Decius's son. Postumus might fall off a horse and break his neck. If you want something risk-free, go buy a farm and grow crops. Then the only risk you have is the weather."

Atticus nodded. "A fair statement of the matter, tribune. But you cannot count on extra legions. We have no doubt but that Gallienius will eventually confront us, and we will need all of the legions we have to defend ourselves. You will have the VI Legion from Norba and whatever forces you can mobilize on your own. Can you make do?"

Publius shrugged. "Do we have a choice?"

"You do not," confirmed Tacitus.

Publius signaled his aide, who brought the two horses to where the three men were standing. He swung into the saddle. "I plan to return to Tarraco to either recruit or neutralize the century in that city. I will alert you to any developments," he said.

Tacitus nodded. "We will give you notice before we move on to Hispania."

Publius and Servius turned their mounts and trotted back down the Via Augusta.

"What do you think, tribune?" asked Atticus.

"That I am not as confident about what the VII Legion will do as he is," answered Tacitus. "I also wonder what kind of ally this Tribune Publius will be."

"How so?" asked the prefect.

"Think about it, Atticus. How trustworthy is a man who would betray his own legion?" said the tribune. "He also does not seem to have much support within the VII, which hardly surprises me. He's an arrogant bastard. We need to do this on our own, prefect. If he can help, fine, but in the end, it will be the VI Victrix against the VII Hispania."

"Do you think it might be possible to divide the legion's loyalty?" asked Atticus.

"They didn't earn the title 'pia' for nothing," Publius answered. Mounting, he began walking his horse north, with the prefect scrambling to catch up.

XVI

Sabina watched Cassius as he carefully picked his way through a field of boulders near the road where the party had halted for rest and food. She remounted her horse and followed him up a gentle slope. "Careful," he said, as she drew close, "the ground here is uneven, which is difficult for horses." She watched him as he drew a wax tablet from his saddle bag and made some quick notations.

"What are you doing, Cassius?" she asked.

He made a few more notations on the tablet, then looked up. "Planning a battle I hope never happens," he said.

"Tell me."

He took off his helmet and ran his hands through his hair, which was dark, curly, and, Sabina thought, quite attractive. Indeed, she found Cassius enticing, especially since they had knocked down the formal barriers the young cavalryman had erected at the beginning of their trip. She was being careful, however. While she thought herself safe, she was alone with young males in a place that she doubted even the gods bothered with.

"If the road to Carthago Nova is blocked, then this is the main road to Corduba, Sabina. Any army moving south will have to come through this pass. From here, the road descends to the upper Baetis River and then to the plain before Corduba," he said.

She looked around her. "So, what would make this a battlefield?"

"It is narrow, Sabina. This field of boulders would be almost impossible to maneuver through, and that ridge," he said, pointing to the other side of the road, "would block infantry from moving across it. It is like the neck of a bottle. An army trying to take it would be restricted as to how many men it could put in the front line, thus neutralizing their superior numbers."

Sabina said nothing for a while, scanning both sides of the pass. "You are good at this, aren't you Cassius?" she said finally. "Is this where Uncle Marcus would fight?"

"I can't speak for the legate, Sabina, and I have only begun to understand how infantry fight. It also might be ground that is too difficult for the VII Legion to fight on," he said.

"Then why fight a battle here?" she asked.

"To buy time and maybe bloody the enemy," he answered. "A legion marching south will need supplies, and those will have to come down a long road from the north. If a blocking force were able to wound that legion and force it to deplete its supplies, then it might think twice about continuing on. And if it did, it might not be in the best shape to fight a major battle."

She shook her head. "War is almost as complex as politics," she said.

Cassius laughed. "I've heard your uncle say that war and politics are much the same, except that politics is bloodier."

"Yes, that sounds like Uncle Marcus," she said with a smile. "So, what did you note down?"

"The distances, the ground, and the places to fall back to if we can't hold the pass," he told her. "I also made a crude map."

She nodded and slipped from her saddle. She looked around for a flat piece of ground and smoothed it out with her foot. Then she picked up a small, sharp stick. "Show me what is going to happen, Cassius."

"Sabina, only the gods know what is going to happen, and they may not be sure themselves."

"Of course," she said, "but show me how you want things to go." One of Cassius's more attractive traits was that he never condescended to her because she was a woman. He talked to her almost exactly the same way he talked to his men, but without the rebukes.

He squatted down and drew a large triangle, wide at the top, narrowing toward the bottom. "This is Hispania, Sabina. Here are Tarraco, Valentia and Corduba," he said, making marks in the soil. "There are two major roads, the Via Augusta, the one we are on," he said, as he drew a line that ran down the coast and pointed to a mark. "This is Carthago Nova. There is a road that runs from Carthago Nova to Corduba," he said, drawing a line that wound around the bottom of Hispania before turning north to Corduba. "That road turns at Antikeria, and the distance to Corduba is short. But if we hold Valentia, then an army will have to leave the Via Augusta at Saguntum and take the inland road, which is much longer."

"And the road goes over this pass," said Sabina, studying the drawing.

"Exactly. Now there is another road to Corduba from the north that runs from Legio south through Lusitania. That was the road the II Century was on when it fought the Lusitanians. But taking that road would require an army to march from Tarraco to Legio before heading south. It would take time and be harder to supply than an army marching directly south from Tarraco." He drew that line from the upper part of the triangle down to Corduba.

"That is why you need to talk with your people, isn't it, Cassius?" she said.

He nodded. "If they join with this so-called Gallic empire, then we will have two fronts and only one legion to cover them." He looked at the map. "We would lose," he said at last.

"Would they do that?" she asked.

Cassius shrugged. "They might. They have no love for the Romans. But this new empire may not be in their interests. If it includes those Romans who are trying to push my people out of the lands they still hold, then they may decide to remain neutral."

"Is that your hope?" she asked.

"It is," he said. "I am fairly certain they will not become our allies. But if they remain neutral, then any force moving south from Legio would have to contend with the possibility that the Lusitanians would take the opportunity to reconquer their lands while the Romans were busy killing one another in a civil war.

Even if cities joined the new empire, my people probably would want to keep the local auxiliaries at home to protect our lands. So, it would be much to our advantage to remain neutral."

Sabina laughed and shook her head. "That is grand politics, Cassius, and more complex than any board game I know."

He nodded, looking at the drawing in the dirt. "A very dangerous game," he said quietly.

XVII

Flavius walked slowly through the camp. Many of the men were in their barracks, while many others were taking it easy, playing dice, or just sitting around conversing and laughing after a morning of drills. He was trying to assess the mood of the VII Legion, and it seemed relaxed. A legion was only as good as its morale, and now its morale seemed fine. He made his way to the principia.

"I take it we have heard nothing, sir," said Flavius, coming into Marcus's office.

"Nothing, optio. But I didn't expect to hear back this soon. The authorities in Carthago Nova will want to consult Roma before they act," said the legate, "and they might decide to do nothing."

"So, we just sit here?" asked Flavius.

Marcus was silent, contemplating a pile of letters and scrolls. "No," he finally said. "We need to act. Getting to Corduba is just the beginning of what we have to do to prepare."

Flavius removed his helmet but remained standing. "What did you have in mind, sir?"

"We will pass through a number of cities on our way to Corduba, and we need to sound out their sympathies."

"Aye. I seem to recall there were some people who didn't think highly of us in Capera," said Flavius.

Marcus nodded. "Counselor Arrius Granius would like to have put our heads on a pilum for sparing the Lusitanians a pointless cycle of revenge after the destruction of the Second Century," he said, "but we had friends in that city, including the head duoviri. There are also army veterans in Capera, and they may stay loyal to the Empire."

"Emerita Augusta is almost an army camp, sir," Flavius pointed out. "The city was founded by retired legionnaires."

"And they sit astride the road from Valentia to Olisipo," said Marcus. "Controlling that road will be essential to holding off this Gallic Empire. We may lose the rest of Hispania, but the south is rich enough to make it on its own."

"May I make a suggestion, sir?" asked Flavius.

Marcus looked up with a lopsided smile. "Since when does my optio ask my permission for suggesting something?"

"Just observing protocol, sir," said Flavius.

"What did you have in mind?" asked Marcus.

"That you send a letter to those fellows from the III Legion Augusta who fought the Mauri with us and are now back in Hispania. See if they want to let some of their old comrades know that if they come over from Mauretania and fight with us, they could get themselves a piece of land."

Marcus sighed. "I tried to get the III Augusta to form again, but my recommendations disappeared into the army bureaucracy. They never should have dissolved that legion, and they treated the veterans shamefully."

"Aye, they did," agreed Flavius. "Which might make our appeal interesting to them. We could certainly use some more trained men."

"That's a very good idea, Flavius. I believe that the former optio we worked closely with—I forget his name—lives near Corduba."

"Quintus Titius, sir," provided Flavius. "He and his tesserarius, Macro Lucilius, went into business together producing olive oil."

"How do you know this?" asked Marcus.

"I asked Rachel to try to find out what happened to the men who came back with us, and she located a number of them. It seems that Quintus has tried to keep the III Augusta veterans together," he reported, adding, "Rachel can find out almost anything."

"An impressive woman," said Marcus. "She demonstrated that in Mauretania and in Roma."

"She helped keep your lady alive when those slavers took them to Mauretania, and she warned us of the assassins in Roma," said Flavius.

Rachel had been a slave when Marcus's lover, Aelia, was taken by the Mauri, and the two had formed a close bond. Aelia had purchased Rachel when they returned to Hispania and had adopted her as a sister. When the assassins attacked them in Roma, Rachel had given them warning and fought off one of the attackers. In the aftermath, Flavius had asked her to marry him, and she had agreed, although that union was not yet consummated.

"I have talked with Tribune Quintus, and he is in agreement about the need for the VII Legion to move south," said Marcus.

"And Tribune Publius?" asked Flavius.

"The last I heard, he was in Barcino," said Marcus. "I have not yet sought out his opinion."

"I wouldn't do that, sir," cautioned Flavius. "I would rather sleep with a viper than let that man know my plans. In any case, I don't think we will see our tribune back here in Legio."

Marcus nodded. "That thought—not the part about sleeping with a snake—ran through my mind as well, optio."

"I would bet a year's pay that Publius is throwing in with those Gallic Empire people, sir. And even if he disagrees with the VII leaving Legio, Quintus and you outvote him," said Flavius. "I would strongly recommend keeping that man in the dark in regards to our plans, sir."

"I agree, optio," said Marcus. "At what stage are our plans?"

"Moving along, sir. I have pulled in our patrols and small garrisons, and we are pretty much at full strength. I am awaiting more mules, and we need to stockpile supplies. Will we be taking oxcarts, sir?" asked Flavius.

"Yes, but they will follow. I want to travel light and fast. Standard 15 days' rations for each man, and we will resupply at Helmantica, Capera, Norba Caesarina, and Emerita Augusta on the way down," he said.

"Any word on our signifer?" asked Marcus.

"Nothing yet. But if we leave before he returns, he can always catch up. I assume Tribune Quintus is not coming with us?" asked Flavius.

"No, Quintus says he is too old for a forced march," said Marcus. "He will stay behind and close up the camp, and then, I suspect, retire."

"What do we tell the men about where we are headed and why?" asked Flavius.

"The truth. That there is a threat to Corduba and we have been sent to counter it. That will explain why we are moving so fast," answered Marcus. "We will take the cavalry and, of course, our Cretian archers."

"And what do we say this threat is?" asked Flavius.

"An invasion," replied Marcus.

"Umm, sir. An invasion would come from Gaul, as the Franks did. The men will be asking why we are moving to Corduba instead of east to Tarraco or Barcino," said Flavius.

"Tell them that we are ordered to Corduba and exactly why is not yet clear. That in the army, we do as we are ordered. You can tell them that if we make Corduba in five weeks, they will receive double pay," said Marcus.

"Really, double pay?" said Flavius. "What if the authorities in Carthago Nova don't approve?"

"Haven't we come into a lot of gold recently, optio?" prompted Marcus.

Flavius chuckled. "Yes, sir, that we have."

"So, begin, optio. I want to be on the road in four days," said Marcus, turning back to his letters and scrolls. "Tell the centurions that we will meet tomorrow at noon and that I will answer questions and fill them in then."

Flavius left, grumbling. "Four days? Have everything ready in four days? No sleep for you, Flavius, or for any of the officers. Four days!"

XVIII

The turmae embarked on the road to Corduba near the head-waters of the Baetis River in the late afternoon. After just a few miles west, they came upon a decent inn. Sabina had thoroughly enjoyed the several nights camping in the mountains, the glorious night sky, and the comradely companionship of Cassius and the men. Over the past two weeks the initial standoffishness of the men—largely impelled by Cassius's stern warnings—wore off under the combination of close quarters and Sabina's natural friendliness and inquisitiveness. She wanted to know everything, about the geography, the flora and fauna, and the people they encountered. And she asked questions of and talked with as many of the men as she could.

But right now, she was ready for a comfortable bed with sheets, a bath that didn't consist of a wet washcloth, and fresh food. Camping had its pleasures, but she needed some civilization.

The trip had been illuminating in a variety of ways. She had never lacked confidence in her intellect, but had not thought much about her body. What surprised her was that she was pretty good at things like riding horses and soldiering through aches and pains. But in some ways what was most interesting was that the men and Cassius clearly thought of her as a woman, not a girl. At first, she found this disconcerting. She really didn't know how to behave like an adult, and her models were not necessarily those that she would choose to emulate. And after her uncle's efforts to marry her off to a senator, thinking about sexuality was disconcerting. While everyone had been studiously polite on their trip, she had caught men looking at her in ways that they would not look at a child. At first, she was embarrassed, but eventually found that it gave her a certain power that was new to her. She learned she was attractive and had the ability to alter a man's behavior with a well-timed gesture or comment.

She was also growing quite fond of Cassius. He was an interesting man who treated her as an equal. In part, she realized, that reflected her status as the niece of his commanding officer, but she quickly came to realize that Cassius was as intelligent and curious as she was, with an easygoing, engaging personality. And he was quite handsome but not at all full of himself.

One day she asked him about the disks he wore on his chain mail. "They are phalerae, Sabina," he said, identifying them as a Civic Crown for saving the life of a civilian and a Hasta Pura for valor. There was no boasting in his telling, however, just a matter-of-fact explanation of their meaning. When she said that the awards meant he was a hero, he shrugged it off. "Officers get the rewards for deeds that their men make possible, Sabina. A unit is only as good as its men."

"How do you mean?" she asked.

He frowned, thinking. "We can issue orders, but how they

are carried out depends on a number of things. First, of course, is are the men well-trained? But that is not enough. Are they happy or unhappy? Are they being treated well or abused? Do they have confidence in their leaders? Morale is as important as skill, Sabina, for without the former, the latter is of little use."

"How do you find out about those things, Cassius?" she asked.

"You need to spend time with the men, eat what they are eating, sleep where they sleep, rub down your own horse, and never ask them to do something you won't do yourself," he said. "Respect for command is earned, Sabina, not granted. And if it were, it would be a frail reed to lean on."

After their talk, Sabina discreetly watched Cassius. He rarely rebuked his men, instead using transgressions as an opportunity to teach. He demanded discipline, but made sure they ate well, that their tents were sturdy and rainproof, and that their clothing was adequate. In fact, Sabina began to think of him more as a strict nanny than as a military commander.

It seemed to work. The men stayed in formation and kept their uniforms well groomed, quietly joked and gossiped as they rode, and at night sang songs around small cooking fires. In short, they seemed contented, more like they were on a recreational outing than a military maneuver.

Sabina had loved the proper bath, the bed and sheets, and the breakfast of fresh eggs, baked bread, and sharp-tasting virgin olive oil, but she was also depressed. Their adventure was ending, and she was headed into—what? A wave of uncertainty swept over her. For the past two weeks, her world had been confined by the exigencies of travel. Rise with the sun, eat, ride, find a place to spend the night. It was all simple and immediate. Now she would be entering a strange household where she barely knew the people. And what would she do? The only thing she was certain of was that she would be more comfortable and less free.

She was finishing her breakfast when Cassius entered.

"We are ready when you are, Sabina. I had your luggage moved onto the mules," he said. "Will you need more time?"

"No, no," she said. "Forgive me, I am finished. Are we near to Corduba?" she asked.

"Just half a day, Sabina. We will arrive in the early afternoon," he told her. "I sent a man ahead to warn Lady Aelia and Rachel of your arrival."

She smiled at him. "You think of everything, don't you, Cassius? I wrote them a letter from Tarraco, but we left before there was a reply. They knew I was coming, just not when."

"It is my job, Sabina," he said. "Much of what I do is just making sure things happen, that there are supplies when the men need them, that there are enough horses and fodder for them. Command is rarely about leading men into battle, it is mostly about organizing things."

"Sort of like housework," she said.

He laughed. "I suppose it is. Not very dashing, is it?"

"Oh, you are dashing, Cassius," she said, "but apparently organization is as important as dash, not something that is obvious to the average citizen." She mounted her horse. "I have learned much on this adventure, and I thank you for it."

Cassius reddened and made a slightly awkward bow. "It has been my pleasure, Sabina."

"Now don't go getting formal, Cassius," she said with a grin. "Lead on, my dashing cavalryman, Corduba beckons." With that, she turned her horse and trotted down the road, followed by Cassius, who scrambled to mount and motioned the men to follow.

* * *

The road led into a broad plain, with the city set on the far side of the river. From a distance, the most prominent feature was an enormous temple on one of the town's high points. City walls were rare in the interior of the Empire, but Corduba was surrounded by 10-foot walls on three sides, prompting Sabina's curiosity.

"Corduba was originally a Carthaginian city, Sabina," said Cassius. "Carthage built walls. When the Romans drove out the Carthaginians, they kept the walls because they were fighting tribes to the south and west."

"Were those your people, Cassius?" she asked.

"No, we are north of here, Sabina. I am not sure who those people were. It was a long time ago," he explained. "The eastern wall was removed many years ago, and the city expanded all the way to the river. It is a major port now."

As they drew closer, the bridge came into view.

Sabina pulled her horse to a stop and Cassius signaled the men behind him to halt. "I have never seen a bridge like that, Cassius."

"Yes, Cordubans are quite proud of it," he said. "It is over a thousand feet long and is said to be one of the longest bridges in the Empire."

The bridge was wide enough for two carts to pass one

another in opposite directions, and as they drew closer, Sabina picked out statues set along the stone railings. There was even room on either side for the horses to bypass the slow-moving oxcarts and thread their way through the traffic that jammed the span. Docks crowded the city side, and gangs of slaves were loading and unloading dozens of ships. When they reached the other side, Cassius called a halt. "The turmae will leave us at this point, Sabina. There is a camp on the southern side of the city. A host of mounted men on the city streets would cause chaos. I will escort you to Aelia's domus. I just need to instruct the men on what to do."

Sabina nodded, looking around at what she guessed was her new home. In general, she liked what she saw. It was obviously a rich city. The streets were clean, the houses painted white with broad red stripes at the bottom, and temples and shrines were scattered on either side of the main road. The streets were crowded, but not like in Roma, where at times it was difficult to walk.

Cassius returned shortly, and Sabina saw the troops head off along a road that skirted the riverbank. She was sorry to see them go. She waved, but none of them looked back, concentrating on not trampling the citizens and slaves going about their business.

Cassius stopped several times to ask directions, but they eventually arrived at a huge domus, almost more like a palace than a house. Sabina's eyes widened. "It is enormous, Cassius," she said.

The cavalryman nodded. "Yes," he said. "I have never seen it, but Flavius and Demaratus described it to me. Lady Dasumi is quite wealthy, Sabina. You will live well."

"I have lived well the past two weeks, Cassius," she said.

"Yes, but, well this…," he said, his voice trailing off.

"Indeed," she said, "I am almost reluctant to knock on that door." It was a huge double door with inset bronze carvings and a bright copper door knocker modeled after a satyr. The two dismounted, and Cassius held the horses while Sabina raised a copper ball attached to the knocker and banged several times.

In a few moments the door opened and Rachel stood on the other side. "Sabina! Cassius! Welcome," she said, flinging her arms around the girl and hugging her. "Please, come in. Aelia is due back soon. She is meeting with some important family." She stood back and looked at Sabina, who was dressed in trousers and simple top with a belt, and bronzed from the two weeks on the road. "Look at you, Sabina. We left you a girl, and you have arrived a woman. And one who has seen something of this land."

Turning to a young slave girl, she said, "Gaia, please fetch some wine, oil, bread, and olives." The girl vanished toward the back of a vast atrium. "Come and sit, but we should wait for Aelia before you relate your adventure, otherwise you will be repeating yourself."

"I need to see to the horses, Rachel," said Cassius. "Is there someplace I can house them temporarily?"

"Yes, of course. There is a small stable beyond the kitchen. I will have someone come and take them there," she said.

"If you don't mind, I would rather someone directed me to the stable, Rachel," said Cassius.

"Whatever you wish," she said, and called out, "Barea!" An

older man appeared shortly, and Rachel explained what Cassius wanted. Barea turned to Cassius, "If you will follow me around the side, sir, I can take you to the stable. It is currently empty, but there is feed and water."

Sabina took the reins of her horse. "Rachel, come with us. I need to take care of my horse as well."

"I will do that," volunteered Cassius.

"No, you will not," insisted Sabina. "As you told me before we began this trip, my horse is my responsibility. She has carried me countless miles with great patience, and each night I have rubbed her down and fed and watered her. This day is no different." And with that she beckoned for Barea to lead the way, and the small party made their way to the stables.

XIX

Flavius was patient—to a point. He had spent yesterday morning meeting with the almost 60 centurions of the 1st through 10th cohorts, calmly fielding questions on supplies, transportation, and the myriad of problems that inevitably arise when you move more than 5,000 soldiers and their equipment hundreds of miles. But now he was getting requests to explain why all this was necessary, as if it is up for discussion when the legate of a legion makes a decision. It was not. That was not the way the Roman army worked, and Flavius expected centurions to know that. But here was a scroll—signed by several of the men—asking to be told why the VII Legion was decamping to Corduba.

He took a deep breath and reminded himself that these were not normal times. When the legion mobilized to fight the Franks, there was an obvious reason. All knew that the Franks had invaded Hispania and taken Tarraco, and it was the job of the VII Legion to defeat them.

This was a lot more complex. There might be an invasion, but this time it would be by a brother legion, not by barbarians.

Their enemy would be speaking Latin, not Frankish or whatever the Goths called their language. The VII Legion had not been involved in a civil war for over 200 years, and while everyone was aware of internal conflicts in other parts of the Empire, these had largely passed Hispania by.

On the other hand, it was not Flavius's job to explain politics. His job was to find at least 1,000 mules and several hundred ox-carts, and to pull all of that together in less than a week. It was Marcus's job to explain why they were doing this, but he had been tied up writing letters to their superiors in Carthago Nova and Roma to lay out what they were doing and why.

Well, Flavius decided, they didn't pay him enough to respond to this scroll, so, busy or not, Marcus would have to deal with it. The optio rolled up the scroll and headed for the principia. There was a crowd around Marcus's office, but the duty officer waved Flavius through. Seated at a table behind a mound of tablets and scrolls, the legate looked harassed. "Well, join the crowd," thought Flavius, as he handed Marcus the scroll.

Marcus scanned it and looked up. "What's the problem, optio?" he asked. "Tell them to follow their orders."

The answer actually surprised Flavius. Marcus was a thoughtful man who tended to see the world in shades of gray, not the simple black- and-white, do-what-you're-told hierarchy of the Roman Army. That he responded the way he did was an indication of the kind of pressure he felt himself under.

"I could do that, sir, but I think it is a bad idea," said Flavius. "We're not going off to fight barbarians, sir. We may be going to fight Romans. Sooner or later, we are going to have to explain that to the men. The centurions have a right to ask these questions."

Marcus gripped his pen and flushed, then forced himself to relax. After a silence of several seconds that seemed longer to Flavius, he asked, "What did you have in mind, optio?"

"We should tell the centurions straight out what is up, sir. This legion is loyal to you. You've led us through battles here and in Mauretania, and you've done it without leaving a lot of men on the battlefield. The men are also proud of that 'pia' designation. We should trust their loyalty," he asserted.

Marcus pushed back his chair and ran his fingers through his hair. "You have become my acting tribune, Flavius, what with Quintus indisposed and Publius off in Tarraco."

"Except I am a lot cheaper, sir," said Flavius.

Marcus grinned at him. "Indeed, you are." He stood and went to the sideboard and poured two small cups of wine, handing one to Flavius. "I agree, optio. Tell the centurions I will meet with them tomorrow morning and answer all their questions," he said, adding, "How is the mobilization coming along?"

"On schedule, sir. It was easy getting the mules, and we aren't taking many in the way of horses. The headquarters staff is happy to go by sea. They will set off to Brigantum once we are underway. The carts will follow us, but it may be a week or more before they catch up with us in Corduba."

"What is the status of the cavalry?" asked Marcus.

"We will have two ala, sir, almost 1,000 men. Cassius is still in the east, but I think he is probably headed to Lusitania by now. The plan is to meet him in Salamantica," replied Flavius.

"Good, I don't want to be without him. He is our eyes and ears," said Marcus.

"I'll drink to that, sir," said Flavius. "Plus, I miss the lad."

Marcus sat down again. "Optio, I have a job for you once we get underway," he said.

"Sir?"

"When we get to the main road south, I want you to leave us and go east to Clunia and then Caesarugusta. We need to sound out where those cities stand. In particular, I want you to meet with the auxiliary commander, Septimius Granius."

"Aye. He was a good one in that fight with the Franks," recalled Flavius. He hesitated. "I am not sure how to do that. This business with the Gallic Empire is kind of delicate. I am not a diplomat, as you know, sir."

"I want you to talk with the military, not the civilians, optio. I want to know how they will react," said Marcus. "If they all join in this breakaway, we will be hard pressed. If they remain loyal, then we can deny the Gallic Empire the west of Hispania."

"If they send two legions against us, we will be hard pressed anyway," said Flavius.

"I doubt they will," said Marcus. "The major threat to any Gallic empire would come from Italia or from some combination of the Goths, Franks, or Alamanni. I don't think they can afford to send more than one legion. If that legion is strongly backed by Hispania auxiliaries, then we will be in trouble. But if the auxiliaries keep their distance or remain neutral, then I think we can defeat an invasion of the south."

"So, staying neutral is something I should talk about?" queried Flavius.

Marcus nodded. "First, talk about loyalty, but if that doesn't work, then suggest that remaining neutral might be a wise choice. Remind them that betting against the VII Legion in the past has been a losing proposition."

"Good point," said Flavius. "What if they want to join up with us?"

"I have been thinking about that, Flavius," said Marcus, rummaging through the papers on his table and finally selecting a map. "Valentia is the key to our strategy. If we hold the city, any Gaul legion will have to retreat to Saguntum, then go north until they strike the road from Caesaraugusta to Libisosa. That will stretch their supply lines and make them march more than 100 miles out of their way. It also means Tarraco will have to send supplies west to Caesaraugusta and then south. If we hold Valentia, we block the shortest route south."

Flavius took a sip from his cup. "I can see that. I would like to take a copy of this, sir."

"Of course, optio. And you need to select at least three contubernium to accompany you. This will not be a trip without danger," said Marcus.

"Twenty-four men is too many, sir. It will make us look like we are on the defensive. An even dozen will do the job. I'll just make sure they are the best we have," said Flavius.

"I leave that to you, optio. You know the men. Just keep in mind that you may find yourself in hostile circumstances," warned Marcus.

"Seems like we've been there a few times, sir," said Flavius with a smile. "And yet here we are, all in one piece."

* * *

The talk with the centurions had gone well. Flavius had been certain it would. Marcus could hold an audience, and by the end the centurions were on board. Marcus had also laid out some of his thinking about how the campaign might unfold. "We are not looking to fight a brother legion," he had said. "We will not seek out war. But we will defend ourselves and the Empire."

That line went over well. No one liked the idea of blood on blood. But defending their homes was another matter. Any legion they fought would be a foreign one, probably the one from Norba, the legion—Marcus reminded them—that let the Franks pass unmolested in an effort to destroy the VII Legion. "They did not act like our brothers and comrades," said Marcus, evoking a growl from the centurions.

And now the VII Legion was ready to march. The mules had been loaded and the cohorts organized by century. Marcus arrived on his enormous fat horse—Flavius thought it was more like riding a couch than an animal—and took his place at the head of the column. The signifer was not back yet, so it was Marcus and Flavius with the legion's golden eagle behind them. Looking over the men, Marcus waved his arm and, like some enormous steel machine, the VII Legion moved onto the road to Asturica Augusta and Corduba.

XX

Sabina rose from her couch when it was still dark and made her way to the small stable at the rear of the domus. The horse gave her a whinny of recognition and she slipped it a fig. As it chewed away, she threw a blanket and her saddle onto its back and cinched them down tight. She slipped the halter and reins over the horse's head and opened the gate to the street. She mounted and rode into the city's center, which was only beginning to stir. There was just a hint of pink in the east.

* * *

The morning had a sharp nip of fall to it, and there was a thin mist on the field near the camp. Astride his horse, Cassius scanned the turmae. The men looked well rested. A few days in Corduba had allowed them catch up on their sleep. The plan was to move north to Metellinium, west to Emerita Augusta, and then north to Norba, from where they hoped the commander could contact the leaders of the Lusitanians. If that went well, the turmae should rejoin the VII Legion near Salamantica.

"Sir," said one man, whom he had designated as his optio, indicating something from the direction of the city.

Turning in his saddle, Cassius saw a single horse carrying a figure muffled in a gray cloak picking its way across the field. As it drew close, he recognized the sorrel, and then the figure threw back her hood and revealed herself.

"Sabina," he said. "What are you doing here?"

Drawing up to him, she smiled. "Saying goodbye and praying that Fortuna will watch over you."

The cool morning had put roses in Sabina's cheeks. The two weeks on the road had deepened the dust of freckles across her nose, and a few drops of mist sparkled in her long hair. He told himself that she might be the most beautiful woman he had ever laid eyes on, and that revelation struck him dumb.

She cocked her head. "I am not used to silence in your presence, Cassius. Am I doing something wrong with Rosa?"

"No," he blurted out. "No, I am sorry, Sabina. I just am just surprised...no, I mean delighted to see you. I did not expect to, and you are alone." The words tumbled out, and Cassius felt awkward and embarrassed and nonplussed in front of his command. He noticed that his optio, Probius, was stone-faced, which, if anything, made him more self-conscious.

"I know when you like to leave, commander, and I did not want to bother anyone at the domus. So, I saddled Rosa and came by myself. The streets are only just coming to life. It is a lovely time to be out in the city, and even better if you are on horseback."

Sabina's little speech allowed Cassius to get a hold of himself. "It is the best time of the day, Sabina, though I have to say, you make it better."

"Shameless flatterer," she said with a grin. "Just what a girl needs to start off the day."

Cassius laughed, noting that Probius was doing his best not to join in.

"How did you know where to come?" asked Cassius.

"If you want to ask directions, it helps to be a woman on a horse," she said.

"I bet they do not see many," said Cassius, adding, "any, in fact."

Sabina was silent for a long moment. "I know where you and the men are bound, Cassius," she said quietly. "I know that you may be putting yourself in harm's way. I did not say anything at the time, but when you scouted that pass, it put a chill in my heart. Like you, I hope there are no battles, but that is out of the hands of people like you and me. Those decisions will be made by the powerful and by the gods." Leaning across her saddle, she touched his sleeve. "Please be careful."

At that precise moment, Cassius Cornelius, commander of the Ala II Flavia Hispanorum Romanorum, fell in love. All he could manage in response was to say, "We will be, Sabina."

She backed up her horse to give the turmae room, and Probius cast a critical eye on the column. Satisfied, he turned to Cassius. "Ready, sir."

Cassius swung his horse around and saluted Sabina. As each pair of riders trotted past her, they turned and saluted as well. And Sabina returned their salutes.

"The men will miss her, sir," said Probius, riding beside Cassius at the head of the column. "She was a good comrade."

"She was," agreed Cassius, turning back to look at Sabina on her sorrel. She waved and turned the horse back toward the city.

* * *

By the time Sabina had reached the city wall, Corduba was coming fully to life. When she had ridden through the streets in the early morning, there had been only a few merchants and shopkeepers afoot. Now the streets were beginning to fill with people on errands and construction workers leading teams of slaves. A number of them glanced at her and then looked more closely. It was a rarity to see a well-dressed woman in pants riding a horse through town.

Sabina enjoyed that double take. She had spent so much time locked up in her parents domus or lost in a sea of Roma's people that it was nice to be the object of interest. She gently pulled on the reins so that Rosa paced, swinging her head from side to side, which drew more attention. She decided that this was something she needed to do more often.

Sabina rode Rosa back to the domus, dismounted, and led the mare around the side to the stable. She took off the saddle, blanket, and halter and rubbed the horse down with straw. She slipped Rosa half an apple.

Aelia, however, was not happy with Sabina's early morning ride. She should have told people she was going. She should have taken a servant with her. It was dangerous to ride a horse in the middle of Corduba. How would it look for an unescorted woman to put herself in the midst of all those men?

Sabina apologized for not letting anyone know, but she had not been about to take anyone with her. "I spent more than two weeks with those men, Aelia, and when they left this morning, they saluted me," she said. "They are going into danger and I wanted to let them know that someone cares."

"Marcus has made me responsible for you, Sabina," Aelia told her. "I take that seriously."

"Aelia, I am sorry and will not go out again without informing you. But they were leaving and going into... I don't know what. Uncle Marcus is as well."

Aelia was silent for a moment. "I know," she said. "I think about it every day. For weeks I have been meeting with the leading families in Corduba and other cities in the province, helping to persuade them to remain loyal to the Empire."

"Can I help?" asked Sabina, happy to change the subject.

"The niece of the commander of the VII Legion might be an attractive asset," offered Rachel, who had stood silently during the initial conversation between Sabina and Aelia. Sabina flashed her a grateful smile.

"Hmm. That is a good point, Rachel," said Aelia. "I am meeting with the Ulpii family this afternoon. They are staunch, of course. A family that produced the Emperor Trajan is not likely to join forces with a bunch of traitors. But they have been quiet, and I am not sure why. They may be speaking with their networks of families, but if so, I have heard nothing of it. I intend to press them a little."

"You can tell them I was sent by Marcus's family to help

you organize support for the Empire," said Sabina. "I will try to look older."

"Yes, pants will not do," said Rachel with a smile.

"I will have to prepare you for this meeting," said Aelia, almost to herself. "I can do that while we are selecting clothes and jewelry for you. Have you eaten? No? Then eat and come to my cubiculum."

* * *

Rachel watched all this from the side of the atrium. Besides those few initial comments, she had been silent, but neither Aelia nor Sabina had seemed to notice. "It is happening," she thought to herself. "There will be less room for me here in the future." Rachel loved Aelia, but she was also uncomfortable with the woman's enormous wealth and recognized that, in addition to the divide generated by her former status as a slave, there was the issue of class. Aelia was of the old equestrian class, while Rachel was a Jew born into slavery. That chasm had just widened.

Rachel was glad that her fiancé, Flavius, was headed toward Corduba. It was time to think about a separate future.

XXI

Tiberius was enraged. He had just learned that his niece, Sabina, had been shipped off to Hispania while he was in the middle of negotiations with a prominent senator over a marriage alliance.

"How dare you do this, Julia!" he shouted. "I have already discussed the union with Senator Publius Mummius Sisenna. There were agreements made! You have ruined it."

"Oh, yes, this senator who you said was in his forties?" she retorted. "I went to the curia and asked someone to point him out. Forties, brother? He is as old as my husband Lucius's father, who I believe once met Caesar."

"What of it? If he dies, she will inherit much of his wealth, and he would have given our family a major boost in status," Tiberius said.

"You know nothing of what she would inherit, brother. The senator already has a pack of children. And, in any case, such things do not interest Sabina. Are you not already a quaestor or some such thing? Isn't that a major boost in status?" she shot back.

"She would have brought in a fortune, you silly fool! The senator was willing to pay an enormous bride price," he said.

"Why not go to the slave market, Tiberius, and buy him a young bride there?" she said, defiantly. "In any case, my daughter is not for sale."

"You have no say in this, Julia. The decision on her marriage is made by Lucius, her father, not her mother. You have forgotten your place, sister," he hissed back.

Julia drew herself up and folded her arms across her chest. "So, now it comes out. 'Raise up the family,' you said? Or buy yourself more influence at the cost of your niece? You have your new position and, I suppose, the emperor's ear. Although that might be a problem, might it not, dear brother? Does whispering into a dead man's ear give you any influence? As a stupid female, I need you to explain that to me."

Tiberius raised his fist, but Julia did not flinch.

"Are you going to strike me, brother? Knock this woman aside and get your way? Just try it!" she challenged. "What nice gossip that will make, the new quaestor tries to auction off his niece to an old man, the niece of a hero to the Empire, the man who brought down the Franks and saved Tarraco, and who asked me to send Sabina to Hispania to be under his care and preserve her from the plague decimating this city! Oh, yes, Tiberius, that will make for a fine story. And what will you do? Send armed guards to bring her back? I suggest many guards, brother. The VII Legion is not to be taken lightly."

"I will not talk with you about this matter anymore, Julia.

I will talk only to Lucius," he said. But he unclenched his fist, letting it drop to his side.

"Lucius is with the boys in Carsulae, and we are of one mind on this, Tiberius. Lucius is a fine husband, but he knows that it is his wife who organizes his life. He also knows that if he attempts to bring Sabina back from Hispania, he will lose that wife," she said.

"You would not dare that," said Tiberius, but he looked uncertain for the first time. "You would be without a way to make a living."

"I dare, brother, and I strongly suggest you do not test my resolve in this matter. It will not come out well for you, and all that influence you have gained will be as fleeting as a nymph," she said, bringing her face close to his. "And now leave this house before I decide to write a long letter to Marcus. Then we will see if a quaestor is a match for a legate."

Tiberius stepped back and tried to keep his surprise and uncertainty from showing. He had always thought of Julia as an empty-headed piece of fluff, not as the intense and determined woman he was facing. And might he come out of this looking bad? There were certainly some in Roma who resented his influence and new position, and Marcus was currently in good stead with the government. And then there was this business of Gaul and talk of a breakaway empire. The VII Legion might be a player in that game. Suddenly, the ground shifted and his characteristic caution took over.

"If I am not welcome in your domus, so be it, sister. I am done with you," he said in a huff, drawing his toga around his chest. He turned, crossed the atrium, and left by the front door.

Julia sighed. "Oh, brother," she said to herself. "You want to be important, but you just don't have the skills or the courage for it. I will not miss you and that is sad, because there was a time when we shared love." Julia sat down on a couch and poured herself a cup of wine. She smiled to herself. "You thought me a kitten, Tiberius, but I have always been a tiger."

XXII

Flavius emerged from the command tent just as Demaratus dismounted his horse. "Signifer," he said, throwing his arms around the Greek. It was a greeting unlike any in the Roman army. "We missed you. Marcus was asking when you might catch up with us."

"I am sorry about the delay, optio, but I had to go all the way to Coventina's village, explain the situation, and then return. By the time I got to Legio, you were long gone," he said.

"How did the visit go?" asked Flavius.

"All right, I think," said the signifer. "Coventina's family is, well, complex, Flavius."

"I want to hear all about it, Demaratus, but first Marcus will want to find out how your mission went." Taking Demaratus by the arm he ushered him into the tent, which was divided into two rooms—an antechamber where a duty officer sat sorting through people who needed to see the legate, and an inner room curtained off by a long strip of canvas. Brushing past the officer, Flavius pushed through into the inner chamber with the signifer in tow.

Marcus, seated at his desk, looked up. "Signifer, it is good to see you." The legate looked tired. Marcus had lost weight, and there were now permanent lines on his forehead. He was surrounded by letters and scrolls, a seemingly permanent condition these days. He pushed his chair back and rose to grasp Demaratus by the forearms, greeting him more as a friend than a subordinate. "Did things go well with Coventina's family?" he asked.

"Well enough, sir. I will tell you all about it after my report," said Demaratus, who was trying to keep his personal life separate from his mission for Marcus.

"Of course, signifer. What is the thinking of the Cantabrians?" Marcus asked, pouring cups of wine for Demaratus and Flavius and taking his seat.

"As you might imagine, the situation is complex," answered the signifer.

"Normal for the Greeks," Flavius couldn't help but add.

"I am afraid you Romans have quite surpassed us in that category these days," said Demaratus. "Trying to explain it all is, well, daunting, optio."

Flavius grunted an acknowledgement.

"Comrades," said Marcus.

"Sorry, sir," said both men.

"We must remember that we may talk of 'Celts,' but the Celts don't think of themselves as a single people, even though they are bound by language and way of life. Coventina's tribe, the Cantabrians, is just one of seven tribes, which include the Gallaeci, Astures, Vaccaei, Arevaci, Vascones and Ceretani."

"Impressive," murmured Flavius.

"Coventina's people are presently at odds with the Astures and the Gallaeci, though it is not what we would call a war," said Demaratus. "They raid one another's herds for cattle, horses and sheep, which occasionally results in a physical confrontation. But people rarely die as a result. If they do, it sets off a blood feud, which is costly and can lead to open war, which no one seems to want."

"But no one person can speak for all of them, or even for a single tribe. There is a sort of king of the Cantabrians, but he has no real authority. He judges matters that are appealed to him, but they mostly concern minor matters, like disputes over grazing rights or breaking marriage contracts. When it comes to something like a cattle raid, anyone can organize one and recruit people to join him. A decision to go to war—and the Cantabrians have gone to war on occasion— is made by all the males gathered in a council," said Demaratus.

"Pretty much the way the Celts did things in Britannia," said Flavius. "And the tribes there were at one another much of the time."

Demaratus nodded. "Which means that even if you got a tribe's headman to agree to something, he wouldn't be speaking for everyone in the tribe, and certainly not the other tribes. There has never been a meeting of all the tribes in Hispania."

"Good thing," opined Flavius. "I am not sure we would want all the Celts in agreement. The last time they all got together they sacked Roma."

"Nonetheless, that makes our life more difficult, optio," said Marcus. "Would they take sides in this Gallic Empire scheme?"

Demaratus gathered his thoughts for a moment. "As I said, it is complex. Coventina says the tribes bear no love for the Romans or for the Empire, but they have learned how to coexist with them. Some of them have grown wealthy trading livestock, and Celtic metalworkers are much sought after. But they are also conscious of the fact that they no longer control the richer land in the north and the west. They still consider the lands on the Douro River to be theirs."

"They haven't held those lands for more than 200 years," said Flavius. "That's a long time to hold a grudge."

Demaratus shrugged. "If someone came and took your land, would you forget about it?"

"Seems to me the Greeks were pretty good at that," flared Flavius.

"They were, and the Celts have not forgotten them either. Forgetfulness is a luxury of the victor, not the vanquished," said Demaratus.

Flavius was about to say something until Marcus broke in. "Comrades, enough. Debate the foils of empire another time. What I need to know is whether the tribes will join with the Gauls against Roma."

"Coventina thinks not, but she is still gathering information," said Demaratus. "To her people, this is a quarrel among Romans. If Romans want to war against Romans, the Cantabrians are fine with that. What they don't want to do is pick a losing side. She is pretty certain they will remain neutral and wait to see what happens."

"Suppose the insurgents in Gaul offer the Celts their old lands back?" said Flavius.

"I don't see that as even a remote possibility," said Marcus. "That would alienate Roman landowners and unite the west against the Gaulish legions. Which doesn't mean they won't try to lure the Celts into joining them by making promises, even if they have no intention of making good on them."

"I put that question to Coventina. She says that her people think that Romans are all liars and utterly untrustworthy. She says no one believes their promises," replied the signifer.

"It looks like neutrality is the best we can hope for," said Marcus. "It will have to do. If it holds, at least we know that we won't have the Celts to deal with."

"When Coventina catches up with us we'll get more information," said Demaratus. "Her brother is sounding out some of the other tribes."

"Fine work, signifer," said Marcus. "Get yourself some food and rejoin us here after you have rested. We will be in Asturica Augusta tomorrow. I have sent ahead a message that we want a meeting with the leaders of the local council. We need to prepare for it. I want you to look into the economic aspects of a divided empire and what Hispania might lose if that comes to pass."

Demaratus saluted and left.

* * *

The meeting with the decurions and leading family members of the local council at Asturica Augusta went pretty much as Marcus had predicted. Yes, people in the city were aware of the possibility of a schism, but no, no one supported it. Marcus did not believe that for a moment. He recognized that no one would be likely to say anything else with a legion camped on the edge of town.

There were pledges of loyalty, but no offers of auxiliaries. Marcus did not really blame them. Any schism would bring about a civil war, and in periods of unrest cities want to keep their auxiliary forces local, not off in Corduba. "What if the Celts take advantage of the strife to fall upon us?" a council member asked. Marcus tried to assure the council that the Celts intended nothing of the kind, but that was met with skepticism. "You can't trust a Celt," one decurion argued, mirroring the Celts' opinion of the Romans.

Demaratus laid out the economic impact of a breakaway. Essentially, it would result in lost trade, particularly by sea. But again, his listeners were hesitant. "They don't want to commit," thought Demaratus. "In a way, I can't blame them."

Some of the town turned out to see off the VII Legion the next morning, but Marcus noted that the mood was somber, as though a storm was brewing. Well, he thought, they have that right.

* * *

While Marcus and Demaratus were at the meeting, Flavius went looking for Manlius Valeranos, centurion of the First Cohort's Second Century. He found the man going over the century's books with his signifer. "Optio, welcome," said the older man.

It was an awkward greeting. While Flavius was an optio who ordinarily would be outranked by a centurion, he was also the legate's aide-de-camp and long-time friend, and had lobbied for Manlius's promotion.

"Comrade," said Flavius, "I need a favor."

"Name it, Flavius," said Manlius.

"I would like to borrow a contubernium from you for detached duty. I have in mind a few men who backed me up during an execution outside of Corduba. Brutus Popilius was one of them," said Flavius.

"That would be the third contubernium, optio. Good men all," said Manlius.

"Can you spare them for several weeks?" asked Flavius.

"Of course. Might I ask what you need them for?"

"Protection," said Flavius. "I am headed for Clunia and then Caesaraugusta to see if I can drum up some support for us, or at least find out how things stand."

"You might need more than eight men for that, optio," said Manlius.

"I don't plan on running into trouble, but if I do, I want to be as mobile as I can be. We will be on horseback. If I need more than that, I would probably need the whole legion, so a single squad will do," replied Flavius.

"Detached duty, no drills, and you get to ride the whole way? I don't think you are going to run into any objections from the Third," grinned Manlius. "Remus," he said to his signifer, "go fetch Brutus."

While they waited, the two talked about how the march was going. It had started slowly because most of the men had not been on a long march for months. It always took a day or so to shake out the kinks and get the men in shape.

Brutus arrived with the signifer and saluted. "Comrade, Flavius here needs a contubernium for detached duty. You and your boys up for that?"

"Yes, sir," said Brutus, a broad-shouldered man, a little taller than the average legionnaire, with a scar running down his right cheek.

"You remember me?" asked Flavius.

"Of course, sir. You asked us to help out when those vigiles were blocking the century down in Corduba. Slapped down that puffed-up twit of an officer right proper, sir. We thoroughly enjoyed it," he said.

"Wherever we go, soldier, we are likely to be outnumbered," said Flavius.

"That won't be the first time for us, sir. We would be honored to be your escort," said Brutus.

"And Brutus, I want you to be my optio."

"Again, honored, sir."

"All right, comrade, go inform your contubernium. We will leave two days from now, when we arrive at the Clunia road."

The man saluted and left with a big grin on his face.

"Looks as happy as a pig in shit," said Manlius.

XXIII

Cassius sat on his horse alongside his cousin Aulus in a field of wheat stubble. An early morning mist clung to the meadow as it sloped down to a small stream. The night was now in full retreat from the dawn. The sky was clear, the east a soft rose color, and the smell of newly cut grass lingered in the air. Off to one side was Cassius's newly appointed optio, Probius. The rest of the cavalry had remained in Norba Caesarina.

Aulus blew on his hands. "They are late," he said.

"Probably not by accident, cousin," said Cassius. "Making the Roman Army wait must amuse them."

"I am not amused, I am cold," complained Aulus.

"This is the best part of the day, enjoy it," said Cassius.

"The best part of a day is a warm bed followed by a good breakfast, Cassius," grumped Aulus.

"You've grown soft, cousin," teased Cassius.

"And I do my best to further that condition at every opportunity. I may be a Lusitanian, but I vastly prefer civilization to this way of life. I love horses, because they make me wealthy. I have no need to ride them anymore," said Aulus.

"What would our ancestors say?" said Cassius with a grin.

"I don't know, and I don't care. You owe me for this, Cassius," said Aulus.

The cavalry commander nodded. "I know, cousin. And it looks like we have visitors."

Coming out of the forest that ringed the field were four men on horseback. Two were armed with lances and shields. The other two only had swords belted to their saddles. All were swaddled in cloaks, with scarves across the lower parts of their faces. Cassius watched as they stopped and surveyed the field.

"Looking for a trap?" asked Aulus.

"It wouldn't be the first time that a peaceful meeting turned into a massacre," said Cassius. "None of us have forgotten what happened to our people at the hands of Servius Galba."

"That was 300 years ago, Cassius," said Aulus. "We are all citizens of the Empire now."

"Romans kill everyone, including one another. Citizenship is no armor," said Cassius, watching the four men.

"Then why do you serve them?" countered Aulus.

Cassius was silent for a long moment. "It's complex," he said at last.

"Well, it's none of my business, cousin. You'll do the talking here," he said.

"I will," agreed Cassius.

Finally, the four men trotted their horses across the field, but those with the spears hung back, taking their mounts off to the side. "Taking no chances," thought Cassius. The two others approached, one mounted on a gray, the other on a calico.

One of the men nodded at Aulus.

"I am Cassius Cornelius, commander of the Ala Flavia and this is my optio, Probius Tarius," Cassius announced, indicating the man holding their horses.

"We know who you are," said one of the men. "We fought you in the meadow and then again later. And we will not use our names."

These words momentarily shook Cassius. These men had been in on the destruction of one of the legion's centuries, a massacre that Cassius had barely escaped when he had gone to warn Marcus's century. In all probability, these men had also fought Marcus and the Second Century the following day. Cassius felt a chill run through him. He was the only survivor of that first battle, a battle that claimed the lives of all his ala comrades.

"We also know why you are here, Roman. Aulus has told us that Romans are about to start killing one another. We think that is a fine idea," said the man on the gray horse.

"They won't stop with the Romans," said Cassius. "They will come for your land next."

"They are already stealing it," said the man on the calico. "If enough Romans kill one another, maybe they will go home and leave us be. Or maybe there won't be enough of them left to stop us from taking back our lands."

"In any case, Roman, why should we care?" said the man on the gray.

"I am not a Roman, I am a Lusitanian just like you," replied Cassius. "I assure you, if the VII Legion is defeated, the victors will come for your land. The VII Legion helped stop a war after you destroyed one of its units."

The man on the calico scoffed. "You wear a Roman uniform, you command other Romans, and you fight against your own people. You may call yourself a Lusitanian, but we call you a Roman."

Cassius made an effort to relax. There was no advantage to getting in an argument. He waited for a few moments, then spoke. "The people behind this civil war have made promises to recruit Roman supporters. One promise is to seize all Lusitanian lands as payment to those who join them. If you think the Romans are going to go home, then you believe in the tales we tell children. But you can depend on the fact that the Romans have long memories. They do not forget."

"Make your point, Roman," said the man on the gray.

"Stay out of it. I am not asking you to join us, I am asking you not to choose sides. If the new empire wins, you may be able to convince the victors that you should be rewarded for that, although I think you will be sorely disappointed. But if we win, you can say that you did not join the treasonous breakaway and remained loyal citizens," said Cassius.

"Citizens! If we are citizens, how can they rob us the way they do?" growled the man on the calico.

"That is wrong, and my commander argued your case in Norba after the fight. I do not defend what the Romans have done and do still. I am saying that your best hope is to remain aloof," said Cassius. "If you join the breakaway empire, or use the civil war as an opportunity to go to war with the Empire, and that endeavor fails, the wrath of the Romans will be terrible."

"You call yourself a Lusitanian and then threaten us?" said the man on the gray.

"No, I merely state the obvious. You must choose what is in your best interests," answered Cassius. "Think about my proposal."

"You serve the Romans," shot back the man on the gray. "Why would we pay attention to you?"

"He spoke for us in the council," argued Aulus. "When Arrius Granius called for revenge, Cassius challenged him and charged him with the murder of our women and children. His speech caused the decurions to back away from all-out war."

The two horsemen were silent. Finally, the man on the gray said, "We had heard that." The two horsemen looked at one another and then back at Cassius. "We will bring your proposal before our council, Roman. We make no promises."

"And none are asked," said Cassius. "Do what you think is best for our people."

The two men turned their horses and trotted back to the tree line, followed by the horsemen with spears and shields.

"What do you think?" asked Cassius.

"I think you made your case. What they will do, I have no idea," replied Aulus.

Cassius signaled for Probius to join them. When they were re-assembled, Aulus asked, "Now can we go get a decent breakfast?"

"Lead on, cousin," said Cassius, spurring his horse to a gentle trot.

XXIV

Fabricius Tuscus, senior magistrate of Norba Caesarina, poured himself a generous glass of wine and popped a grape into his mouth. "You must try these, Marcus. The summer was generous and the grapes are sweet." The magistrate was a large man, once well-muscled, now given over to fat. He had aged and was heavier than Marcus remembered him, but still a commanding figure. "Now let us think about this so-called empire in our midst."

"You are aware of it?" asked Marcus.

"Of course, legate. Nothing happens in Norba that I don't know about, or at least nothing of importance," he said, pulling another grape off its stem. "And I believe you are acquainted with some of the actors already."

"Who?" asked Marcus with a frown.

"Arrius Granius and Tiberius Porcius, whom you humiliated before the council two years ago, for starters. And they have a circle of allies throughout the city," Fabricius replied, adding, "Arrius bears you a special enmity."

"How widespread is their support?" asked Marcus.

"Not as wide as they think," said the magistrate. "Norba has many veterans living here, some of them former members of the VII Legion. There were mixed feelings about you after that unfortunate business with the Lusitanians, but when the VII Legion crushed those Franks, the city declared you one of its own. Norba is loyal, Marcus, but I am not sure that counts for much."

"How do you mean?" asked Marcus.

"In uncertain times, legate, we first will see to ourselves," said the magistrate. "There is talk that the Lusitanians may try to take advantage of the unrest to settle old scores and retake the lands they lost. That means the city will keep its auxiliaries close. If you are looking for support, it will be of the moral variety, not with swords and shields."

"I am not looking for soldiers, magistrate. What I want is for Hispania Ulterior to remain loyal. If cities like Norba refuse to have anything to do with the Gallic Empire, it forces those in Gaul to spread their resources more thinly. That makes it harder for them to concentrate against the VII Legion," said Marcus.

"You will get neutrality from Norba and Emerita Augusta," said the magistrate. "You may even get some troops from Emerita. The city is basically a retired army camp. I can't speak for Capera or Salamantica."

"What will you do if there is an effort by Arrius and his supporters to challenge that?" asked Marcus.

Fabricius chuckled and took another grape. "We know with whom he meets and when. I know how to take care of my city and our Empire, legate."

"This is good news, sir. Cassius, the young cavalryman who took over the council meeting two years ago, is meeting with some Lusitanians," said Marcus.

"That would be important," said the magistrate. "If they go to war against us, it will accrue to the benefit of Arrius and his lot. They have been arguing that Roma doesn't care for Hispania, that it allowed the Franks to invade and take Tarraco, and that a Gallic Empire would better defend us."

"It was the supporters of the Gallic Empire that let those Franks march through Gaul unmolested," countered Marcus.

"Yes, I figured that out," said Fabricius, "but the whole thing is murky, and it is uncertainty that allows lies like those Arrius is pushing to take hold. What of the Celts?"

My signifer is working on that problem, but we have yet to hear anything solid," said Marcus. "If they just stay neutral, that will serve our purposes."

"Let's drink to that, legate," said Fabricius, refilling his glass.

* * *

In a small meadow south of Clunia, Flavius gathered the men around him. "I want to keep you up on where things stand, comrades," he said. "If something happens to me, I want you to be able to report to our legate in Corduba."

"Things not going well?" asked Brutus.

"Not all bad, not all good," replied Flavius. "These Gallic Empire sorts have got their claws into a lot of people. I was a little surprised by the kind of support they are getting. The local auxiliary commander told me it was the Empire that set those

Franks against us, and that the only thing keeping the barbarians from overrunning us are the Gaul legions. I pointed out that those legions had been mysteriously absent when the Franks marched through Gaul, but he was having none of it. 'You take our taxes and give nothing back,' he told me."

"We heard some of that, too," said a young legionnaire. "But I didn't say anything, just let them talk. There were also some who argued the other way."

"Yeah, I heard a pretty heated argument in the forum about it, with about the same number of people on each side," another legionnaire put in. "I also stayed quiet, didn't want to draw attention to myself."

"That's good," said Flavius. "You're here to listen and back me up if I need it. I thought I might need help at one point, because things got pretty hot with that auxiliary commander, but I backed off. What I know is that we can't expect much support from Clunia."

"So, do we not say anything, sir? I mean, some of the talk sounds like treason to me," said Brutus.

"Put this thought in their heads. In the last civil war, parts of Hispania threw their lot in with Pompey against Caesar. Then, when they came out on the losing side, it wasn't pretty. Just suggest that staying neutral might be the smart choice," said Flavius. "But we don't want to draw a lot of attention to ourselves. Someone might think we're spying for the Empire and decide to eliminate us."

"I'd like to see 'em try," growled one legionnaire.

"The information we collect for the VII Legion is more important than winning an argument or beating up some local auxiliary. Put that thought about the last civil war in their heads and keep yours down," directed Flavius.

The men nodded. "If you're concerned about yourself, sir, shouldn't we be with you when you talk with these auxiliaries?" asked Brutus.

"No," said Flavius. "Again, any information you can glean is more important than any one of us. If we stick together, we stand out, which makes us a target. If I don't come back from one of these meetings, scatter and get yourselves to Corduba. Is that clear?"

The men nodded again.

"It will take us a little more than two days to get to Caesaraugusta," said Flavius. "There is a good auxiliary commander there, Septimius Granius. He did a fine job backing us up in that fight with the Franks. I want to see where he stands. And if something happens to me, Brutus is in command. If something happens to Brutus, Remus is in command. But if it comes to that, you should probably fall on your swords."

The quip raised a laugh. The group mounted and headed east.

* * *

"Sir?" said Demaratus putting his head into the inner command tent. "Coventina has returned. Do you wish to speak with her?"

"Yes, send her in," said Marcus, rising and pouring a cup of wine. He handed it to her as she joined them. She drank it straight down and held out the cup for a refill.

"Hard journey?" asked Marcus.

"Long," she replied, taking a sip. For having ridden for six days straight, she looked surprisingly fresh. But Coventina was strong, and tough as well, as she had demonstrated on their trip to Roma the past summer. An assassin had made the mistake of underestimating her. He had paid with his life.

"Can you tell us where the Celts stand in this matter of the breakaway empire?" asked Marcus.

"My people were largely unaware that such a thing is being contemplated. A few had heard rumors when they went into the cities to trade, but they didn't pay them any mind. They are much more focused on fighting—or getting ready to fight—one another. My people are at the brink of war with the Autrigones, and the Astures and Vaccaei are raiding one another's horse herds," she said.

"But it is on their minds now," she continued, looking for a place to sit down. Marcus pulled his chair out from the desk, and she sat down with a sigh. "Our world is small, Marcus. We have been pushed to the margins and it is over those margins we squabble. Suddenly, people are aware that something major might happen that could upend that world, and they are not clear what to think about it."

"In this they are not alone," said Marcus.

"I have talked with some of our elders about it, and they, in turn, have talked with some of the other tribes, especially the Gallaeci and Ceretani. Their views? Uncertain. Some see a civil war as an opportunity to reclaim our former lands. Others see a civil war as a disaster, with our people caught in the middle."

"Is there talk of staying out of it?" asked Demaratus.

"There was after I raised it, but what does that mean? If my people remain aloof, will both sides punish us? Whoever wins, we are not sure we won't be the losers," said Coventina.

"If the Celts remain neutral, the VII Legion will speak up for them and say that they did what we asked them to do," said Marcus.

"I mean no disrespect, Marcus, but you are only one legion among many. The decision of what happens to my people will be made in Roma, not Corduba," she said, "and those that make it may or may not listen to you. And, what is more, that assumes we will all survive the next several months." Coventina put down her cup and stared off into the distance. "Dark times are upon us, I fear, and where they lead is known only by the gods."

Marcus put his hand on her shoulder. "You did the best you could for us and for your people, Coventina."

She shrugged. "We will see. In the meantime, I am tired, Marcus." She gave him a wan smile. "And I need my Greek."

XXV

Tiberius Cicero trotted swiftly across the plaza to the VII Legion's headquarters in Tarraco. There was no sentry at the entrance. He strode through the empty anteroom, knocked on the door, then entered without waiting for a response. Antonius Crispus, centurion of the Third Century, 10th Cohort, sat behind a desk, his elbows resting on a pile of scrolls.

"Sir," said Tiberius, coming to attention, breathless. He was young, but had gone through the siege of the Franks and had proved to be steady and level-headed. The old centurion liked him.

"Report," said Antonius.

"Sir, the VI Legion Victrix has crossed the border and taken Emporae. According to my report, there was no resistance. It appears the VI Legion is preparing to march on Barcino."

"Then Rhoda will be next, followed by us," said Antonius. "My, the lads are energetic, aren't they?"

"And Tribune Publius Felix has arrived from Barcino and is on his way to headquarters," added Tiberius.

"Is he?" asked Antonius. "And are the arrangements made?"

"Yes, sir. We have most of four centuries, a little over 300 men," answered Tiberius.

"Good work, lad. Now slip your pugio behind your back and let's wait for the tribune to show up," said Antonius, rising and sliding his officer's knife out of sight.

"Sir?" The tesserarius awaited further orders.

"The tribune will have an aide with him. That is your job," said Antonius.

"What job, sir?" said a confused-looking Tiberius.

"I think the tribune is going to try to commit treason, tesserarius, and he is my problem. Yours will be to watch his aide, and to stop him if he tries to intervene," said Antonius quietly.

"What are you going to do, sir?"

"Well, if I turn out to be right, then I am going to kill our tribune," replied Antonius.

"What!" said Tiberius, clearly startled.

"Just follow my lead, lad. If the aide doesn't try anything, then we will talk with him. But if he does, then stop him. Is that clear?" asked the centurion.

Tiberius nodded his agreement.

"Good lad," said Antonius.

The two did not have long to wait. The tribune must have ridden directly to the plaza rather than first to the stables. The door to the office opened and in strode Tribune Publius Brutus, accompanied by an aide Antonius recalled was named Servius.

"Sir," said Antonius respectfully.

"Centurion, the VI Legion Victrix will soon be arriving in

Tarraco. I want your cohort to prepare to welcome them. Please see to it," said Publius briskly.

"Now why would a brother legion from Narbo be coming to Tarraco, sir?" asked Antonius. "We already whipped the Franks, so they are a little late to the party, aren't they?"

"The Empire allowed those Franks to invade Hispania, and the VI is coming to our support. All of Gaul and Britannia have declared that, since Roma can no longer defend them from the barbarians, we will do it ourselves," said Publius. "We have 12 legions and the VII Legion Hispania will be the 13th."

"And who is this 'we,' sir?"

"The Gallic Empire will be led by the governor of Germania Inferior and Superior, Postumus Marcus Cassianius Latinius, centurion," said Publius.

"Given up the title of Imperial Legate, has he?" asked Antonius. "Yes, I suppose that would be difficult when you're committing treason, wouldn't it, sir?"

"It is not treason to defend our people, centurion. In any case, this is none of your business. I am in command here, and I order you to prepare to welcome the VI Legion," said the tribune.

"That is a problem," said Antonius. "You see, the VII Legion has 'pia' as part of its title, and, as you know, sir, that means loyal. So, I don't think I can do that."

"Your job is to follow the orders of a superior officer, centurion. If you refuse, I will arrest you. Is that clear?" said the tribune.

"Well, I wouldn't want that, sir," said Antonius, slipping his pugio out from the back of his belt. He slammed the blade upwards at the fifth rib, driving it into the tribune's heart. The man gasped, staggered backwards, fell on the table, and finally rolled off onto the floor.

His aide stood stock-still. Tiberius had moved behind him.

"Now what are you going to do?" asked Antonius quietly.

"Nothing, sir," said Servius.

"You part of this Gallic Empire stuff?" asked Antonius.

"I was just following orders," said the clearly terrified aide.

"That you were, lad, that you were. So do you want to wait here with our late tribune, or take a little boat ride with us and meet up with our boys from the VII?" asked Antonius.

"I would like that fine, sir," said Servius.

"Good," said the centurion. "Tiberius, you and Servius head for the docks. I have a few things to gather and will join you soon," Antonius continued, starting to fill a satchel with scrolls.

Both men saluted and left. Antonius finished gathering up the papers and glanced at the tribune. "Well, Publius, you were a useless prick anyway, tribune. The VII Legion is the better for your absence." Taking one more glance around, he headed out and across the plaza toward the docks.

* * *

Gaius Porcius, the late head duoviri of the city of Tarraco, lay crumpled in the forum, blood staining his toga and spreading out onto the stones of the plaza. Two men stood over him, while several others held back a growing crowd.

"Who is it?" one man asked.

"The duoviri," replied another.

"A good man. What happened?" asked still another.

Pointing at the two men, a woman said, "Those two stabbed him. In the back. A bunch of cowards, I say."

"Here, here, back off," one of the assassins ordered. "This man opposed the new empire. He would have opened our borders to the barbarians."

"New empire? What's that?" someone in the crowd asked. "The duoviri got us through the Frankish occupation without a lot of bloodshed. What are you on about?"

Lucius Thorius pushed forward. "I am now head duoviri and I ask you to disperse. In a few days the VI Legion from Narbo will be here to defend us."

"Defend us from who?" shouted a woman toward the back of the crowd. "Where was this Narbo legion when the Franks came through? It was our VII Legion that saved us, not one from Narbo."

As the crowd grew, the atmosphere got tenser and angrier. The men holding off the crowd were not soldiers. They had neither shields nor armor. And there were not that many of them.

"I think we should get out of here," one assassin whispered to Lucius, who looked nervous and unsure of himself. The assassination had gone badly. The plan had been to kill Gaius in a quiet place with no one around, but the duoviri had grown suspicious of the men tailing him and had dashed into the forum. Instead of waiting, the men had struck, and now a crowd had gathered.

"Maybe you are right," whispered Lucius. "Grab him and take him with us."

"You grab him," the man said. "This is getting ugly. I thought you said the city would welcome the men from Narbo."

Lucius backed away from the crowd, followed by the team

of assassins, leaving the head duoviri's body on the plaza. The crowd closed around him and the assassins took the opportunity to exit the forum.

Once out of the forum, one of the assassins grabbed Lucius by his toga. "You said people would welcome that man's death. Instead, here we are running for our lives. You lied to us."

"They will come around," said Lucius. "And I didn't tell you to kill him in the middle of the forum."

"We didn't have much choice. He was onto us, and he started to call out that he was in danger. We had to act in case people came to his aid," said one of the men. "But I don't see much enthusiasm for the VI Legion out there. And aren't there soldiers here? I don't want to be fighting any soldiers."

"The tribune is taking care of that," said Lucius. "You don't have anything to worry about."

"Another one of your lies!" sneered the other man. "As for me, I am getting out of this town until the VI Legion shows up."

"You can't do that," said Lucius. "I also hired you as bodyguards."

"Yeah, but under false pretenses," an assassin protested. "I didn't sign up to take on a city. You are on your own, duoviri," he said.

Lucius watched the men walk away, then looked back at the angry crowd in the forum. He turned and fled.

XXVI

Flavius sat patiently in the outer office. He and the men had arrived two days before, and the optio had spent most of that time trying to see Septimius Granius, the commander of the auxiliary legion that had fought with distinction against the Frankish invasion, After the third excuse, he began to suspect that the commander was avoiding him, but he persevered. Much of the rest of the time he was listening, although he had to rein in some of his men. There had been several fistfights in the city's taverns.

"Comrades," he told them, "We're here to see where things stand, not fight a war."

"But the town is full of lies, sir," protested Brutus. "They say the Empire let the Franks invade Hispania because of a bribe!"

"And some even accuse the VII Legion of letting the Franks invade," said a man with a bruise over his eye. "They claim the proof of that is that the Franks didn't get turned into slaves after they surrendered. They say it was all a plot to make the VII Legion look good."

"We lost good men fighting those Franks," said Brutus angrily.

"I know, I know. I have heard a few of those stories myself," said Flavius, "and I can't say I wouldn't want to punch someone in the face for them. But that is not why we are here, comrades. We need to find out where the city stands."

"What I don't understand is why so many people here are talking about this, but we didn't hear anything in Legio," commented a man with swollen knuckles.

"Because Legio is out in the middle of nowhere," said Flavius. "The VII Legion is there because a long time ago the Celts were troublesome, and because that is where the gold is. Well, the Celts aren't troublesome anymore, but the gold is still there. Add to that army commanders who don't like to see anything change, and there you are."

"I don't think everyone is buying this Gallic Empire stuff, sir," said the bruised man. "I heard people say it will kick off a civil war, and Hispania didn't do well in the last one."

"Other of you hear stuff like that?" asked Flavius.

Several of the men nodded. "I think many would rather not get involved, sir," said Brutus. "Although I have to say, this nonsense about a conspiracy is everywhere."

"Yeah, people like conspiracies," said Flavius. "They would rather believe them than what they see with their own eyes. But I want you to listen and then put in that maybe the big plot is just hot air. And don't tell them you're in the VII Legion."

"We aren't stupid, sir," said the swollen-knuckled man.

"I don't know," said Flavius. "You joined the army, didn't you?" which brought a round of laughter.

* * *

And now Flavius was sitting in the office of the city's auxiliary commander, trying to find out where the man stood.

An aide poked his head out of the inner office and said, "Sir, Commander Septimius Granius will see you now."

Flavius rose and followed the man into the inner office, where Septimius sat behind a desk that was surprisingly free of scrolls and tablets. "Sir," said Flavius, saluting. It was a nice gesture. Flavius was regular army, Septimius an auxiliary. And Septimius knew that Flavius was more than a simple optio, but rather the principal aide to the legate of the VII Legion.

"A cup of wine, Flavius?" said Septimius, reaching for two cups.

"A pleasure, sir. How are you?" inquired Flavius.

"Well enough. Not quite the excitement of a Frankish invasion, but at my age, I can do with fewer of those," said the commander, handing Flavius a cup. Ordinarily, the optio would have toasted the Empire, but he decided that would be inappropriate, especially if Septimius was leaning toward backing the independent breakaway empire. "Confusion to our enemies," Flavius decided was a neutral choice.

The two sat and exchanged news. Septimius already knew that the VII Legion was headed to Corduba, but allowed as that he didn't know why. No, he hadn't heard about Marcus's trip to Roma and was glad to hear that Lusitania appeared to be calm.

Flavius finally decided to come straight out. "Sir, you know this business about the Gallic Empire? I have been hearing a lot about it in the city."

Septimius took a long pull on his wine and sighed. "Yes, I heard about it."

"And they are saying that the invasion was the fault of the VII Legion," Flavius continued.

"Yes, I have heard that one, too, Flavius, and others as well," said Septimius, turning his wine glass in his hands.

"It's a lie, sir," said Flavius. "We lost good men to the Franks."

Septimius nodded, "I know. We lost men too, Flavius."

"Do you think the VII Legion or Roma let those Franks invade?" asked Flavius.

"The VII Legion? Of course not. First, you were off in Legio and nowhere near the invasion. How did it happen? Of that I am less sure. How did the invaders pass through Germania and Gaul without challenge? Someone told those legions—at my last count, 11 of them—to stay in camp. Who else but Roma has that power, Flavius?"

"I don't know, sir, but why would the Empire do that? What would be the payoff? Doesn't it make more sense that someone in Gaul or Germania is behind this? Cutting out their own empire would be pretty lucrative. And we caught some of them trying to smuggle the Empire's gold into Gaul. Why would the Empire do that?"

"Hmm. I hadn't heard that," said Septimius. Shaking his head he said, "I don't know, Flavius, this is all over my head."

"Well, you aren't alone there, sir. But we are looking at civil war, and as I recall, the last one with Pompey and Caesar didn't turn out so well for the province," said Flavius.

"No, it didn't, and I am no booster of civil war, Flavius," said

Septimius. "But then again I am just an auxiliary commander, so my opinion doesn't carry a lot of weight."

"It does if you join, sir," said Flavius quietly.

Septimius was silent for a long moment. "What are you here for, Flavius?" he asked at last.

"The VII Legion needs help if it comes to a fight, sir," said Flavius.

"The VI Victrix crossed the border, Flavius, and last I heard they were headed to Rhoda. Tarraco will be next," said Septimius.

"I hadn't heard that," Flavius said.

"A rider came in this morning. It is not general news yet, but by tomorrow it will be," said Septimius.

There was a dead silence that went on for a long time. Finally, Flavius asked, "What are you going to do, sir?"

"I don't know, Flavius. My men are not regular army. Most are married with children and vocations. They rose to the occasion with the Franks, but this is different. Are you asking me if they want to fight a brother legion? Of course not, and I suspect that goes for both the VII Legion and the VI Legion."

"Except one is from Gaul and the other from home," Flavius pointed out. "And it was that Gaul legion in Narbo that let those Franks pass by. They are not the same."

"I know that, Flavius, but I don't know that the men know it," said Septimius.

"You could tell them," Flavius said.

The commander shook his head. "I can't ask them to leave their families to go to Corduba. It was different when the Franks took Tarraco. That was a threat to us all. The Gaul legion is only a threat if we fight it."

Flavius bit back the words that were on his tongue, refraining from asking, "You would commit treason because it is convenient?" Realizing that there was nothing to be gained by taking that tack, he softened his tone. "No, I am asking you not to fight either one of us. I am asking you to keep your troops in Caesaraugusta. Tell the VI Legion you need to keep the troops here because there is unrest in Lusitania. I don't know. Tell them what you want, but don't get involved."

"How long can we do that, Flavius? said Septimius. "What happens if this Gallic whatever is a success? Then we would be punished for standing on the sidelines."

"I don't think so," said Flavius. "It looks like they only sent one legion into Hispania. They can't afford to antagonize people who initially don't want to get involved. If the VI Legion goes up against us and wins, then do what you want. I'll be dead, honor preserved." Septimius winced at the word "honor." Flavius continued, "I don't think their odds are too good. They will be a single legion at the end of a long supply line, and if you know my commander, you know he will figure out something that will make them wish they had never crossed that border."

"And then you come north and punish us?" reckoned Septimius. "This sounds like lose-lose to me."

"Why would we do that? I have been authorized to tell you that not joining an invasion of the south will be considered a patriotic act," said Flavius, knowing that he had no such authorization, but it seemed reasonable, and Marcus was always reasonable.

"Really?" said Septimius giving him a sidelong glance.

"Yes," said Flavius. "You keep the men at home and that will be fine with us."

"What happens if they try to force us?" asked Septimius.

"Look, I can't cover every contingency, commander. Tell them if they try, your men will desert. Whatever works," said Flavius, trying to keep the exasperation out of his voice.

"Hmm. I might be able to do that. I certainly don't want to fight Marcus. He is a pretty dangerous man to be on the wrong side of," said Septimius.

"Very dangerous," said Flavius firmly.

Septimius stood and proffered his hand. "I will do what I can, Flavius. And my best to Marcus."

Flavius knew when he was being dismissed, which was fine with him. He was sick of this conversation.

* * *

Flavius surveilled his men. They had mounted and were free of the city. "All right, comrades, we did what we came for," he said.

"What are the auxiliaries going to do, sir?" asked Brutus.

"The best we can hope for is that they sit it out, optio," he answered.

"Sit it out? That still sounds like treason to me," said Brutus.

"Well, things are a bit complicated these days, optio," said Flavius. "If we can just make it us against the VI Legion, we come out ahead."

"Their heads on a pilum is how this should end," growled one of the men.

"It may come to that, but you know we have a legate who wins battles without a lot of people getting hurt. Let him figure this out. We're heading south. We are going straight to Libisosa, then Corduba. I want to avoid the cities. We need to deliver what we know to the VII Legion, and maybe meet up with some of our old friends from the III Augusta."

"Really? We owe those lads an amphora of good wine for covering our asses in Mauretania," piped up the bruised man.

So, the contubernium turned and trotted south on the road to Corduba.

XXVII

The atrium was mostly full and Aelia was holding forth on the current state of affairs in Corduba. Seated next to her was Sabina, who had become Aelia's constant companion over the past few weeks. The crowd was a mix of men and women, most of the men in expensive togas and the women in finely made stollae. Trays of food and drink were scattered on small tables throughout. "There are merchants who are not present," she said, "but I have letters from them declaring that they will abide by what is decided here."

Rachel silently corrected her sister, who clearly meant "major merchants." The people filling the atrium represented most of the wealth and power in the city and included the powerful Ulpii and Aelii families. There were no small shopkeepers in this crowd.

"When is the VII Legion due?" asked a man whom Rachel knew to be a wealthy banker.

"It should be here within a few weeks," answered Aelia. "My last letter from the legate was two days ago, so I know they have reached Norba. They plan to spend a few days in Emerita Augusta helping to organize the defense of that city. Emerita has many veterans, who will be an important part of defending our province."

It was odd for a woman to be holding forth on military strategy, but then the "legate" was Aelia's companion, and everyone in the room knew the stories behind the two of them getting together and the expulsion of Aelia's brother to Tarraco. It was wonderful gossip, but not the kind one made reference to in a meeting like this.

"Can you enlighten us more about what the VII Legion intends and who it is recruiting as allies?" asked another man. Rachel thought he was a member of the Aelii family, exporters of garum and olive oil and owners of the largest copper mine in Baetica.

"As I said, Legate Marcus Favonius is currently organizing allies as the VII Legion marches south. He has also sent envoys to Clunia and Caesearaugusta, as well as Évora, Pax Julia, and Olisipo. He plans to build a defensive line from Valentia in the east to Olisipo in the west so as to wall off the richest provinces in Hispania from the traitors."

There was a moment of silence while the crowd digested this piece of political and military geography. "That may work," said a man near Aelia whom Rachel knew was an Ulpii. "It is a natural barrier."

"But what of more soldiers?" asked another man. "Is Roma sending a legion?"

Aelia hesitated and Rachel stepped in. "The Empire has no legions in Italia to send. Roma is likely to use its Pannonia legions to confront the usurpers in Gaul. But the VII Legion is in contact with the old III Augusta in Mauretania and is requesting it send some of its soldiers."

"The III Augusta? Aren't they the disgraced legion that was disbanded for disloyalty?" asked the man.

"The men of the III Legion made it possible for the VII Legion to rescue the citizens of Hispania from the Mauri slavers," said Rachel. "We owe them a great deal."

"How do you know this?" asked the man.

"I have been passing letters between the legate's close aide and the leader of the III Augusta," she replied.

"How many men are we talking about?" the man pressed on.

"That is not clear. I should say that they have been promised land in Hispania if they come," said Rachel.

"How much?" asked one well-dressed man, adorned with rings on all of his fingers and a heavy gold rope chain around his neck.

"I do not know, sir. You will have to ask that question of the legate when he arrives in Corduba," said Rachel.

The man uttered an incoherent mumble as he withdrew, but others stirred. "We can't give away the province," said one man.

"We won't have anything to give away or to keep if that Norba legion comes to Corduba," said another, and a spate of back-and-forth comments and arguments temporarily disrupted the meeting.

Aelia let them go on for a bit before breaking in. "We need to organize our own troops to aid the VII Legion and, as for the cost, we are all in business. Besides air and sunlight, nothing worth having is free. Please, let's continue."

The discussion veered off to how to recruit an auxiliary and what it would do, and then to getting contributions from some of the more reluctant members of the community.

Rachel watched the meeting for a while before slipping away. She gathered a few bags and left the domus, headed for the forum and the market. There was nothing she really had to buy, but she felt stifled by the gathering in the atrium. As the liaison between Flavius and Quintus Titus, the former optio in the III Augusta, her part of the meeting was, in any case, done. Rachel wanted to wander among the people to look and listen, so as to measure the mood about the coming crisis.

* * *

The three ships bearing most of the VII Legion's Tenth Cohort cleared the harbor entrance of Tarraco and spread their sails, tacking south, headed for the Pillars of Hercules and Corduba.

XXVIII

Maximus Clodius, legate of the VI Legion Victrix, stood in the forum at Barcino flanked by two of his tribunes, Annius Fabius and Tacitus Agrippa, as a curious crowd of merchants, slaves, and ordinary shoppers looked on. A delegation of men dressed in expensive togas approached. Tall and bearded, with a full head of gray hair and broad shoulders, Maximus was every inch a legate. He and his tribunes were dressed in everyday uniforms. They had just completed the march from Rhoda, arriving only hours before at Barcino, and Maximus had not had the time—or the interest—to change into something more formal. He didn't need credentials, he had over 5,000 legionnaires behind him.

The delegation halted and saluted him, the leader introducing himself as Julius Dasumi. Maximus recognized the family name —it was among the most powerful and wealthy in the province. "Welcome to Barcino," said Julius. "Hispania awaits the Gallic Empire and sends greetings to Marcus Postumus."

Maximus nodded. "I will see that the emperor receives your greetings, Julius. Would you be so good as to introduce me to your companions?" What followed was a round of handshakes with politicians, local businessmen, and civic leaders, including Remus Pedani, the head of Barcino's richest family. It was a group the legate needed to pay attention to. Their support was essential for recruiting Hispania to the new empire.

Eventually, the crowd thinned out and the delegation invited the legate and tribunes into a library, where Maximus could ask and answer questions.

"What do you know of the VII Legion?" Maximus asked the group.

"The VII Legion has left Legio, sir, and my sources tell me it is on its way to Corduba," one man volunteered.

"When was that?" asked Marcus.

"A little less than two weeks ago, sir. It will take about five weeks to reach Corduba," the man answered.

Maximus considered. The VI Legion would spend two days in Barcino, then march to Tarraco. But he had only a vague idea of the distance between Tarraco and Corduba. In any case, the VII Legion had gotten the jump on him, which suggested that the Gallic Empire's plans had leaked out.

He was hoping to take Tarraco, then march west to Caesaraugusta, pinning the VII Legion in place at Legio. Even if the VII had left for Corduba, the assumption of his leaders was that any resistance in Hispania would be concentrated in the wealthy Baetica Province. And the VI Legion was actually closer to Corduba than the VII was. Maximus had thought he could either catch the VII on the march or arrive before it had an opportunity to prepare its defenses. But that plan was no longer feasible.

"They are afraid of you, sir," said Julius Dasumi. "Like whipped dogs, they slunk off to Corduba."

Maximus was not inclined to explain that the VII Legion had actually outmaneuvered him and shown commendable initiative by heading south. "Those dogs did a pretty good job fighting the Franks," he admitted.

"Barbarians!" Julius spat. "They won't stand a chance against a real Roman legion." Maximus said nothing. The man was a fool. He changed the subject.

"What is the status of Tarraco?" His question was addressed to the group as a whole.

There was some back-and-forth cross discussion among the delegates. Then one of the duoviri answered. "The city is divided, but my last report was that the VII Legion cohort had left the city by boat."

Maximus frowned. "I was given to understand that a tribune of the VI Legion...." A soldier from the VI leaned forward and whispered in his ear, and he continued, "...a Publius Brutus had arranged for the cohort to join us. What happened?"

There was some shuffling among the delegates. Finally, one spoke up, "He apparently was killed by someone in the VII Legion is what I was told."

The legate did not like that. "Are you certain about this?" he asked.

The man shrugged. "It is secondhand, but I have no reason to doubt it."

"Will there be resistance to the VI Legion?" Maximus asked.

"No," said Julius. "I arranged for the elimination of the one man who might have caused difficulties, sir. The city is divided, but they will not resist."

"Not just a fool, but an arrogant one," thought Maximus. Was his information to be trusted? "How do you know this?" the legate demanded.

"I have extensive contacts among the leading families and merchants in the city, and there is general enthusiasm for the Gallic Empire, sir," said Julius. "Tarraco is open to you."

Maximus nodded, but he told himself that the VI Legion should assume it would be going into hostile territory and would have to take the requisite precautions—full marching camps, aggressive cavalry patrols, and full readiness by the legionnaires. The legate had asked for three legions for the invasion, but with the new Roman Emperor, Gallienus, gathering the Pannonia legions and preparing to march on Postumus, nothing more could be spared. The Germania legions were busy with the northern barbarians, and the Gaul legions had to remain in place to fight Gallienus should he invade. The VI Legion was on its own. There was a need for caution, Maximus concluded.

* * *

"Is it done?" asked Postumus.

"Done, sir," answered Prefect Aconius Calpurnius.

"The Gauls are out of hand," complained Postumus.

"Yes. Killing the son of the Roman Emperor and a prefect of the Praetorian Guards right here in Colonia Claudia," Aconius said, keeping a straight face. "Barbarians."

"Hmmm," said Postumus. "I am not certain they will believe that in Roma. But then, they have no choice, do they?"

"The emperor may march on Norba, sir."

"I have no doubt but that Gallienus will march on Norba, but it will take him time to gather the Pannonia legions, and we will be waiting for him near Mediolanum," said Postumus. "I am leaving tomorrow to join the legions."

"How many?" asked the prefect.

"I will have four," he replied. "The VI Victrix has crossed the border into Hispania. And I will have the II Adiutrix, the XIV Gemina, the XV Primigenia, and the XVI Gallica. I also have several cavalry ala and some auxiliaries."

"Will that be enough?" asked Aconius.

"It will have to be. The men are motivated, even more so since I distributed the loot the Juthungian had stolen from their invasion of Italia," said Postumus. "And great rewards always involve risk, prefect."

"Have you heard anything from the VI Legion in Hispania?" asked Aconius.

"No. But I do not expect to hear anything until I get to Norba," Postumus replied. "The VI Legion is a good one."

"So is the VII Hispania," the prefect noted.

"Yes, it appears to be. But what can two legions do? If the VII is defeated, then Hispania is ours. If it is not, or if there is a standoff, we will still harvest the province's gold. A single legion cannot hold a province as large as Hispania. If our VI Legion is defeated, I suspect the VII will remain in the south to defend the richest part of Hispania. That means the province will be divided, but we will have the gold in the north. I am not much concerned, prefect," said Postumus.

"What will you do with the bodies of the Praetorian and the Emperor's son?"

"We will send them to Roma with all honors and our sincere regrets that the barbarian Gauls would do such a thing," said Postumus. "See to it."

"Yes, sir," said Aconius, saluting as he left.

Alone, Postumus perused a map of Gaul. "Well, the die is cast now, my friend," he said to himself.

XXIX

Marcus had halted the VII Legion outside of Corduba. It was important to make an impression, and the southern province had not seen a full legion in at least a hundred years. The legionnaires' baggage was loaded onto mules, and the nine cohorts—the 10th was still scattered among the eastern cities—lined up. The Second through the Ninth cohorts each made sure their six centuries were aligned and that each century's 80 men were properly uniformed. The First Cohort, with its 160-man centuries, led the way with the legion's golden eagle. The Legion had left Tribune Quintus Junius at Legio—he was too old and ill to travel—and Tribune Publius Brutus was absent, somewhere in the east, either Tarraco or Barcino. So, Marcus led with his great fat horse, while Flavius and Demaratus followed at the rear of the legion.

Almost 5,000 strong, the legion was impressive— the men in armor, marching in step, holding their great scutum shields and pila spears, each century led by a centurion and a signifer clothed in wolf-skin who hoisted its unit's banner. An optio with a hastile, accompanied by a tesserarius, brought up the rear of each century. Musicians beat drums and blew cornus horns. They had diverted the mules to camp, as 1,000 braying animals would have detracted from the drama of the event.

Crowds lined the streets, cheering—there was even an occasional shower of rose petals. Marcus paid close attention to their reception. The spectators seemed excited to see the legion. Maybe even relieved. These were uncertain times, and if anything showed stability, it was a Roman legion.

After many weeks on the road, it was good for the men's morale to see a cheering crowd, bringing back memories of the way the VII Legion had been greeted in Tarraco after it defeated the Franks. Morale was something any commander worth his salt paid close attention to.

As the legion rounded a corner near the forum, Marcus spotted Aelia in the crowd. Next to her were his niece, Sabina, and Aelia's sister, Rachel. A wave of affection and loneliness swept over him. He had not seen Aelia since they had returned from Roma, and he realized how much he had missed her. He waved and gave her a very un-legate-like grin, which she returned with a blown kiss. Sabina waved and clapped her hands.

Eventually the legion reached the river, following its banks to the camp south of the city's walls. The mules had already arrived, and within a week the first of the oxcarts would join them. Now the centurions broke up the centuries, sending men to the barracks, while the tesserarii assigned men to guard duty. What Marcus wanted most of all was a bath followed by a visit with Aelia, but there was a mountain of things to do before that was possible. The staff who had made the trip to Corduba by sea had already organized his headquarters, and when Flavius and Demaratus arrived, the three retreated to his inner office.

"What's the plan, sir?" asked Flavius.

"The plan? Right," said Marcus. "The plan is for me to spend two days here in Corduba and then head to Carthago Nova. We need to know what the people of Roma are thinking right now and whether we can expect any reinforcements, although I don't expect much."

"Why is that, sir?" asked Flavius.

"Roma has nothing to send other than the Praetorians, and no emperor is going to give them up. I think it will be up to the Pannonian legions to challenge the new empire, and we will need all of them if we are to succeed."

"What about the legions in Mauretania and Tripolitania?" asked Demaratus.

"In times of unrest, I suspect the governors will keep their legions close, signifer," replied Marcus.

"Our friends from the III Augusta may join us," said Flavius. "I have been in correspondence with Quintus Titius, and he says many of the old legion members would be interested in coming to Hispania if it will get them some land. We can also train some locals, put together an auxiliary cohort or two."

"Aelia is negotiating with the authorities in Corduba and Gades to see if we can arrange land grants," said Marcus. "As for locals, we will see what we can do, but I do not think we have a great deal of time. Untrained men are more likely to get in the way than to be of help."

"I will try to round up some veterans, sir," said Flavius. "They may be able to help us with training. I know it might create problems, but we may have no choice. We don't know what they are going to send against us. I did my best to try to convince the auxiliaries to stay neutral, sir, but I don't know if that will hold."

"What about cavalry and specialty troops?" asked Marcus.

"We have our Cretian archers and some Balearic slingers, sir, and I will see what we can put together from other cities in the province," said Flavius. "As for cavalry, do we know when Cassius is due back from Lusitania?"

"His last message was from a week ago," said Marcus. "He was gathering horses and men, and trying to keep the Lusitanians neutral."

"Any luck?" asked Demaratus.

"Not sure," answered Marcus. "He thinks he might have been successful, but we will have to await his report. He did say he thought we would have a good-sized cavalry force."

Marcus paced back and forth. "All right. We need to give the men time to rest. No training for the next three days, and give them extra rations. Signifer, pay the men some of their stipendia and arrange for them to have some leave time in Corduba. I want them content and rested before we start to make serious preparations. I should be gone a week."

"We will start things on this end, sir," said Flavius. "I will send messages to city duoviri asking for veterans. Can I say they will get paid?" asked Flavius.s

"Yes," said Marcus. "Tell them they will get paid the same wage as when they mustered out, plus a bonus."

"Can we do that?" asked Demaratus.

Marcus shrugged. "If we win, we will have all that gold from Legio. If we lose, it won't be our problem. We will be dead."

"Roman logic is very different than Greek logic," said Demaratus.

"And which do you prefer?" asked Flavius.

"The part about plenty of gold," said Demaratus.

"All right, comrades, let's go to work," said Marcus.

* * *

Cassius watched as his men mounted their horses outside of Metellinum. He had recruited cavalry in Norba Caesarina and Emerita Augusta, and he now had almost 200 men. He also had 700 horses—good ones. Because Cassius was paying for them in gold, his cousin had managed to round up horses from all over Lusitania. The price was maybe a little high, but considering the quality of the mounts, it was a bargain. And Cassius was leaving his cousin considerably wealthier than he had been a week ago.

As for his mission, Cassius was hopeful that his argument for neutrality had made an impression. Of course, he would now have to sell his approach to Marcus, but Cassius thought the proposal would be acceptable. Marcus was a pragmatist and neutral Lusitanians were considerably better than hostile ones.

He began mentally counting his forces. The men he now surveilled, added to the ala in Corduba, would bring the count to around 700 men. He was confident that he could get more cavalry from Gades, Italica, Hispalis, and Malaca. He wanted a force of at least 1,000 men before going into battle. What the auxiliary cavalry in Clunia and Caesaraugusta did would be pivotal. He would be up against the 1200 to 1500 cavalry that any legion would be expected to have, and he felt confident he could deal with that. But if the Clunia and Caesaraugusta auxiliary cavalry were added to the opposing fighters, he would be outnumbered two-, or even three-to-one. That would be a problem.

He signaled to his optio to round up the horses and start down the road to Corduba. The more experienced men were in charge of the herd, and they efficiently moved it off the meadow, where the animals had been grazing, and onto the road. The rest of the command led the way.

Cassius was also thinking about Sabina. She had been in his mind since the morning the turmae left Corduba. He had a vivid mental picture of her mounted on her sorrel, with the mist burning off the Field of Mars, and waving as his command moved out.

It was madness, of course. She was the legate's niece from a well-to-do family—a Roman family. He was a provincial commander of horsemen who lived from stipendia to stipendia. He had no home, and a family that was happy to take his silver but was embarrassed by his presence. "You work for the enemy," one nephew had said to him—while mounted on a horse that Cassius's pay had purchased. And above all, he was a Lusitanian. Their only common ground had been the two-week adventure from Tarraco to Corduba. She was as unattainable to him as a goddess.

But a young man can dream.

XXX

The two days had flown by. Marcus managed to squeeze in time with Aelia, but both of them were extremely busy. There had been no time for Sabina, about which he felt guilty, but his niece and Aelia seems to have established a working relationship. Aelia had managed to round up an impressive number of wealthy and influential people who, for their part, had begun recruiting auxiliaries and setting aside land for the veterans of the III Augusta from Mauretania. How much land was still under discussion, but there was an agreement in principle.

He, in turn, was at the center of preparing the VII Legion for a possible fight. All he knew at this point was that the VI Victrix had crossed the border and taken Emporiae, Barcino, and Rhoda. Marcus suspected it was already in Tarraco, although he had no firm confirmation of that.

He assumed the VI Legion would attempt to augment its forces by recruiting auxiliary in Clunia and Caesaraugusta. That would take time. The latter was a two-day march to the west, and Clunia three days beyond that. He was hopeful that Flavius's expedition would keep most of the auxiliaries at home. If they joined with the VI Legion, however, the VII Legion would have a problem.

He was confident that he could either defeat or neutralize a single legion. He had the advantage of local support, while the Victrix would be at the end of a long supply line. He had sent out messengers to estates along the route, requesting that they move their supplies to a safe place. Since the VI Legion would simply confiscate any foodstuffs from the big latifundia, that took no great persuasion. He aimed to starve the invader, or at least put him on short commons.

He didn't need to actually defeat the VI Legion, just to fight it to a standstill. While he could draw on local supplies, the VI Legion would be in hostile territory, its supply lines distant and at risk.

Well, there was a proviso to that. His defense strategy depended on holding key points and forcing the enemy to bypass strongholds to obtain supplies. He would try to get Carthago Nova to augment its garrison of the city, bolstering its ability to hold off invaders, rather than sending him reinforcements. He would urge Roma to blockade all ports north of Valentia, so that supplies for the VI Legion would have to come by oxcart all the way from Tarraco. The VI Legion would then have to siphon off men to guard the road, reducing the force that Marcus might have to fight near Corduba.

Flavius had taken on much of the legion's organization, and Demaratus controlled its treasury. Given that this now included the gold seized near Lucus Augusti, there was a considerable sum of money. He had been able to give Cassius gold, rather than the silver diluted with bronze that passed for money these days, to purchase horses. When merchants balked at fully financing an auxiliary legion, Demaratus stepped in and paid the bills. The VII Legion was probably one of the wealthier legions in the Roman army.

Flavius had already sent along a formal invitation to the veterans of the III Augusta, but Marcus would be gone by the time there was a reply. He needed to get to Carthago Nova as quickly as possible.

* * *

Coventina had come to fetch Rachel after the midday meal. "Doctor Timotheus has asked me to recruit volunteers to help in the valetudinarium in case there is a battle," she said. "Would you be interested?"

Rachel leaped at the chance to get out of the domus, where she had felt increasingly marginalized as Aelia and Sabina organized the local merchants. Rachel felt she had nothing to say to the wealthy Romans who cycled through the house. Ignored, she tended to sit to the side and watch. She had hoped to see more of Flavius, but he was caught up in preparing the legion for war and, with Marcus leaving for Carthago Nova, his tasks had tripled.

"Have you ever taken care of wounded?" asked Coventina, as the two women approached the legion camp.

"Not really. I fixed the cuts and scrapes of the children I watched over when I was a slave, and I helped Flavius when he was poisoned and then wounded in Roma, but besides that, I know little of medicine," she admitted.

"The doctor and his assistants will administer most of the medical care. Your job will be nursing," said Coventina. "But if it comes to a fight, some of the wounds will be difficult to look at."

"If you are asking if blood bothers me," Rachel said, "it does not. Nor does pain. I can be useful, more so than by sitting at home."

"Good. I want to show you the valetudinarium so you are familiar with the layout and how we deal with the wounded. You know Doctor Timotheus?" asked Coventina.

"Yes. I met him after we were freed from the Mauri, but I only know him from the short voyage from Mauretania to Hispania," she replied. "I remember I liked him and that he was Greek."

Coventina nodded. "He is Greek. Like mine, but not as pretty. He is better than most doctors, who generally see themselves as gods."

The valetudinarium sat in the middle of the camp adjacent to the principia, the legion headquarters. Rachel had never seen one before, so she was curious. Coventina ushered her in by the main door. The building was a single story with a central garden, much like an atrium. The garden was flanked by raised corridors surrounded by single rooms with portable walls, so that a patient could be alone or in the company of several others. The permanent walls were double thick, which served to reduce noise and provide insulation. The outer walls had high windows, and the central garden was roofed over, but with an opening to allow for air to circulate.

The building was mostly deserted, although a few cots were

occupied by patients, and several legionnaires rested on benches in the garden. Coventina was pointing out that the garden was planted with herbs and medicinal plants when Timotheus appeared.

Rachel reintroduced herself to the doctor, who ushered them to an inner office and poured three cups of wine. "You are most welcome, Rachel," he said. "If it comes to a battle, the more people I have helping out, the better it will be for our patients."

"I warn you, doctor," said Rachel, "I have dealt with little more than cuts and scrapes."

"Once my staff, Coventina, and I have repaired their wounds, all they need is quiet, rest, and water. There is no magic here, just care," said the doctor.

"I saw Coventina sewing up Flavius in Roma. It was amazing," said Rachel.

"Yes, she is quite skilled, more so than most of my staff," he said. "Have you ever seen the results of a battle, Rachel?"

"Only the wound that Flavius received in Roma," she replied.

"His wound was typical of the kind we will see if it comes to a fight," said Timotheus. He hesitated for a moment. "But there will be much more serious wounds, Rachel. They can be quite distressing. These are mostly young men, and some of the wounds will be quite terrible to look at. And some will not survive. Your job will be to ease their journey."

"Understood," said Rachel. "They must be cared for."

"Indeed, that is what mostly happens here. Many times, a soft hand and sympathy can do more than knives and splints," said Timotheus.

"I can do that, doctor," she said.

"Good. Then I will get back to my work and leave you to Coventina to finish the tour," he said, rising. He gave both women a short bow and left the two standing in the office.

"Do you think it will come to a battle?" she asked Coventina.

The Celt shook her head. "I don't know. If it can be avoided, Marcus will find a way. He is not as bloody-minded as most Romans. But I have no high hopes."

"We both have men who will be in the middle of it," said Rachel. "I do not want to be a widow before I am a wife."

"Our men are survivors," said Coventina. "And Marcus has yet to lose a battle."

"He only has to lose one," said Rachel softly.

XXXI

Marcus was not used to waiting. On the contrary, he had grown used to other people waiting for him. But here in Carthago Nova he was waiting in an outer office. It was an odd and not entirely comfortable position to be in. Decimus Domitius was a consul, who, in theory, was a superior officer. But Marcus was the only legion commander in Baetica Province. A consul could tell him what to do, but had no means to enforce his directives. The other man he had asked to see was Potestas Remus Mindius, who represented the civilian side of the government. Having to wait to see two men who had virtually no power over him was irksome, but Marcus could be patient. He needed to maximize unity in the province if the VII Legion was to survive the next several weeks.

Finally, the door opened and an aide beckoned him in. Both men were seated behind a large table covered with scrolls and wax tablets, glasses and plates. Both looked gray and tense as they rose to greet Marcus.

"Legate, forgive us, but we have received disturbing news and were only just told that you had arrived," said the consul. "I am afraid our aide was caught up in our distress and it slipped his mind that you were waiting. We have spoken to him quite sharply."

"What is this news?" asked Marcus, ignoring the apology and the despondent young man off to one side.

"That the commander of the auxiliary legion at Valentia, Publius Maximus, has declared for Postumus and brought the city over to the side of the enemies of the Empire," said Potestas. "Apparently some among the auxiliaries refused to accept the order and have fled the city to take refuge in Lucentum. But we are not certain of how many or what they intend."

Marcus was silent for a long moment. He then reached into his bag and, without a word, shoved the scrolls and tablets aside and spread out a map, which he anchored with glasses and plates at its corners. The two men leaned closer to the table.

"The news from Valentia is not good, but it does not alter what I propose to do," he said. "If you look at this map, you can see a natural defensive line that runs from Lucentum in the east to Olisipo in the west. This line controls the main east-west road, as well as those that come down from Salamantica, Caesaraugusta and Tarraco." He traced the line of mountains and passes and roads with a stylus he plucked from the desk.

"Valentia is important because it might have blocked supplies from coming down the Via Augusta and forced our enemy to take the longer route through Caesaraugusta, thus stretching their supply lines. Without it, supplies can now come south to Valentia and then inland to Libisosa and then Corduba," he said.

Potestas Remus ran his hands though his hair, of which there was very little. Consul Decimus looked grim. "Have we lost already?" he asked.

"No," said Marcus. "It is the opening gambit in a complex game. We have many moves."

"What moves?" asked Remus.

"First, we need make sure they cannot come south by the coast road. If they do, they will have a backdoor entrance into Baetica Province and can attack Corduba from both the south and the north. That means Carthago Nova must hold at all costs. I believe we can defeat one legion, even one supported by auxiliaries. But we cannot divide our forces to deal with two enemies. As long as this city holds out, it will force them to attack from the north only."

The men looked at one another, and then the consul said, "We will hold this city, legate. We can draw on forces in Acci and Urci to augment our garrison."

"Even so, with the auxiliary legion, they will be much stronger than you, Marcus," opined Remus.

"They will outnumber us, but that does not make them stronger. First, if your information is correct, the auxiliary legion is divided. And even those who have gone over to this Gallic Empire may not be enthusiastic about fighting somewhere other than home. Auxiliary legions are local. They rallied against the Franks because they were facing foreign invaders. This is a civil war, and, as I recall, Valentia was on the losing side of the last one. How eager do you think those men will be to risk their lives in another?"

"That coin has two sides, Marcus," said Decimus. "How eager will our people be to support us?"

Marcus shrugged. "I can't answer that. As you know, I am not native to Hispania. But the VII Legion is not like other legions. It is all Hispanian. The VI Victrix is from Gaul. They are the invaders. I think that will make a difference. In any case, we have no choice but to proceed in this way."

"What do you propose, legate?" asked the consul.

"That you focus on two things. One, holding the Via Augusta and Carthago Nova. And two, communicating with Roma and urging them to blockade Valentia and Saguntum by sea," Marcus said, pointing to the two ports on Hispania's east coast. "Even if only partly successful, it will force the VI Legion to draw on supplies from further north."

The consul shook his head. "The navy is much degraded these days, Marcus. I am not sure they can handle two ports, or even one, for that matter."

"It is important that they show up and declare a blockade, even if they can't fully impose one. Those cities will not be very eager to send their supplies south if they think they may be on short commons themselves. Just the threat may be enough for them to refrain from feeding a foreign legion," said Marcus.

"Our strength is that we are local," he went on. "The VII Legion will be able to draw on Corduba and the surrounding cities for support. The VI Victrix will be in hostile territory with a long supply line. I am going to try to cut that supply line, or at least require them to protect it with forces that they then will not be able to use against us. The countryside from Valentia to Corduba is not well populated. There are few farms and estates the VI Legion will be able to draw on, and I have sent out riders to instruct those that do border the roads to send their supplies elsewhere. I want the VI Legion to face a land barren of people and provisions."

Decimus nodded. "You have planned well, legate. And we will urge Roma to establish that blockade. In the meantime, we have several warships here in Carthago Nova, and I will send messages to Malaca, Baelo Claudia, and Gades to send theirs to us here. We might have the ability to blockade Valentia on our own, or at least threaten to do so."

"That would be deeply appreciated, consul," said Marcus. "Haste is important."

"Yes, yes, of course," said Remus. "And we will keep you apprised of our communications with Roma and let you know how many auxiliaries have deserted from the Valentia legion."

Marcus rose. "Then I will take leave of you and return to Corduba. We all have much to do and not a great deal of time to do it in."

* * *

Flavius stood by the banks of the Baetis and watched the barges slide into the riverside docks. The boats were loaded with men carrying bundles, shields, and some pila, with helmets and swords slung over their shoulders. He spied Quintus Titius, the former optio of the III Augusta, and his tesserarius, Macro Lucilius. He tried counting the men and then gave up, striding down to greet Quintus.

"Welcome back to Hispania," said Flavius, reaching out his hand. Quintus took it, and the two embraced. Flavius continued, "It is good to see you, comrade. You are much needed."

"We have just short of a thousand men, Flavius," said Quintus, "although a number of them are not exactly battle ready." He paused and patted his own stomach. "Somehow this got larger since we were mustered out."

"Not a problem, Quintus," said Flavius. "Fat guys always hit harder than skinny guys."

The two Augusta officers chuckled. "Then the enemy doesn't have a chance," said Macro.

"Were you satisfied with the land offer?" asked Flavius.

"Generous. I hear that pretty lady worked out the details," said Quintus.

"Aelia," said Flavius. "Keep in mind that that 'pretty lady' is our legate's companion."

"So noted," said Quintus.

"How is our old friend Domitius Antonius, the governor?" asked Flavius.

Both men laughed. "Not well, not well at all. It seems like someone in Hispania supplied the Mauri with some pretty good Frankish infantry," said Macro. "They have been making the governor's life very difficult."

Flavius affected a look of innocence. "Must be that the gods no longer favor the governor. I should send him my regrets."

"So where are we bound, comrade?" asked Quintus.

"We have set up barracks for you and the men. I'll show you the way."

Quintus shouted out to his officers, who assembled around him. "Organize your units, men. Flavius here will show us where we are bound. It's our new home, comrades."

XXXII

Flavius watched two centuries maneuver. Since it was the First Cohort, there were 320 men, double the size of two normal centuries. Flavius had passed on Marcus's instruction that the legion's cohorts should train on replacing and relieving frontline troops. In the event of a battle, it was essential to rotate fresh men into the front lines without disrupting the formation. It was tricky and took perfect coordination. But it would allow troops to battle all day, if necessary—a half hour in the front line, then at least half an hour to rest in the rear.

Cerficius Nonius, centurion of the Fifth Century, was rotating the men onto the line of battle, while his optio was moving the fatigued troops to the rear. It was all going smoothly. Cerficius was young—he was previously known as the "pup"—but competent, and the exercise was going well. It is, of course, one thing to rotate troops on a training field and quite another in battle, when the enemy is looking for an edge to attack. Rotating troops was a delicate and dangerous maneuver.

In another part of the field, the Second, Third and Fourth

centuries were practicing the same movements. The First was resting off to one side. For the past several days the VII Legion's 10 cohorts had been perfecting this maneuver, and Flavius had to admit they were good at it.

They would break for the midday meal soon. After that the entire legion, all 5,400 men, would take the field. Flavius had arranged to deploy some of the support troops, the slingers and archers, in the rear, and Cassius would deploy the cavalry on the flanks. It would be the way the legion would look if it came to a battle.

The VII Legion was not at full strength. The Tenth Cohort had been split up among various cities, and only Tarraco's three centuries had most of their men, but Flavius was filling the gaps with retired veterans and better-trained auxiliaries. Within a few days, the Tenth should be at full strength. Antonius Crispus of the cohort's Third Century had managed to deploy three centuries all the way to Corduba. Their ships had come through the Pillars of Hercules and up the Beatis River directly to the city. A few other centuries had made their way south when they got the news that the VII Legion was abandoning Legio and heading to Corduba.

Antonius had done more than successfully extract the three centuries, he had also killed the tribune who had betrayed the legion, a man widely disliked in the ranks. The old centurion had become quite a hero when the story came out. In a previous battle, when the Franks had invaded Tarraco, he had successfully kept his Third Century intact and safe, and had ended up playing an important role in the final liberation of the city. Flavius was happy to have the man.

Sometime in the next day or so, veterans from the old III Augusta from Mauretania were due to arrive, although Flavius was unclear as to how many men that would involve. Any experienced reinforcements would be welcome, however many.

The training of the auxiliaries was proceeding, but more slowly than Flavius was comfortable with. Marcus would probably deploy the auxiliary troops on the flanks, backing them with cavalry to stiffen them. But flanks were always a concern, one that Roman legions had special expertise in exploiting. What worked in the VII's favor was that it would be facing a single legion, one that would have problems with its own flanks. Flavius was hoping for a straight-up fight, century to century, and seeing who wore out first. Given that the VII Legion would have local support and short supply lines, that tipped the balance in its favor. Provided, of course, that the two sides were approximately equal. If the VI Victrix showed up with many extra men and auxiliaries, that would be a different story.

The centuries were breaking up, and the men were stacking their shields and spears and preparing to march back to the camp and food. They appeared at ease, radiating a quiet competence. All in all, Flavius was pleased. The VII Legion was ready for a fight.

* * *

Rachel was lying on her palla and preparing to leave when Sabina intercepted her at the front door. "Can I come with you?" she asked.

"Doesn't Aelia need you, Sabina?" asked Rachel.

Sabina sighed. "Not really. She has mostly finished lobbying people, so there is no real reason to have the niece of the VII Legion's commander around to show off. Aelia does not want me to ride alone, so I have been spinning yarn and reading, and I am bored."

"Do you know anything about working in a valetudinarium or taking care of wounded people?" she asked.

"No, but before you began going off with Coventina, did you?" said Sabina. "I want to be helpful, too. I can fetch things, can't I?"

Rachel smiled. "Of course, and I am sure you can do more than that. The doctor will be happy to have you, and being Marcus's niece won't hurt."

"I am rather tired of that title," said Sabina with a grimace.

"Nonetheless, Sabina, it is useful. I am certain your patients will appreciate it," she said.

"Are there patients already?" asked Sabina. "There hasn't been any fighting, has there?"

"The valetudinarium treats everyone who is ill, Sabina. There are soldiers who are sick from various ailments, and some who fake symptoms to get out of drill or guard duty. Not many, but enough to practice on," said Rachel. "And you can familiarize yourself with the clinic and its procedures. Plus, I would like the company."

"Oh, thank you," said Sabina, hugging her and dashing off to get her cloak.

As the two women walked through the town headed for the camp, they fell into a conversation. Sabina wanted to know about Flavius.

"In truth, I haven't seen much of him, Sabina," said Rachel. "With Marcus gone, he is spending all his time making sure the soldiers are properly trained. It all sounds complicated, and I can't follow much of it. We have not had much time to talk. But what of you? Have you heard from your dashing cavalryman?"

Sabina shrugged. "I have not heard anything since I saw him off weeks ago, although he is back in Corduba. I really don't know what to think," said Sabina, sounding unhappy.

Rachel was silent for a bit, then said, "You know, it is complex for a man like Cassius."

"Why?" asked Sabina." "Why is it complex to write me a letter? It is as if I did something wrong."

Rachel stopped and took Sabina by the shoulders. "Have you looked at yourself recently, Sabina?" she asked.

Sabina looked puzzled. "Yes, probably too much."

"You are becoming a beautiful woman, Sabina," she told her.

"I don't agree, I am too fat." she said. "And what does that have to do with anything?"

"It is possible that Cassius looks at you as more than a friend," she said.

"I don't understand. What...." Sabina paused and her face reddened. "Oh," she said.

Rachel smiled. "I suspect that you have not heard from Cassius because he does not know how to approach you."

Sabina was silent for a long time. "But if what you say is true, why wouldn't he write me a letter?" she asked plaintively.

"Sabina, you are the niece of the commander of a Roman legion and a much-hailed hero throughout the province. You are the daughter of a well-to-do, high status Roman family. And you are beautiful," said Rachel patiently. "Cassius is a brave and talented cavalry commander, but I doubt he has much in the way of wealth, and he is not even a Roman. Whatever the young man has in his heart, his head likely tells him that you are far beyond his reach. He might as well be in love with Venus. In short, to him, his situation must seem hopeless. Isn't that reason enough not to write a letter?"

"But Rachel, I am just me," said Sabina. "I am not all those other things, and they don't mean anything anyway."

Rachel sighed. "I am going to say something, but I do not want you take offense. I want you to listen and think about it before you react. Can you do that?"

Sabina nodded mutely.

"It is only those who have wealth and status that can dismiss it as unimportant. If you have neither of those things, they mean a great deal. Remember, Sabina, I was a slave most of my life. Those without power are acutely aware of its absence. Those with power take it for granted and have the luxury of suggesting it is not important. To a man like Cassius, it is supremely important, and not because he wishes it to be so. My impression of Cassius is that he is not full of himself, nor does he seek to wield power over others outside of his command responsibilities. But if you were Cassius, wouldn't you be hesitant about writing a letter to someone like you?"

"Oh, Rachel, that is awful," Sabina said, putting her hands to her cheeks. "I must seem like a spoiled, out-of-touch rich child to you."

Rachel laughed. "Not at all, Sabina. In fact, you seem genuinely unaware of your high status. I have never seen you use it to intimidate or silence anyone. But Cassius has none of those assets, hence he must always be acutely aware of them lest he transgress some forbidden barrier."

"What do I do?" asked Sabina.

"In this case, take advantage of your status. Write him a letter. He can't fail to answer it. To ignore it would certainly transgress one of those barriers. But you should expect something formal and careful in reply," warned Rachel.

"Yes," I will do that," said Sabina. "And when he answers I will insist he take me for a ride. And I will tease him."

Rachel laughed "Men need a good tease now and then. When we get back, we can talk a little about what you should say in your letter."

"I would like that," said Sabina.

XXXIII

Marcus and Flavius stood side by side, watching the men of the III Augusta. "They're a little rough around the edges, sir, but given that they haven't trained in more than three years, they look pretty good," said Flavius.

"Agreed, optio. And they are just a few short of two regular cohorts. We can use them," said Marcus.

"There is another concern, sir," said Flavius. "They want to serve as a separate unit. They don't want to be part of the VII Legion. And they want their own eagle."

Marcus looked over at him. "I don't care about the eagle. I am sure our blacksmiths can make one up. But we can't have them maneuvering separately from the VII Legion. It would be a divided command, and that is always a bad idea. We are going to have to be precise and disciplined if we are to defeat the VI Victrix. Almost 1,000 men moving independent of us is a formula for chaos."

"I know, sir. But Quintus is adamant. When they were dissolved for getting involved in politics, they lost more than pay, retirement, and their eagle. They lost their honor, and they want it back."

Marcus sighed, took off his helmet, and ran his fingers through his hair. "Our centuries and cohorts don't just follow our orders, optio. They watch what other centuries and cohorts are doing and adjust their movements based on what they see. A unit moving independently could throw that off, and we cannot afford that. They have to be under the command of the VII Legion or else they cannot stand in the line of battle. It is just too dangerous."

"There might be a solution, sir," said Flavius.

"Hmm. Why do I think you had that solution worked out in advance of our little talk here?" said Marcus.

"Just doing my duty to advise, sir," said Flavius.

"So, advise," said Marcus.

"We could hold them in reserve behind the VII Legion's First Cohort. If there is trouble on the flanks, they could be sent in as a unit," said Flavius. "They would have to agree to take orders on where to go and what to do, but I don't think that will be a problem. They want to fight as their own legion, under their own officers and eagle."

Marcus nodded. "That is a good suggestion."

"Or...," said Flavius.

"Or?" asked Marcus.

"We mount them on mules and assign them to accompany Cassius to that pass of his. That way, if things get too hot, Cassius can hold off the VI Legion long enough for the men of the III Augusta to climb back on those mules and return to Corduba," said Flavius. "It has the added advantage of taking them and the confusion they might bring to our training away from the area of operations."

"A certain cavalryman mentioned this idea to you?" suggested Marcus.

"Well, the boy is full of ideas, sir, as we know," said Flavius.

Marcus was quiet for a bit. "What do you think of that plan?"

"I like it, sir. Two cohorts could do some damage at that pass, and if we can bloody the Victrix before they get here, all the better," said Flavius. "Although they will probably send their auxiliaries, rather than regular troops, sir."

"It doesn't matter whom we bloody, as long as it means we face fewer soldiers here at Corduba," said Marcus. "And it just might make the auxiliaries shy about throwing themselves into the next battle. Let's talk to Quintus about it," said Marcus.

"Oh, I've already done that, sir," said Flavius. "He was pretty enthusiastic. I think the III Augusta would like to get out of being little more than reinforcements for our legion."

Marcus looked exasperated. "Given that you have already made all these arrangements, why bother to tell the commander of the VII Legion anything?"

"Oh, we would never do anything without your approval, sir. We just thought you would appreciate a little initiative on our part," offered Flavius.

"I assume you both made the requisite sacrifices to Laverna, the goddess of deceit, optio?" said Marcus.

"Sir," said Flavius, sounding wounded. "We know how busy you are. It is our job to make your life easier."

Marcus sighed. "All right. Let's hope they are successful. Now send for Cassius. I need to speak with him.

* * *

There was quite a crowd in Marcus's inner office at the principia. Besides Marcus, Flavius, Quintius and Cassius, there were the senior centurions from each cohort, plus three of Marcus's aides.

Marcus was seated with his elbows on the desk in front of him. It had been swept clean by the aides, who had piled the scrolls and tablets on a sideboard. "Cassius," he said, "please outline your plan."

"Yes, sir," said the cavalryman, taking a deep breath. "The pass is halfway between Corduba and the crossroads between Libisosa and Metellinium. It is narrow, with steep slopes on either side. The only way through it is the road, unless you are willing to climb one of the mountains on either side to bypass it. Horsemen could take that route, but it would take a legion a day or more. The III Augusta could hold the road, and the cavalry can cover the flanks. If things get too hot, I can drive the Victrix back with a charge, allowing the III Augusta to retreat, mount the mules, and head back to Corduba."

"What if the VI Legion attacks with its cavalry?" asked a centurion.

"I have been monitoring them since they left Tarraco. They don't have enough cavalry to overwhelm us. I suspect they have kept some in reserve to protect their supply line down the Via Augusta. We can hold them at bay while the III Augusta makes its escape. And I doubt they will follow us too far down the road. They will be wary about an ambush," said Cassius. "I know I would be."

Marcus turned to Quintus. "What will you need?"

"We don't have enough shields or pila, sir. And some of the men will need helmets and armor," he said.

"Flavius will see to that, Quintus. I am also sending two contubernii of archers. You will find them very handy," said Marcus. "Can you think of anything else?"

"An eagle," reminded Quintus.

"Our blacksmiths have been working on it. I suggest you take a look at what they have done and see if it meets your approval," Marcus suggested. "Cassius, bring at least two weeks' rations. We don't know how long it will take the Victrix to reach you."

"Already done, sir. We're bringing tents as well. The weather can be changeable this time of year," said Cassius.

"Then I leave it in your hands, commander. May Mars and Fortuna favor your endeavor."

Cassius saluted, and the crowd, aides included, left.

When they were alone, Marcus turned to Flavius. "I worry that our cavalryman is overconfident, optio. I think it will be a lot more difficult to extract the III Augusta than Cassius believes."

"For all his enthusiasm, he is a careful man, sir. He keeps his head. Remember how he rescued us from the Mauri? He may be the most competent man in the legion. I mean, besides yourself, sir."

Marcus grinned at him. "I am glad you added that, optio. I was beginning to feel hurt."

"Of course, sir. As long as you have me and our Greek, you are the best," teased Flavius.

"The gods quail on their mountain, optio."

"As well they should, sir."

XXXIV

Marcus, Flavius, Demaratus, and Cassius studied the map laid out on the long table in the legate's office. It was rough, with few details, but it included the network of roads leading to Corduba and the mountainous terrain that ran as a band across the northern edge of Baetica Province. The map had a crude line drawn from Valentia in the east to Olisipo in the west.

"This was my original plan," said Marcus. "It would have forced any legion coming south to take the inland route, where there are fewer resources for it to draw on. We have now lost our eastern anchor," he said, putting his finger on Valentia.

"Will Carthago Nova hold?" asked Flavius, indicating the coastal city south of Valentia.

Marcus shook his head. "They won't be coming that way anyway, optio. If I were commandeering their legion, I wouldn't, and I have to assume they will see the same thing," he said, demonstrating the obstacles on the map. He showed them that following the Via Augusta south through Carthago Nova, the road shifted westward, left the coast and passed through a series of cities—Acci and Antikeria—and mountainous terrain before reaching Corduba. "This is one of the most densely populated sections of the province, with a host of cities we can draw on—Malaca, Medina-Sidonia, Ronda, Baelo Claudia, Gades, Hispalis, and Italica. Remember, they are only one legion. No, I expect them to turn west just south of Valentia, take the road to Libisosa, and be able to draw on resources here, here, and here," he said, pointing to roads coming south from Segóbriga. "And maybe from Toletum."

"Then the loss of Valentia was not as serious as I thought it was," said Flavius.

"Serious, but not critical. Its loss does allow them to shorten their supply line," said Marcus.

"What about blockading the port?" said Demaratus.

Marcus looked up and nodded. "I have requested that, but I am sure you are familiar with the weakness of the Roman navy, signifer."

"I doubt the Gallic empire has much in the way of ships either, sir. Even a partial blockade would be helpful," said Demaratus. "Anything that slows down their supply line will hurt them."

Cassius broke in. "Before I left Emerita Augusta, I arranged for an auxiliary ala to try to interdict the road from Libisosa. I told them to take engineers with them and to dismantle as many bridges as they could. It won't stop supplies from getting through, but it will slow them down."

"Excellent, commander," said Marcus.

"And we can certainly both delay and bloody them at this pass," said Cassius.

"Hmmm," said Marcus. "How can a cavalry stop a legion?"

"It would take infantry as well, sir," replied Cassius.

"Infantry we can't afford, commander," said Flavius. "Our ranks are thin enough as it is."

"What about the III Augusta, sir?" asked Cassius.

"It just would be throwing away good men," declared Marcus.

"They don't have to hold the pass, sir. All they have to do is buy you more time to train the auxiliaries here in Corduba. I can arrange to have mules for any infantry, and if things go badly, they can always get out," said Cassius.

"It does have some merit, commander. If the VI Legion could be bloodied, that would be helpful. In the meantime, send a rider to Emerita, and activate that ala to interdict the VI Legion's supply line."

Cassius left, only to return shortly. "A rider is on the way, sir," he told Marcus.

"Good. Now, comrades, let's look to our deployment in case it comes to a battle." He moved the map to one side and set out some small blocks of wood. "Our right flank will be covered by the river. I want three cohorts of the VII Legion in the front line, with three backing them up, and two cohorts in reserve. On our left, I want two cohorts of our best-trained auxiliary troops, backed by the power of the First Cohort. Our cavalry will anchor the far-left flank, one ala in front and another in reserve. I want the slingers and archers on that left flank, just behind the auxiliary cohorts and in front of the First Cohort."

Flavius leaned over the table and tapped the two blocks representing the auxiliary cohorts. "They will try to turn that flank, sir, and trap us by the river."

"That is why I have the special troops and the First Cohort

on that flank, optio. And remember, we can also turn a flank. If they concentrate too much on our left wing, the First Cohort can hold them, and we will use the reserve cohort to turn their flank by the river." said Marcus, manipulating the blocks of wood. "I think they will be cautious, optio. I know that in their place, I would be. We can afford to make a mistake and fall back if we need to. They cannot."

"I hope you're right, sir," grumbled Flavius.

Marcus ignored him. "Cassius, can you speak to the cavalry?"

"Yes, sir. I will have a little more than two ala, sir. They are quite competent. I have also arranged for a special unit to be armed with the contus, sir," said Cassius.

"The contus?" queried Flavius.

"Yes, sir. Do you remember that lance I had when we fought the Mauri cavalry? The contus has its problems, because once you use it, you have to get rid of it. And it is too long to use in close quarters. But several turmae armed with contus lances are pretty intimidating, even for experienced troops."

"You always have something up your sleeve, commander," grinned Flavius. "I do remember now, and I would agree that I wouldn't want to face a lot of horsemen armed with those things."

There was a long silence. "Well," Marcus finally said, "we have a plan. Let's hope it survives contact with the enemy."

* * *

Sabina's head was spinning with information about bandages, the treatment of wounds—a heavy dose of colostrum is essential,

Doctor Timotheus had stressed—and what to watch for in case bleeding starts. "Check the bandages," he'd said. "If the blood is bright, it means it is fresh and needs to be dealt with. Immediately come to get me or one of my assistants."

"You can assume that anyone who has suffered a grievous wound to the large intestines will not live," he told her. "In that case, your job will be to administer poppy juice and make the patient as comfortable as you can. Sit with them. No one wants to die alone."

Sabina nodded. Would people really die? She didn't know what to think about that. And maybe it wouldn't happen. They surely wouldn't give her the most serious cases anyway. But death was not a concept that she had dwelt on very much. She put it out of her mind and concentrated on the bandages and what the patients could have, water, and what they couldn't have, food.

She was now versed in the choreography of battle. The wounded would first be handled by the capsarii, medical helpers who would bind wounds and carry the wounded to the rear. The wounded were then transported to the valetudinarium, where doctors would perform surgery and medici would see to it that patients were bandaged and assigned a bed. Then helpers like Sabina and Rachel took over, monitoring the men and giving them poppy juice for their pain. "Not too much. Too much can kill," the doctor stressed. He laid out the number of drops each patient could have. "If they are still in pain, come and get me or an assistant to help out."

"What about the ones that are, uh, well, going to die?" she asked.

Timotheus shrugged. "If we tell you a man will not make it,

give him whatever he needs. Death is enough of an insult. No need to add unnecessary pain."

It was all a little scary, but also exciting. And she felt she was making a contribution, something she had been missing for the past several weeks, ever since Aelia had concluded her lobbying campaign.

She sought out Rachel, and the two women left for the forum to shop for food.

XXXV

A hawk circled overhead, searching for thermals in the early morning light. It wheeled across the pass, skimming over the men gathered below before catching an updraft that spun it out over the valley.

"An eagle. A good sign, commander," said Quintus, squinting at the bird. It was a goshawk, but Cassius did not correct him. Eagles were a big deal for the Romans, so let the man think it was an eagle.

"Good ground you have here," he continued. Cassius, Quintus and Macro, plus several III Augusta centurions, had dismounted and were surveying the pass to which Cassius had led them. The road ran up from a valley and through a low spot in the mountains. Shoulders on both sides narrowed the passage to no more than 100 feet or so. The shoulders were not overly steep, but too steep for a unit to maintain a formation while maneuvering. In essence, anyone trying to take the pass would be reduced to employing a frontal assault, which could be expensive.

Macro chuckled. "Like those Spartans at Thermopylae, sir."

"Right. We can hold this front with two centuries, Macro. We just have to be careful how we rotate the men in and out," said Quintus.

"Could cavalry get around our flanks by going up the mountain?" asked a centurion, surveying the upper parts of the pass

"I will have cavalry on both flanks," said Cassius, "and archers as well. My information is that they do not have a lot of cavalrymen, not enough to force us away. I am confident that the flanks will hold. Do you intend to fortify the pass?"

Before Quintus could answer, a horseman called out to Cassius. "Sir?" he shouted, pointing.

A bloc of cavalry was moving through the valley below, heading for the pass.

"Well, looks like our friends are here, commander," said Quintus, "so it looks like we don't have a lot of time to fortify this ground. We need to get ready." He called the centurions to form a huddle, while Cassius mounted his horse and gathered the leaders of the ala's turmae, assigning units to cover the flanks and others to stay ready in reserve.

The Victrix cavalry was clearly surprised to see themselves facing this force. They milled around for a while before a bloc of horsemen started up the road to scout the pass. As they were only about 30 men, Cassius let them get within a half mile, then led two turmae forward to challenge them. The Victrix cavalry backed off. Cassius kept the unit in place until he saw the first of the infantry. The VI Victrix Legion was in the lead, its eagle in the front ranks with two officers at their head. Cassius assumed one of them was the legate. A man on horseback raised his arm and called a halt. Cassius watched several men come forward to hold a discussion. "Didn't expect us, did you?" thought Cassius.

Eventually, orders must have been issued, because a much larger body of cavalry came forward and began to move up the road to the pass. Cassius watched them for a time, trying to judge who they were. They looked competent enough, but also tentative, clearly not quite sure what to do. "We'll show you soon enough, boys," thought Cassius, signaling to his men and leading them back to the pass.

"Is that the Victrix legion, commander?" asked Quintus.

"It is. I saw their eagle. And they were surprised. I imagine their cavalry commander is in for some rough language about not scouting ahead," said Cassius.

"The surprises have only begun, commander," said Quintus.

"Any idea about the auxiliary?" asked Macro.

"It has to be the I Ausetanorum. Its base is Valentia. We fought with them against the Franks," said Cassius.

"Any good?" asked Quintus.

"Not as good as the auxiliary legion from Caesaraugusta," said Cassius. "They held back a bit. But I am not really an expert on infantry."

The III Augusta centuries were organized into blocs, the men gathering their armor, pila, and scutums. Two centuries moved up into the pass behind an eagle carried on a long staff, while others gathered behind them. The centurions put their heads together and worked out how to rotate the units. While this was happening, Cassius gathered his cavalry commanders together and sketched out how they would deploy.

Below them in the valley, the VI Legion was assembling. Off

to one side were the auxiliaries, which Cassius was busily count-ing. There were many more than they had expected. It looked as if the VI Legion had managed to recruit an auxiliary legion of several thousand.

Cassius returned to the front line and took Quintus off to one side. "There are more auxiliary troops than we had figured on, Quintus," he said. "You should be ready to withdraw if you need to. I will keep the mules close to the front lines to speed up any retreat."

"Retreat is a bit premature, commander," protested Quintus. "Yes, they are many, but they can only put two or three centuries in their front line. And we can match that."

"But for how long?" asked Cassius.

Quintus shrugged. "No one can predict how a fight will go, commander. You just have to see what happens and be ready to adjust. We know how to do that."

"I wouldn't presume to tell you your business, Quintus. All I want to do is have things ready in case we need to depart," said Cassius.

The optio nodded. "You do your job, commander. We will do ours."

"Sir?" said a legionnaire, stepping back from the front line. "There are a couple of men coming up to the road. Looks like they want to talk."

Cassius and Quintus pushed through the front line and waited as two men on horseback made their way up the road. The men rode to within a spear's throw of the line and dis-mounted. Cassius and Quintus moved away from the line of shields, stopping about 10 feet from the men.

"I am Tribune Tacitus Agrippa and this is Prefect Atticus Aemilius. We would like to talk," said one of the horsemen.

"Who do you represent?" asked Quintus.

"We represent Postumus Marcus Cassianius Latinius, Emperor of the Gallic Empire," said the tribune.

"Hmm," said Quintus. "Never heard of him." Turning to Cassius, he asked, "How about you, commander?"

"Neither have I. You are in the province of Baetica, Hispania, part of the Roman Empire. Our emperor is Gallienus. Maybe you should go back to where you came from," said Cassius.

"The Gallic Empire currently controls most of Hispania," said the tribune. "We have also given you our names, and we would like the same courtesy."

"Cassius Cornelius, commander of the Ala II Flavia Hispanorum Romanorum," replied Cassius.

"Quintus Titius, optio, III Legion Augusta," said Quintus.

The tribune frowned. "The III Augusta does not exist. It was disbanded for treason. It lost its eagle and its honor."

"And yet here we are, tribune," said Quintus, crossing his arms.

"Let us put aside these matters, comrades," said the prefect. "We would like to avoid the shedding of blood. We do not threaten Roma. We merely want to protect Hispania, Gaul, and Britannia from the barbarians. Roma cannot do that these days. The Goths have killed an emperor, and they threaten us all with invasion and pillage. The Gallic Empire will protect everyone. Let us join as brothers."

"Well, brothers don't normally come to visit with a legion behind them, prefect. We would be happy to talk as soon as you turn that legion around and go back to Gaul. The VI Victrix is a little out of its jurisdiction, isn't it? I seem to recall that the VII Legion Hispania Pia is in charge here."

"We can't do that," said Atticus.

"Well, then we have a problem, don't we?" said Quintus. "You see, we don't fancy treason."

"Treason? This from a non-existent legion that lost its honor and its eagle for treason? Stand aside, and we will forget this disagreement," said the tribune.

"You want this pass?" asked Cassius. "Come and take it."

"This is your last chance," said the prefect, as he and the tribune mounted their horses. "There will be no quarter."

"Let's see who emerges from this field with honor," challenged Quintus.

The prefect and the tribune trotted down the road to where the VI Legion was deploying. But it was the auxiliary legion that pushed forward and began climbing the road to the pass.

"Sending in the fodder, are they?" said Macro.

"Well, we figured they would," said Quintus. "Let's give them a warm welcome, shall we?" Turning to the front line, he addressed the men, "They say we are a legion without honor, comrades. What do we say to that?"

There was a low growl that seemed to erupt from the ground on which the III Legion was standing. "Cassius, we will take it from here. See to those flanks," said Quintus.

Cassius saluted, mounted, and rode back through the III Legion, rallying his men behind the legionnaires and assigning them their places. Most of the cavalry were to be held back as reserve.

The auxiliaries had deployed three centuries who now were slowly making their way up the road, shields locked together. The line was a little ragged, and the men jostled one another, sometimes leaving gaps in the shield front.

"No pila," observed Macro.

"Not surprising," said Quintus. "Takes a lot of coordination to add spears into the mix. Also, they may be short of spears, reserving them for the VI Legion."

"What should we do?" asked Macro.

"Let's hold off as well. We don't have many, and we are going to need them when we eventually face the Victrix," said Quintus. He strode forward and called for the three centurions to convene. After a short discussion, they nodded and began to return to their centuries. Quintus moved over to where Macro stood. "They agree," he announced.

A centurion turned to look back at Quintus. "We're going to advance when they get close. They won't be expecting that. The men want to send this lot packing."

"Have fun, Paullus," rallied Quintus.

When the front line of the auxiliary legion got within 10 feet of the III Augusta, the legion's frontline centuries suddenly surged forward, slamming their shields into the auxiliaries and stabbing at the men with their gladius swords. Out of the corner of his eye, Quintus saw arrows strike the auxiliary's reserve line.

It was clear the auxiliary legion was not expecting an attack. They had been told they would be assaulting a defensive position. Not only were they surprised, but the line of replacements behind them was thrown off balance when the centuries fell back under the assault. Legionnaires tripped over one another, and, falling, dropped their shields and scrambled to get out of the way.

Within minutes, the leading cohort of the auxiliary legion was in panicked retreat, spreading chaos among the reserve cohorts. It was not that the attack did any great damage. There was a scatter of wounded, a few fatally, but the attack had been disrupted, and the auxiliary legion had been routed.

"Go home to your mothers," some of the III Augusta men shouted at the fleeing centuries of the I Ausetanorum.

The III Augusta centuries pulled back and firmed up their formation, while the auxiliary legion began re-forming. After about 20 minutes, the three centuries of the I Ausetanorum began to advance again, but their line looked tentative. This time, the III Augusta let them get close, then advanced sharply, stabbing through the gaps between shields. The auxiliary centuries did not panic and fought back, though not with great enthusiasm. It turned into a standoff, the auxiliaries unwilling to push hard, the III Augusta happy to hold their position. There were a few casualties on both sides, but not enough to discomfort either formation.

Eventually, the auxiliaries pulled back and rotated their centuries, and the III Augusta did the same. For the next hour and a half, the legions performed a lethal pas de deux, but in the end, the pass stayed in the hands of the III Augusta, while the I Ausetanorum held its position on the road.

"I wonder what that's about?" said Macro to Quintus. He was referring to a small gathering of officers in the meadow where the VI Victrix was deployed. Quintus could make out the prefect, the tribune, and another man, whom he assumed was the legion's legate. Several auxiliary officers were part of the mix, and whatever the discussion was, it grew heated.

"I think our friends from Gaul are none too happy with the youngsters from Valentia," quipped Quintus.

The discussion apparently concluded, the Victrix officers turned and looked up at the pass. Eventually, the man Quintus took to be the legate motioned to some men in the field, and several centuries began forming up.

"It looks like we're about to find out just what that Gaul legion is made of," said Macro.

Quintus nodded. Turning to one of the junior officers, he said, "Go tell Cassius the VI Legion is about to get into the fight. And warn the reserves we will be needing them." The man saluted, slipped through the front rank, and disappeared.

Turning to the front line, Quintus spoke loudly enough for all three centuries to hear. "All right, comrades. We spanked the striplings and home they went. Now our friends from Gaul would like to take this pass. What say we make that real expensive."

Again, there was a growl, but more subdued than the last time. The III Augusta had no illusions about what they were facing.

It took almost half an hour for the Victrix centuries to form up and move into place. They were armed with pila. Quintus knew the drill, advance and throw the heavy spear. Its point would bend after penetrating the scutum, making the shields temporarily useless. Behind the frontline centuries, replacement shields were already in place. The shields pierced by the pila would be passed backward, the fresh shields moved forward, and the shields with the spears would be sent to the rear to be cleared.

But two could play that game, and the lead centuries for the III Augusta took up their spears as well. In the end, it would come down to man against man, each armed with a gladius sword.

As the Victrix centuries moved up, the centurions instructed the men to prepare to throw their pila. It was a delicate moment. Too soon, and the spears might not reach the enemies' shields. Too late, and the men would be trying to shift shields and throw their spears at the same time. When both lines were about 30 feet apart, the centurions of the III Augusta centurions gave the word and a cloud of pila engulfed the Victrix's centuries. Most buried themselves in the shields, which were rapidly exchanged for ones from the rear. The Victrix threw their spears, and there was a mirror set of movements by the III Augusta.

And then the six centuries came together with a crash.

The fighting was now continuous, and, for the first time, serious casualties began filtering out from the battle. Medici had set up a primitive first aid station a hundred feet back, and they began bandaging the wounded as the capsarii carried them away from the fighting. The more seriously wounded were set off to one side. There were only three medici, and they were soon overwhelmed. Several cavalrymen dismounted and lent a hand.

The centuries were rotating with regularity on both sides of the line, but after two hours the ranks of the able-bodied among the III Augusta were growing thin. At one point, there was a break in the line. Reserves eventually firmed it up again, but Cassius could see where things were headed. The Victrix cavalry didn't even attempt to take action on the steep flanks. His two ala had nothing to do but watch.

Cassius dismounted, handed his reins to his aide, and went forward to find Quintus. Finding him helping a wounded legionnaire to the rear, he waited while Quintas delivered the injured man to the make-shift valetudinarium.

"Quintus, we should move the mules up, and your men should get ready to retreat. We will attack the Victrix and hold them in place until you can extract your men," said Cassius.

Quintus was silent for a long moment. "No, I don't think that is what we are going to do, commander."

"What? You can't continue for long, Quintus. You should get out while you still have a fighting force," urged Cassius.

"And what do we do about these men?" Quintus asked, indicating the field of wounded men. "I am not about to leave them."

"I can begin putting them on mules now," said Cassius. "I will have the men double up with the more badly wounded."

Quintus shook his head. "They won't go, commander. And I don't think you can keep this lot at bay long. I have to say, they are pretty good."

"Sir, they said they won't give quarter," said Cassius.

Quintus grinned. "Sir? I like that, commander. I doubt any optio in this army has ever been called 'sir' by an ala commander before. I like the sound of it."

"Sir, you will all die," said Cassius.

"Aye, we will. But you know something, commander? We don't have much control over our lives. I don't know if that's the work of the gods or just the nature of things. But there is one thing you can control—how you die. And if you can do that with honor, then it's a life well-lived," he said. "You take your cavalry and get back down to Corduba. Be sure to take those mules or else cut their throats. Leave nothing for these bastards. It's been a pleasure serving with you, lad." He grasped Cassius by both wrists, then thumped him on the chest, turned, and walked back to the front lines.

Cassius shook his head. He had never quite understood this thing the Romans had about honor, but there was obviously nothing he could say to dissuade the III Augusta from choosing its fate.

He mounted and signaled for his officers, who gathered around him as he laid out what would happen next. The group broke up, two turmae taking control of the mules and herding them down the road, followed by most of two ala in formation. Cassius kept a turmae with him and moved off to one side. The archers were abandoning their positions on the flanks and mounting mules. They followed the two ala down the road toward Corduba.

The drama at the pass was playing itself out. The III Augusta continued to rotate their centuries, but there were fewer men to fill the gaps, and many of the wounded were making their way forward to rejoin the ranks.

The left flank of the III Legion began to fold, and there were no reserves to send in to stabilize it. The center and the right flank retreated to avoid getting outflanked by the Victrix, but that widened the front. More men were needed to hold it, but there were no more men.

Cassius watched as the III Augusta collapsed. Its men threw themselves on the VI legion, but fresh troops came forward to push them back. Cassius watched as the VI Victrix soldiers put to the sword the wounded from III Augusta. He witnessed Quintus bring down two legionnaires, then vanish in a sea of scuta and swords.

He waited until he saw the VI Legion's cavalry push through the pass. Then he turned and led the turmae down the road at a lope. The victorious cavalry saw him and set out in pursuit. Cassius kept just ahead of them until the road went through a small forest. There he turned and was joined by most of an ala. The men were armed with the long lance, the contus. Cassius took one up.

The Victrix cavalry slowed when they saw the ala, continuing on at a trot. They clearly outnumbered Cassius and his men. Uncertain about why he was being challenged by an inferior force, the commander of the Victrix forces hesitated.

He soon learned why.

Cassius formed a front with the lances and charged. The second ala sprang forth from two ravines lining the road and struck, taking the VI Legion cavalry on both flanks. The Gaul cavalry was so packed together that there was little room to maneuver. Cassius's cavalry slammed into them, the long lances sliding by the small shields and unhorsing the riders. While the numbers on both sides were fairly even, the Victrix cavalry were not able to maneuver most of its men into action. Surrounded as they were by the Corduba cavalry, they could not free their horses from the packed center.

It was not much of a fight. The VI Legion cavalry panicked. Riders began spurring their horses to the rear to escape, knocking over other riders and throwing the fighting men off balance.

Eventually, the press of panicked cavalrymen to the rear forced Cassius's men off to one side, and a stream of Victrix cavalry fled back in the direction of the VI Legion. They left behind more than 200 dead or wounded.

Seeing what had happened at the pass, the Corduba cavalry put the Victrix wounded to the sword. When the Hispania cavalry had finished, there were no wounded Gauls to treat.

Cassius assembled his officers and signaled them to take control. He assigned two turmae to keep watch over the Victrix and to report back to him on a regular basis. He sent a rider to inform Corduba that the pass had fallen, and the III Augusta had been destroyed. "The Gaul legion has lost most of their cavalry," he messaged. "They will be blind. Let's keep it that way."

* * *

Legate Maximus Clodius, Tribune Tacitus Agrippa, and Prefect Atticus Aemilius stood on the road and watched the remnants of their cavalry stream past. The pass was covered with the dead of the III Augusta, and some Victrix men were finishing off the last of the wounded.

"What's the butcher bill?" asked the legate.

"Too high," said the tribune. "At least 400 dead and more than 500 wounded, a lot of them too badly to recover by the time we need them. We are down almost two cohorts. And from the looks of things, our cavalry just took a beating."

"And the I Ausetanorum was less than impressive," said Atticus.

"Well, on the plus side, they were pretty much unscathed by

the fighting. But on the downside, they showed no great interest in mixing it up," said Tacitus.

"But we're stuck with them, and we are going to need them. Those III Augusta were fighters," said Atticus.

"They were," said the legate. "And we have paid a price for it as well. Let's rest the men for the night. We can start toward Corduba in the morning. The real fight is yet to come."

XXXVI

Aelia was angry. She was sitting alone in the garden—well, not exactly alone, there were the servants—and feeling ignored. For the past two months, she had been the center of attention, organizing Corduba's wealthy families to remain loyal to the Empire. She had wined, dined, cajoled, persuaded, and occasionally browbeat the leading merchants and politicians to resist the spread of the Gallic Empire. She had also raised a good deal of money to raise an auxiliary militia, buy medical supplies, horses, and the thousand other things such a mission requires.

And now she was alone and no one had time for her.

Rachel and Sabina were gone most of the time, volunteering for work at the valetudinarium. When Sabina had gone on about learning how to bandage wounded men during dinner one night, Aelia snapped at her and made her cry. She was short with Rachel as well, who had taken to ignoring her, just smiling and changing the subject. It was impossible to argue with the woman!

Marcus was no better. He was rarely there, and when he was,

his mind was elsewhere. Aelia could understand this, but he seemed oblivious of her fears and insecurities. If the VII Legion were to be defeated, she had no illusion of what this would mean for her. Her brother would not be satisfied with killing her, he would first humiliate her publicly.

She picked up a book, then lost track of what it was about, and threw it on the couch. She called for wine, then complained to the servant for being too slow. When the servant apologized, she became even more upset. And the angrier she grew, the more she felt sorry for herself.

Eventually, she put on a palla and left the domus. Shopping near the forum generally made her feel better, but today the whole city was tense. She could feel it on the streets. Knots of people in the forum were talking about the coming battle with a legion from Gaul. After wandering for some time, she found a park bench and settled in to watch people as they passed.

Surprisingly, she began to feel better, or at least not so sorry for herself. Many people in the city were frightened, and some were packing to leave, traveling south to Hispalis, Ossonoba, or Gades. Some were even booking berths on ships to Italia.

She would stay. If the VII Legion was defeated, Marcus, whom she genuinely loved, would probably be dead. She would share his fate, but not one designed by her brother. And rather than depressing her, this decision brought her relief. She stood up, walked back to the domus, and planned a dinner party. Dinner parties always improved her mood.

* * *

Sabina carefully wrapped the bandage around a thick branch, working on how to keep it tight without constricting the wound. She glanced at bowls of vinegar, powdered aloe, and bottles of colostrum to treat the wounds, and made sure she could reach them easily. She neatly tied off the bandage, then admired her handiwork.

"Well done," said a voice.

She turned and saw that Timotheus had been watching her. "Thank you doctor. I have been practicing."

"Excellent. And you know how to use these?" he said, pointing to the bowls and the bottle.

She nodded. "First, vinegar on the wound, then the powered aloe, and finally the colostrum. Don't wind the bandage too tightly, but tight enough to put pressure on the wound to stop the bleeding," she set out.

"Exactly, and what about a wound in the abdomen?" he asked.

She frowned. "I would put the vinegar, aloe, and colostrum on it, but I have no idea how to bandage it."

The doctor took a bandage and folded it over several times. "First, make a pad. Press it on the wound. Then you need to wrap the bandage around the body. That might be hard for you because you are smaller than any of your patients. If they are conscious and can move, ask them to sit up and hold the pad while you wind the bandage around the body to keep it in place. If they are unconscious, call a medicus, who will help you."

Sabina nodded. "I can do that," she said.

"Good. Would you like to sit in on a class I am holding on the extraction of arrow shafts, sling missiles, and bone fragments?" he asked. "Coventina and Rachel will be there."

"Oh, I would like that very much, doctor, thank you," she said.

He smiled at her. "Medicine is interesting, isn't it, Sabina?"

"Are there any women doctors?" she asked.

"None I am aware of, but women like Coventina work much like doctors," he said. "Who knows, maybe Sabina Aquillius will be the first woman doctor in Hispania. It is a field without competition."

She laughed, rose, and followed the doctor to where, for two hours, Rachel, Coventina, and several medici watched as Timotheus demonstrated how to use forceps to remove pieces of bone and how to use a tool specially designed to extract arrowheads and lead missiles.

Sabina found the arrow extractor particularly ingenious.

"It is called the Spoon of Diocles," said the doctor, opening a box and taking out a long tool with two hooks ending in a spoon-like device with a hole in its middle. "You push the spoon between the flesh and the arrow, rotate it, then fit the arrow point into the hole. When you extract it, the hooks will keep the flesh apart and the arrow can be extracted without doing great damage to the patient."

Coventina shook her head. "We have nothing like that spoon. You Greeks are clever."

"It is a clever device, but we only have two of them. If there are many arrow wounds, we will have to use our standard tool," said Timotheus. He passed around a tapered wooden cone made from tightly woven willow branches, flexible but strong. "Slide the narrow part of the cone over the arrowhead, rotate it, and then pull. The barbs will embed themselves in the willows, and the arrowhead can be removed. It does more damage to the tissue than the spoon, but it is better than trying to dig out an arrow head with a scalpel."

"My people have the willow cone. I have used it myself, but it is nothing like that spoon," said Coventina.

Sabin touched a saw. "What is this for, doctor?"

"We use it to amputate a limb. It is a dangerous operation and many do not survive it, but when it is necessary, we have no choice," he said.

Sabina shuddered at the thought of someone sawing off an arm or a leg. "Isn't it painful?" she asked.

"Yes, but we are liberal with the poppy syrup before we cut. The key is to be swift and quickly cauterize the wound," said the doctor.

When the instruction was done, Sabina and Rachel left for home as the evening began to darken. They carried small lamps, which they did not need, arriving at the domus before nightfall.

* * *

Rachel and Sabina chatted as they walked back to their domus. Sabina had sent a letter to Cassius, but the cavalryman had already left for the pass with the men from Mauretania. She had heard nothing and was anxious about it. Rachel urged her to be patient, reminding her that Cassius had a lot on his mind.

She enjoyed talking with Sabina, but her thoughts were elsewhere. She had seen very little of Flavius for the past several weeks. He had been so caught up in preparing the VII Legion for what now looked like an inevitable clash with the Gaul legion. She was concerned, but she had seen the VII Legion in action and simply could not imagine that it could be defeated. Her major worry was Flavius's tendency to put himself in the forefront of battle.

Rachel was patient. Slaves had to be, she thought, and while she was free now, she remembered slavery's primary lesson—you are not in charge. What the future would bring was beyond her control, so she sealed it in a box. Again, an old slave strategy—set aside what you can't control, focus on what you can. For Rachel, the focus was on becoming a skilled medicus.

She knew that Aelia was unhappy and why. For so long, she had been at the center of things in Corduba, but now events had passed her by. She had difficulty not being in control. But there was nothing that Rachel could do about that, other than not to react to her sister's bouts of ill temper. She also knew that Aelia was afraid, afraid for Marcus and afraid for herself if the VII Legion were to be defeated. These were not abstract fears, but very real. Her own brother would be quick to kill her—although he had best bring a stout bodyguard with him. Rachel had seen Aelia kill two men, one a Mauri warrior, the other a Roman assassin.

When they reached the domus, Rachel sought out Aelia and drew her into a discussion about their future. After some back and forth, Aelia admitted that she had a responsibility for Sabina that made her consider moving to Gades if things did not go well. And, yes, she knew she had a life she could rebuild in Roma, but she didn't want to talk about it anymore tonight. Rachel left satisfied that she had moved Aelia toward being more sensible. Rachel hoped she would see Flavius soon, but if it didn't happen, then it didn't happen. She could be patient.

* * *

Marcus had a headache, and it was not from too much wine. In fact, he hadn't had a decent cup in more than two days. Being the legate of a legion preparing for war meant a thousand meetings—with the centurions, with the junior officers, with Flavius and Demaratus, with Doctor Timotheus, with the leading merchants, with the decurions, with the suppliers, and with the officers sent by his superiors in Carthago Nova. Then there were the auxiliaries and the militia the town had organized. While Flavius did much of the heavy lifting on this issue, Marcus still had to make appearances, listen to complaints, sympathize with how difficult their lives were, and tell them whatever would keep them happy. It also meant reading through endless scrolls, letters, and tablets, because no matter how many aides he had, the decisions were his to make.

Lastly, he also had to deal with a very unhappy lover. This was probably the most difficult of his tasks. He was awkward with women, and Aelia was not the simplest of people. In his opinion she was considerably more challenging than planning to fight the VI Legion.

And those plans were in constant flux. He was still trying to absorb the news of what had happened to the III Augusta at the pass. He liked those men. They had been a valuable part of his expedition to free the Roman slaves from the Mauri. Now they had been butchered on some nameless pass in Hispania, and he was responsible for having sent them there. He wanted to take time to mourn those men, but there was no time. His centurions were clamoring to know the plan to fight the VI Legion Victrix, and he had not yet fully formulated one.

The result was a headache, and he was tempted to ask the doctor for something to moderate it. But anything that moderated the headache would also slow down his thinking, so that was not an option. He had the germ of a strategy, but it would have to wait. Flavius was doing his best to keep the various constituencies at bay, but he could only do so much.

Marcus did not want this fight. He did not feel good about fighting legionnaires in his own army, even if they had defected. But he also knew he could not lose this fight. There was far too much riding on its outcome. He was worried about Aelia—he had no illusions about what her brother would do to her if the VII Legion were defeated,—but when he suggested that she consider moving to Gades and be prepared to take a ship to Roma, she almost bit his head off.

He took a deep breath and told Flavius to send in the next *Absolutely Important Person* who wanted to talk to him.

* * *

Flavius was overworked and exhausted, but he had not the slightest worry about what the outcome of the coming fight would be. "Marcus doesn't believe in losing," he told Demaratus, when the signifer indicated he was nervous about the coming clash. Flavius's only real concern was Rachel. He barely saw her these days, but when he raised this with her, she had kissed him on the cheek and told him not to worry, she knew he was busy, she was as well, and everything would come out just fine.

Flavius had come to admire how unperturbable she was. She was not demanding or jealous of his time. Her stance could be summarized as, "You are busy now, Flavius, and so am I. In the end we will spend our lives together."

Flavius took things at face value, and if there was one thing in life he could trust, it was Rachel. Well, Marcus and Demaratus, too, but that was different. So, he refused to worry about their love, turning his attention to triaging the next set of *Important People Who Had to See the Legate!*"

* * *

Unlike their friends, Demaratus and Coventina did have time to see one another. The signifer was busy distributing the gold seized by the VII Legion and paying off suppliers, but it wasn't all that different from his customary job. Coventina had become a major asset for Timotheus, spending long hours at the valetudinarium, but there was only so much the medical corps could do in the absence of a battle. They would soon be very busy, but that was sometime in the future.

So, the two managed to meet, eat together, and even sleep together on occasion.

"So, Flavius said we have nothing to worry about?" queried Coventina, as the two lay in bed.

"Not to worry is not quite what he said. He said Marcus doesn't lose a fight, and I have to agree with him. I have seen the man in action, and he is formidable. Like the Greeks of old," said Demaratus, tracing her eyebrows with his finger.

"Didn't the Romans win and the Greeks lose?" she countered.

"Well, yes, but our current generals were not as good as our generals in the past," said Demaratus, moving his finger down her cheek and tracing her jaw line.

"Hmm. As I recall, we sent the Greeks packing," said Coventina, "and we are just barbarians."

"Those were merchants who hired mercenaries," said the signifer, "and not very good ones at that."

"You are the most charming *and* the most irritating man I know," said Coventina. "Of course you are the only Greek lover I have ever had. But I think that pretty much sums up your race."

"I would not disagree," he said, kissing her. "So how is Marcus's niece doing at the valetudinarium?"

"Quite well. I have come to really like her. She is smart and quite capable, and she is learning how to be a healer. I think, too, that she is in love," said Coventina.

"Really?" said Demaratus, propping himself up on an elbow. "Who with?"

"Our dashing commander of the cavalry," said Coventina.

"By the gods," exclaimed Demaratus. "That might get complicated."

"You mean a liaison between a well-to-do Roman who is the niece of a legate and a Lusitanian with only a handful of denarii to his name? What's complex about that?" teased Coventina.

"Everything you just said."

With mock seriousness, Coventina continued, "You mean like a barbarian Celt and an educated Greek?"

"Oh, not that complex, but almost," said Demaratus, pulling Coventina to him. "I just don't want Cassius to end up with a broken heart. I like that young man, and he has saved us on several occasions."

"I think you underestimate Sabina. Like her uncle, she doesn't believe in losing," said Coventina.

* * *

Cassius was trying to organize his thoughts. Marcus would want a report, but Cassius's mind kept returning to having watched the III Augusta be overrun and to the image of Quintus throwing himself into the grasp of the Mauretania legion. All those brave men gone, men whom he knew the VII Legion was banking on having at its side in Corduba.

But at the same time, the fight at the pass was not a defeat. The Victrix had hoped to use the I Ausetanorum to push through the pass, but that had been a fiasco. Instead, the auxiliary legion had taken a beating that had almost certainly demoralized them. It was also clear that the Gaul legion had been hurt. How much, he didn't know, but he had witnessed a stream of wounded moving to the rear. And there were no replacements for those men.

Lastly, the auxiliary cavalry had been seriously weakened. He doubted they had more than two or three hundred men, and his Corduba cavalry could match that three-to-one.

But he couldn't think of the fight as some kind of victory. He had come to really like Quintus and his quiet second-in-command, Macro. Now they lay butchered on the ground, left for wolves and vultures.

He sighed. His report would be that the VII Legion would face a possibly demoralized auxiliary legion, a wounded Gaul legion, and a much-depleted cavalry force. If we defeat them, he said to himself, he would return to the pass, gather the bones of his comrades, and give them a proper funeral pyre.

XXXVII

The rain arrived in the early morning hours, and the VII Legion cavalry turmae huddled under a large oak tree on the top of a hill overlooking the road into Corduba. It was now approaching noon, and everyone was wet and miserable.

"Sir?" said a mounted trooper. "Something is moving down there. Should we send a rider to Corduba?"

Rufius Atticus had been a turmae commander for almost a year now. He had seen action against the Franks and the Gaul legion. He was not one to jump to conclusions.

"Let's wait, Barea. We want to be sure. If it's just cavalry, there is no need to alert anyone at this point," he said.

His men were restless. It was hard to blame them. They had seen the destruction of the III Augusta at the pass, and they were nervous. Again, hard to blame them. They might soon be facing the men who had crushed the III Legion. But he wanted to make sure it wasn't just some cavalry scouting ahead.

The riders halted, milling around, and within minutes a

column of legionnaires appeared, led by several mounted officers with their eagle in the vanguard.

Bad use of cavalry, thought Rufius. They should have been way in front, scouting for potential ambushes and making sure hostile cavalry was not able to observe them. But then, maybe they didn't have much left in the way of cavalry. They had lost many of them in the ambush at the pass.

"Barea, you and Paullus go. Tell Corduba the VI Victrix has arrived," he said. Barea and a companion turned their horses, rode down the back side of the hill, and galloped west.

Rufius pulled his horse around and said, "Follow me. Let them see us." The 27 horsemen fell in behind him and began to parallel the men on the road. He saw the VI Legion's cavalry point them out. "Yeah, ride up here to scare us off," he thought. Two more turmae were hidden in a stand of trees a few hundred yards from where Rufius's troop was pacing the road. He was hoping they might try to attack him, but the VI Legion didn't take the bait. The Gaul cavalry stayed on the road.

Ahead of them was half an ala, enough to keep the Gaul cavalry from doing much more than escorting the foot soldiers. Rufius would shadow them and keep his superiors informed. Their orders were to gather intelligence and to keep the enemy cavalry from forging ahead of the legion. The VI Legion was still a day and a half from Corduba.

Because the Gaul cavalry could not push through the screen of the VII Legion cavalry, the VI Victrix was essentially blind, unable to scout out what the Hispania legion was up to.

* * *

The pilus prior centurions were arguing with one another and with Marcus, although he kept silent. It was best to let people talk themselves out before stepping in. The pilus prior centurion of the Ninth Cohort, Paullus Acilius, was objecting to being placed in reserve. "My men fought with distinction against the Franks," he said. "Why are we banished to the rear of the battle?"

Marcus refrained from sighing out loud. He also recognized that the two leading centurions of the Ninth and Second Cohorts were reflecting the unhappiness of their cohorts' other five centurions, who in turn were representing their own optios, tesserarii, and signifers, all of whom had picked up on the grumping among the ranks. In that sense, they were doing their jobs.

Marcus finally intervened. "No one is being banished. Every cohort will have its moment if it comes to a fight." He pointed out that the First Cohort was in reserve to the auxiliary legion. But the primus pilus centurions of the First Cohort were none too happy about that placement either.

"We do not know how this battle is going to unfold," said Marcus. "I am quite aware of the Ninth Cohort's record, Paullus, which is why I want them where I have placed them. If there is trouble, I need my best units prepared to step in and stabilize things."

He had diagramed the order of battle on a sheet of papyrus that was pinned to a wall—the First through Seventh and Tenth were deployed in two layers, with the river on their right flank. The Ninth was in reserve behind this core. The First was on the legion's left behind the auxiliaries, with the cavalry guarding the left flank.

"According to my optio, our auxiliaries are pretty good, but they have not seen battle yet. That is why we need to have the First Cohort backing them up. Then if things really go wrong, we can throw in the Ninth Cohort to support them. We need to have that flexibility, and the Ninth is perfectly placed to come to our relief, or to the relief of any cohort in the main battle line. Since the ground is more uneven in front of the auxiliaries, I think the Victrix will initially avoid making a major push there."

Paullus grumbled, but he also backed off, mumbling, "I just don't see why it has to be the Ninth Cohort."

"Because if it were the Third or the Sixth, I would be having this discussion with Felix and Aconius. I thought the two of you would see the strategic necessity for this formation," answered Marcus. "And I want one of my best units in reserve. It could be the difference between victory and defeat."

The compliment ended up silencing both centurions, who each would take those words back to their centurion council. Being a legate not only meant being responsible for everything, it also meant keeping people happy. The latter had not been part of the official job description.

When both had left, Marcus turned to Flavius. "Next?"

"This one's a pleasure, sir. Our boy Cassius wants to finalize what the cavalry will be doing."

"Send him in, optio," said Marcus, going over to the sideboard and pouring himself a small cup of wine, which he downed in a single shot.

Cassius came in looking slightly disheveled. He was wet and

covered with mud, and he clearly had not bathed or shaved for several days.

"Sir," he said, with a smart salute.

Marcus smiled at him. There was something about the young man that always made him feel slightly uplifted, in part because Cassius was good at his job. "Give me some good news, commander," he said, taking a seat behind the desk.

"Well, the Gaul legion doesn't have much left in the way of cavalry, sir, which means they have no idea what we are up to. I also had a report from Emerita Augusta that the city is sending cavalry to try to disrupt the VI Legion's supplies coming down from Valentia."

"What do you think their chances are?" asked Flavius.

"Good, sir. I told them to avoid confronting any supply columns and concentrate on dismantling bridges. With the rains coming, some of those rivers will be difficult to cross without a bridge. I don't think it will stop the supplies, but it will slow them down," said Cassius.

"And maybe force them to divert men to guard the supply wagons," said Flavius.

Cassius nodded. "Yes, sir, I thought of that. I told the cavalry to avoid a fight, but to be sure to show themselves. I doubt the supply trains will take chase, as they won't want to risk an ambush. I am sure they've heard what happened at the pass by now."

"Excellent, commander," said Marcus. "Have you looked at the plans I've made for deployment if it comes to a fight?"

"I have, sir. I am certain that it will come to a fight, and I see no problems with the plans. I will keep a special reserve armed with the conti. The long lances are not very useful for hand-to-hand combat, but they are intimidating in a charge. I think they would make any unit flinch and retreat, giving time for our reserves to get into position," said Cassius.

"Do you need anything, commander?" asked Marcus.

"No, I think the two alas are ready. I will make sure the men are fed and rested before a battle. I will also keep a cavalry screen between Corduba and the VI Victrix. I want them to know nothing about us before they get here."

"Fine work, Cassius. Please let Flavius know if you require anything," said Marcus. "Now, go take a bath and relax a little."

"Sir," said Cassius, saluting.

After he left, Marcus said, "Why aren't they all like Cassius?"

"They broke the mold with that one, sir," said Flavius.

A wave of depression swept over Marcus. Cassius reminded him of the III Augusta. Their loss was more than a reduction of the men he would have for the coming fight. He had liked those men.

Marcus took a deep breath. "Who's next?"

* * *

Coventina, Rachel, and Sabina were huddled in the garden of the valetudinarium eating lunch, taking a break from preparations for the coming battle.

"Have you two given any thought to what happens if the VII Legion is defeated?" asked Coventina.

Rachel was silent. Sabina looked startled. "But they are not going to be defeated. My uncle never loses a fight."

"My Greek would call that hubris, Sabina, the most dangerous thing a person can feel, because it always draws the ire of the gods," said Coventina. "No one can predict the turn of battle."

After a pause, Sabina admitted, "No, I never considered it."

Coventina looked over at Rachel. "And you?" she asked.

"Of course," said Rachel.

"And?" pressed Coventina.

"If the VII Legion falls, so will Flavius. That is hard for me to contemplate, but it is a reality. I am nobody, so I could simply blend into the population of the city and disappear. Slaves are good at vanishing. But the complication is my sister. Aelia will be in mortal danger from her brother. I have urged her to flee, but I am not sure she will. I have impressed on her that she is responsible for Sabina. If she does flee, I will go with her, probably to Roma. I will not, however, die with her if she decides to stay or take her own life. Life is too precious to cast aside," said Rachel. "And you, Coventina?"

"If my love dies, I will be deeply distressed, but I agree with Rachel. Life goes on. I would go north and be with my people in the mountains. If Demaratus survives, I will try to take him with me, but I am not sure of his mind on that subject. While he has strong ties to Marcus and Flavius, Demaratus has no great loyalty to the Roman Army or the Empire. If they fall, I believe he would go north with me. But I have not thought beyond that."

Sabina shook her head. "I have no idea what to do."

"We need to think about it, Sabina," said Rachel. "You are the niece of the commander of the VII Legion, and Romans have a long reach when it comes to revenge. I have argued with Aelia that she has a responsibility to you, regardless of what happens to Marcus, and that she should be prepared to flee with you to Gades or some port in the south. You have your family in Roma, and Aelia has resources independent of her brother. Her recent agreement with a senator on trade with India promises to be very lucrative. And since her brother has apparently thrown in with the Gallic Empire, he has lost any chance of the Senate overturning his father's will dividing his estate between the two of them."

Sabina looked slightly dumbfounded. "Why has this never come up until now?" she asked.

"Because we were not clear there would be a battle. After the fight at the pass, it is almost certain there will be," said Rachel.

"I feel stupid," said Sabina. "I've thought of none of this. And you, Rachel, even have a plan to save me. This morning, I was feeling like a grown-up. Now I feel like a child."

"You are both, Sabina," said Coventina. "These are not the kind of things a 13-year-old thinks about, and I curse the world in which you have to. I think Rachel's plan is a good one, so you must play along and support her with Aelia."

Sabina nodded. "I will." But there was icy ball in the pit of her stomach.

XXXVIII

Marcus eyed the deployed legion. To his left were the two cohorts of auxiliaries and the reserve cohorts that would provide their backup. On their flank, set back several hundred feet, was a block of cavalry. To his right, the Second, Third, and Fourth cohorts had deployed a century apiece. Altogether, he had 480 men in the first line, with 480 cavalrymen on the flank, backed by another ala of 480. He could not see the special cavalry unit armed with the long contus lances, but Marcus assumed Cassius was keeping that unit out of sight. Surprise was a major weapon.

A plan had formed in his mind, and he was running through its variations. He would talk with Servius Junius, the Primus Pilus of the First Cohort. As the lead centurion he, in turn, would brief the four other centurions that made up the Primi Ordines, the body that oversaw the First Cohort. He would need the commander of the auxiliaries, Avidius Hadrianus, in on that discussion. Avidius was a former centurion in the VII Legion, but he had not seen any active fighting. Marcus's impression was that the man was solid and dependable, which is what he needed. Flavius and Cassius had to be at the meeting as well.

Flavius had left to round up the various commanders, and Marcus had nothing much to do but reexamine the plan, looking for flaws. Plans on paper rarely revealed flaws, it was when those plans were translated to the battlefield that the problems showed up.

One by one, the men filtered into his office, milled around, and made small talk until Cassius and Flavius finally arrived. "Comrades," said Marcus, "let me outline my strategy for the coming battle." Marcus had sketched out the deployment on a sheet of papyrus, and he gathered the others around it.

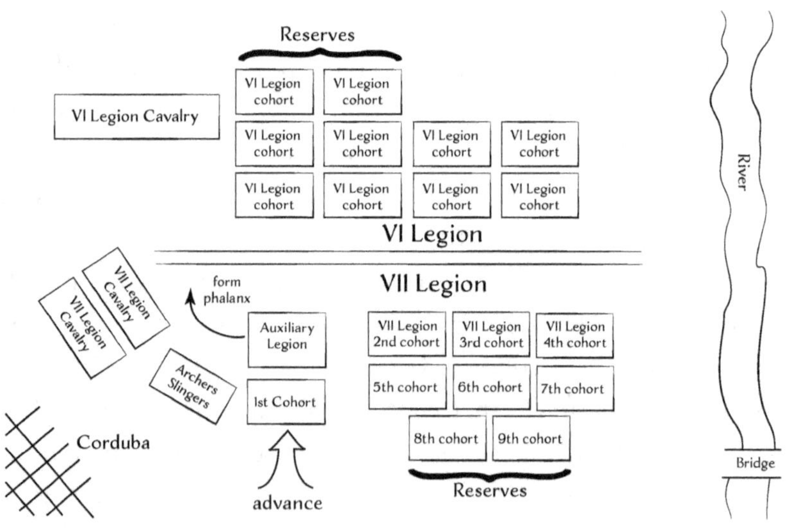

"On the right side of our line will be the Second, Third, and Fourth Cohorts. Behind them will be the Fifth, Sixth, and

Seventh Cohorts. In reserve will be the Eighth and Ninth Cohorts, and the First Cohort will be behind the auxiliaries, with the cavalry on their left. Any questions?" asked Marcus.

The group was silent. It was not the first time they had seen the deployment plans, and many of their initial questions already had been answered.

"Now, if I am the commander of the VI Victrix, I am going to look at this deployment and ask myself, 'Do I see any weak spots?'" said Marcus.

Centurion Servius of the First Cohort turned to the commander of the auxiliaries. "No offense, Avidius," he said, "but if I were the VI Legion, I would go after your auxiliary on our left wing."

"None taken, comrade," said Avidius, a stocky man, a little past his prime, but still looking like he could handle himself in a brawl. "I would do the same thing. I have put my vets up front with a lot of strong, young men to back them up. If they think we are going to fold and run, they are in for a surprise."

"At a certain point, they will retreat," said Marcus. "Please explain what you're planning for the auxiliaries, commander."

"For the past week, we have been working on how to form a phalanx, comrades. We will have long spears stashed off to our left, and when we move off the front line, my men will retrieve them and form a phalanx. At first, my men were confused, but when the legate's scheme was explained, they became rather enthusiastic about it," said Avidius.

"A phalanx?" said Servius. "They are going to fight as a phalanx? Didn't we demonstrate that the phalanx is no match for the maneuverability of a legion when we whipped the Greeks?"

"We're not exactly going to fight," said Avidius. "What we want to do is make it impossible, or at least difficult, for the VI Legion to flank our position. The phalanx can't move very well, but it is difficult to fight. It's a big block of men armed with long spears. Getting past it is not easy. Any Roman legion would eventually defeat it, but we just want to have a hard spot on the battlefield.

"If the VI Victrix decides it wants to go after us as a way to turn our flank, it will take men and effort. And the First Cohort will be in position to move up and attack. The Victrix will, in effect, have two fronts, one fighting the First Cohort, the other trying to overcome our phalanx. And we won't just sit there, we will move to attack the VI Legion, just slowly and deliberately. I mean it won't be on us to win the battle, but they will have to deal with us."

"Huh," said Servius. "They won't be expecting that."

"And surprise is an ally," said Marcus.

"The trick will be getting the auxiliaries out of the way, so the First Cohort can move up," said Servius.

"The reserve cohorts and centuries behind the front line will exit to their left first. Avidius has been practicing the maneuver along with forming the phalanx," said Marcus. "I don't expect it will all go smoothly, but I am confident that the First Cohort can handle it. They will already be deployed behind the auxiliary front lines, and when the front line falls back, the First Cohort will move up."

"Lots of pieces to line up and move, sir" said Servius. "The best of plans tends to go awry when the blood starts flowing.

If we botch up the maneuver, the VI Legion may see that as an opportunity to attack."

"Which is where we come in," said Cassius. "If there is any problem, two ala will attack, distracting the VI Legion long enough for the auxiliaries to get into place, and for the First Cohort to move up into position."

Servius nodded. "That sounds good, commander. Is the idea to turn their flank and drive them toward the river?"

"Ideally, yes," said Marcus. "The two reserve cohorts—the Eighth and Ninth—will move up and attack the right side of the Victrix's front line, the section closest to the river. Both wings of the VI Legion will be under attack. But even if the First Cohort cannot break through, I think the VI Legion will have to retreat and realign its front units."

"And since that will be fairly late in the day," said Cassius, "the Victrix may decide to retire from the field. That will give us time to replace our losses. They, however, have no replacements, and they are far from their home base. They may decide not to continue the following day."

"What then?" asked Servius.

"That, comrades, depends on many things that we can't know at this point, such as what their casualty lists and ours will look like," said Marcus. "But I want everyone to be clear what our plan is."

"It's clear enough, sir. Whether it works or not is another matter. I guess we will find out in the next few days," said Servius. "I would like to run this by my Primi Ordines."

"Of course. However, I expect the fight to begin no later than the day after tomorrow, maybe earlier. It is important that your men get plenty of food and rest."

The group was a lot quieter now than when the meeting had begun, and they exited silently, with only Servius pulling Avidius aside to continuing the conversation.

* * *

The group of horsemen were gathered on a small hill watching the VI Legion go by. The legate, Maximus, and his two tribunes, Tacitus and Annius, sat side by side, with prefect Atticus slightly behind them. "What's the report on the wounded?" asked Maximus.

"The problem, sir, is that we have no real valetudinarium," said Annius. "Many of them are recovering, but the more seriously wounded can't be moved. We left them back at the pass. Some should improve enough to join us eventually, but not for a week or so."

"Supplies?" asked the legate.

"We do have a problem, sir," said Tacitus. "It seems that two bridges were dismantled. The supply column had to unload the oxcarts, pull them across the rivers, and hand-carry the supplies. They are getting through, but slowly."

"What's happened to our cavalry?" Maximus asked.

Annius shrugged. "Not enough of it, sir. We lost many at the pass, and some of the auxiliary cavalry have melted away. We don't have enough to guard the bridges and still try to scout ahead of the legion. We even lost some cavalry that we sent out as messengers."

"Lost?"

"Well, not exactly lost. Several horses came back with only the heads of their riders tied to the saddles," said Annius. "It seems some of the locals have developed animus toward us."

"And we know nothing about what lies ahead," said the legate, as much to himself as the others.

"No, sir. The screen of Corduba cavalry is thick and aggressive. We have fought several skirmishes with them, to no avail I am afraid," said Annius.

"The fight at the pass was more expensive than I had counted on," said Maximus. "We need to halt for a day outside the city and give the men a chance to eat and rest. I don't think this VII Legion will be easy."

XXXIX

Marcus and his officers watched as the VI Legion Victrix deployed. It was said that when the natives first encountered Claudius's legions in Britannia, the Celts thought they were seeing an animal of some kind, not a gathering of men. But what he was seeing reminded Marcus of a machine—smooth, precise, and menacing.

The Gaul legion had arrived the day before and had camped a few miles from the city. Cassius's men had kept it under surveillance while the Victrix built a marching camp and bedded down for the night. In total numbers, the VI Legion and the I Ausetanorum together outnumbered him, but it was also clear that the Gaul legion had taken casualties at the pass. Cassius estimated that the Victrix was slightly below 5,000, which meant it was down close to a cohort. And from what had Cassius told him, the Valentia auxiliaries did not account for much in their fight with the remnants of the III Augusta.

The VII Legion was in formation behind him, the auxiliaries to the left, closest to the city, with the cavalry on their flank.

He was nervous. He always was before a battle. Standing next to him were Flavius, Demaratus, Avidius of the auxiliaries, and Cassius. All looked tense, Flavius particularly so. It was hard to tell with Demaratus, ever the master of his emotions, but Marcus watched him finger his sword. He, too, was nervous.

A group of men from the Victrix camp was moving toward them.

"Sir?" said Cassius

"I see them, commander. It appears they want to talk," said Marcus.

"They wanted to talk at the pass," said Cassius. "They asked for our surrender and told us there would be no quarter if we didn't. They butchered all those good men, sir."

The Victrix delegation halted some distance away.

"The tall one is a tribune, sir. I think his name is Tacitus. The man standing next to him is a prefect, Atticus by name. The other man must be the legate. We saw him, but never talked with him," said Cassius.

"Let's meet them halfway, comrades, and see what they have to say," said Marcus. The officers of the VII Hispania approached the men from the VI Legion, stopping when they were 10 feet apart.

"I am Maximus Clodius, Legate of the VI Legion Victrix," said the man whom Cassius had not named. "And these...."

Cassius cut him short. "We know who they are. We have met, if you recall."

"Do you let a Lusitanian cavalryman speak for you?" asked Tacitus.

"You are acquainted with our cavalry commander, I believe,"

said Marcus. "Your cavalry knows him intimately, much to their regret. What are you doing here?"

The question seemed to take the VI Legion officers aback. After a pause, the legate said, "We represent the Gallic Empire and our Emperor, Postumus Marcus Cassianius Latinius, former Governor and Imperial Legate of Germania Superior and Inferior. We call on you to join us. Help us keep the barbarians from despoiling our lands and sacking our cities."

"The VII Legion has already done that by defeating the Frankish invasion," said Marcus. "So, we suggest you go home, which I believe is Gaul. We can take care of Hispania. We have no need for your help."

"Hispania is already with us," said the tribune. "We were greeted by friendly crowds in Emporiae, Barcino, Tarraco, and Valentia. We have come to liberate Hispania and unite our people against the Goths and the Franks. Roma can no longer do that. They merely take our taxes and build lavish palaces."

"Baetica is with the Empire," said Marcus, "and the VII Legion is proud of its name, 'Pia.' If you do not return to Gaul, we will fight you."

"You are one legion against 20," said Maximus. "All of Britannia and Gaul is with us. You stand alone."

"It looks to me like you have one legion and whatever you call those men from Valentia. They did not conduct themselves with great courage or skill at the pass," said Cassius.

"Again, a Lusitanian horseman speaks for you?" challenged Tacitus.

"We all speak from one mind here, tribune," said Marcus. "Commander Cassius Cornelius has earned that right on the battlefield against the Mauri and the Franks. He wears his awards on his armor. I see none on yours, tribune. So, yes, our Lusitanian horseman speaks for us, as we do for him."

"If you join us, we will depart and the VII Legion will rule the province in the name of the Gallic Empire," said Maximus. "There is no need for bloodshed."

"Blood has already been shed," said Marcus. "Good men died at the pass, men we fought alongside in Mauretania."

"They were men without honor from a dishonored legion," said Tacitus. "You shame yourselves by standing with them."

"An interesting way of thinking, tribune," said Marcus. "You decry the men of the III Augusta as without honor because they revolted against an emperor with no claim to the throne. Yet you claim honor after revolting against an emperor anointed by the Senate. Let us say that we in Hispania have a very different definition of honor. We prefer ours to yours."

"This is your last chance," said Maximus.

"Or yours," said Marcus.

Maximus glared at him and signaled to his men, who turned away and walked back to the deployed legion.

"So, war it is," said Flavius quietly.

* * *

The VI Victrix made the first move. Five centuries deployed in a broad front, shields locked as they advanced. The centuries from the auxiliaries and the Second, Third, and Fourth Cohorts awaited them. When the two lines came together, the cornus war horns on both sides blew a trumpet, and the morning rang with the clash of swords and shields. Almost immediately, casualties began filtering back from the front lines to the rear. Carried by capsarii, the wounded were laid out to be triaged by a medicus ordinarius. Minor wounds were treated on the spot, while others of the wounded were directed to the valetudinarium. For the more seriously wounded, stretcher-bearers were deployed.

As the wounded trickled into the hospital, Sabina and Rachel helped them to cubicles to wait for the doctor or his assistants to attend to them. The vast majority of injuries were sword cuts that needed to be sutured and bandaged. Some of those men returned to their units. But others, which included almost anyone with leg wounds, were bedded down on cots, to be cared for by Rachel, Sabina, and other volunteers, who brought them water and saw to their comfort.

Slowly, the valetudinarium filled. Sabina soon found herself overwhelmed by the sheer number of casualties. There were over 100 wounded men. As their numbers increased, Doctor Timotheus pulled her aside.

"Sabina, there is a soldier for whom I am afraid we can do nothing. The wound is deep in his inner organs. Would you be willing to sit with him and see that he is well supplied with poppy juice. I must warn you, this may be difficult."

"Of course," she said.

Calling for one of his medici, the doctor had him lead Sabina to a young man lying on a cot, a large bandage wrapped around his abdomen. "His name is Aconius," he told her.

The man was quiet, but awake, and he gave her a wan smile. She sat near him and pulled the blanket higher on his body, then offered him water. He took a sip and whispered, "thank you."

For almost an hour he said nothing, but then he turned toward her. "I am glad you came, sister," said the man looking at her. "When I am well, we can go to the sea. I know you love the sea."

Sabina started to tell the man he was mistaken, that she wasn't his sister, but he continued. "We will eat the shellfish you like so much, and maybe even take a boat ride. You wanted to do that once, and mother said we couldn't, but we won't tell her."

She bit back her denial.

"Talk to me, Octavia. How is our younger brother? Is he paying attention to his studies?" he asked, reaching for her hand.

Sabina took his hand. It was cold. "Yes, he is diligent and being a good boy, Aconius."

"Oh, he was always a good boy. You and I were the trouble-makers, Octavia," he said. "But we had so much fun. We can do that again."

"Yes," said Sabina, fighting back a sob.

Aconius was silent for a long time, his breathing shallow, his eyes closed. Sabina noticed a growing stain on the bandage.

"Is it night, sister? It is so dark," he said. "And I am cold. Mother, why am I cold? Don't I have a banket?"

Sabina looked around for another blanket and, seeing none, put her cloak over the man. "Mother," he whispered. "It is getting darker. You know I am afraid of the dark. Come hold me, mother, please."

Sabina put her arms around the soldier. "Oh, mother, I am so glad you are here," he said, and Sabina hugged him tighter.

Death arrived silently. Sabina sensed the stillness and looked up at Aconius. The young man's eyes were open, but there was no spark in them, so she gently closed his eyelids. She felt numb. Eventually, a medicus arrived, took her by the hand, led her to the inner garden, and sat her on a bench. He returned with a cup of wine, but all she could do was stare at it.

Somehow, she had always thought of war in terms of honor and courage, the Empire's noble legions holding the barbarians at bay. But it also meant blood and pain and death, and a young man calling out for his mother as he slipped into the great darkness.

* * *

Throughout the afternoon, the two legions ground away at one another, with neither gaining more than a temporary tactical advantage on the battlefield. Each time there was a potential breakthrough in the lines, reinforcements moved up and sealed the breach. The casualties on both sides were mounting, but not to the point that either legion had an advantage.

The archers and slingers took a toll, but their impact was marginal. The auxiliaries fought well, but they were growing tired. Marcus decided it was time to put his plan into action. Calling Flavius over, he issued instructions for the attack on the right flank of VI Legion. He then slipped off to the left flank, consulted with Cassius and the auxiliary commander, Avidius, and returned to huddle with the centurions of the First Cohort.

The move began surreptitiously, with auxiliary reserves sliding to their left and re-organizing on the flank. When most of their reserves were in position, the frontline auxiliary legionnaires backed away. Marcus watched carefully for what the VI would do. There was clearly some initial confusion among the ranks of the Gaul legion. Then, as Marcus watched, fresh troops moved up into position to take advantage of the auxiliaries' retreat. The Victrix advanced, throwing troops out to its right in an effort to turn the VII Legion's left flank and drive it to the river.

To their surprise, the VII Legion's First Cohort advanced and slammed into the new troops, driving them back several steps, as the auxiliaries reorganized and picked up several hundred very long lances. Rather than retreating, the auxiliary legion now formed a compact body of troops defended by a forest of long spears. From what had looked like a disordered withdrawal, the auxiliaries now had turned into a very bristly porcupine blocking any attempt to turn the VII Legion's flank.

The VI Legion made a stab at dispersing the phalanx, but that would have required more troops than it had, particularly since the VII Legion suddenly threw several fresh centuries at the Gaul legion's other flank, pushing it back. The few centuries it had in reserve were left to stabilize the Victrix's river flank.

And then the VII Legion's cavalry attacked, led by some 100 horsemen wielding long contus lances. The cavalry attack was not as dangerous as it was surprising, and the lances intimidating. The legionnaires knew how to handle cavalry, but they flinched as the lances slammed into them. Rather than advancing and turning the VII's flank, the VI Legion found itself backing up, forced to concentrate on preventing the cavalry from breaking through.

The Victrix eventually firmed up its lines and trapped several members of the cavalry who had managed to smash through the front line. Surrounded, their lances useless, they had nothing but their long spatha swords and small shields. There was little chance any of them would survive.

Led by Cassius, several turmae attacked in an effort to free the trapped horsemen. But the Victrix tightened their lines, and Cassius's horse stumbled, tossing the commander to the ground. Two legionnaires attacked him, one driving his gladius into Cassius's right side, the other opening a slash on his left leg. A counterattack by several horsemen drove them back, and two cavalrymen jumped from their horses, grabbed Cassius, and dragged him back toward the rest of the massed cavalry.

The combination of the cavalry attack, the advance of the First Cohort, and the increased attacks on the river flank forced the Gaul legion to back off and reorganize its lines. Marcus sent out orders for the VII Legion not to advance, largely because the legion was played out. It had been fighting for several hours, and most of the troops were exhausted. Since the VI Victrix made no effort to advance, Marcus assumed it was in the same shape.

The day was a stalemate.

* * *

Sabina sat in the garden, her wine untouched. After a time, she felt a hand pressed on her shoulder. She looked up to see Rachel.

"I cannot, Rachel. I am sorry, but I can't do anymore," she said.

"It's Cassius," said Rachel softly.

"By the gods!" cried Sabina. "Where, how badly is he hurt? He isn't dead, is he?" she said, sitting up and dropping the wine.

"No, he is not dead, Sabina, but he is gravely wounded. The doctor is with him now," she said.

"Take me to him, please," pleaded Sabina.

Rachel led her back to the cubicles where the most seriously injured were housed. Cassius was lying unconscious on a cot, the doctor hovering over him. Sabina could see that he was tying off sutures. A medicus placed a bandage on the wound.

"Doctor?" said Sabina.

Timotheus looked exhausted, his hands and clothes stained with blood. "Sabina," he said. Rubbing his hand across his forehead, he sat down on a small stool next to the cot. "His wounds are bad, and he has lost a lot of blood."

Cassius was pale, with dark rings under his eyes. It was hard for Sabina to think of him as other than the deeply tanned, animated horseman with an easy smile, wild hair and quick wit that she had come to know on her trip to Corduba. The pale, drained man on the cot seemed almost a stranger.

"How bad, doctor?" she asked.

He shrugged wearily. "It is hard to say with loss of blood, Sabina. He is young and strong, but I must warn you, he might not survive. The next 12 hours will be critical. If he is still alive in the morning, he has a chance."

"I will sit with him, doctor," she said. "Is there anything I can do?"

"Watch that bandage, Sabina. If there is a flow of fresh blood, come and get me. Otherwise, just be with him," he said. "I need to tend to others, but do not hesitate to call me. We all owe this young man a great deal."

"Do you want me to stay with you?" asked Rachel.

"No, no, Rachel. There are others who need you. I will be all right here," said Sabina.

Rachel kissed her on the cheek and left.

"Don't die, Cassius," she said softly, putting her hand on his arm. He felt cold, so she covered him with a blanket, careful not to disturb the bandage.

She said a prayer to Asclepius. "I will not let you have him, Pluto," she whispered.

XL

◯⣿⣿◯

"Report," said Marcus.

"Casualties serious, but not critical, sir," said Flavius, reading from a wax tablet. "The VII Legion had 1,800 wounded and 423 dead, although the doctor says the count is sure to go up. The auxiliaries took 900 casualties, 243 dead. Again, the doctor says that number is not final. We lost some cavalry. I haven't gotten the figures, but I don't think the losses are heavy."

"How are the men?" asked Marcus.

"They feel like they won today, sir. It was the other legion that backed off," said Flavius.

"Still, we have lost one-third of the legion. Can we fight tomorrow?" asked Marcus. "And where is Cassius?"

The group clustered in the principium included Flavius, Demaratus, Primus Pilus Servius Junius of the First Cohort, and Avidius Hadrianus, commander of the auxiliaries.

"No question, sir, we can fight tomorrow," said Flavius, and the auxiliary commander nodded his agreement. "And Cassius, uh, he is in the valetudinarium, sir. I hear he was pretty badly wounded, but I haven't had time to follow that up."

"That happened during the charge?" asked Marcus.

"I think so, but I am not sure, sir," answered Flavius.

"I will go check on him, sir," said Demaratus. "I don't have much to contribute here in any case. I will send you a message when I find out more about his condition."

"Thank you, signifer. We need that man," said Marcus. "Now about tomorrow. I propose sending a message to the VI Legion asking to meet with its legate. I would rather avoid another day of bloodshed, but only if the Gaul legion departs. Does that sound acceptable?"

"Aye," said Avidius. "If we fight tomorrow, I think we can defeat them. But if they leave, that would be a lot simpler. Back to Gaul?"

"I don't think that is a real possibility, commander, but we can demand that the Gallic empire stays north of Valentia. That will ensure the security of Baetica. It will mean a divided province, comrades, but I do not think the VII Legion by itself can force the Gallic Empire out."

* * *

The command tent of the VI Legion was cold. The evening had turned chilly, and the men crowded around a brazier of burning wood. The group included the legion's legate, Maximus, tribunes Annius and Tacitus, the prefect, Atticus, and several aides clustered by the tent's back wall.

"Report," said Maximus.

Tribune Annius perused a wax tablet. "These figures are not complete, legate, but they give us a sense of where we stand. We lost 2,200 men, of which a little more than 700 are dead. The doctors say that figure will rise. Casualties were light among the auxiliaries, mostly because they did very little fighting. Our cavalry—what is left of it—largely stayed out of it."

"Morale?" asked Maximus.

"I think good, sir. They know we didn't lose today, but it was hard fighting and they need rest," said Annius.

"What about the VII Legion?" asked Maximus.

"Not certain, sir. Their wounded were quickly removed, and no one took the time to do much counting. I would judge that they had a similar rate of casualties," answered Annius. "Their auxiliaries fought better than ours," he added.

"They tricked us into committing our reserves too early with that phalanx maneuver," said Maximus. "The VII Legion was well handled."

The men around him were silent.

"Can we fight tomorrow?" asked Maximus.

There were murmurs and some cross discussion until Atticus spoke up. "Yes, sir. The legion is intact."

"Between the fight at the pass and today, we have lost almost half the legion. I do not think we can depend on the Ist Ausetanorum for much of anything, and, without cavalry, we are blind. Our enemy has superior support troops and limitless supplies. It may be restocking its ranks with fresh men at this moment. That being the case, if we fight, can we win?" asked Maximus.

There was a long silence.

"Your silence is most eloquent, comrades. In any case, this is my decision," said Maximus. He slumped onto a camp stool and ordered an aide to serve wine.

"I have never seen one of those," said the prefect.

"A phalanx? No, not much reason for them these days. We could have defeated it, of course, had their cavalry not attacked," said Maximus, taking a long draw on his wine. "It was inventive and surprising, which is what I think the VII Legion legate intended. Throw us off balance by seeming to retreat, we over-commit, they counterattack. He is good at his job."

The group fell into a discussion of the day's battle, until an aide arrived and handed the legate a scroll, announcing, "This was brought through the lines by a horseman, sir." He saluted and left.

Maximus fingered the scroll. "I suspect this is from our recent foe." He unwrapped the scroll. "He is asking for a truce and a parley," he said.

"Maybe they are in worse shape than we assumed," suggested Tacitus. "They may be asking for conditions."

"Or they may be dictating theirs to us," said Maximus. "Well, it can't hurt to talk. I will send back a message asking them to meet us in an hour."

* * *

Demaratus entered a world of pain. The valetudinarium was crowded with patients, some waiting patiently to be seen by the doctors, others lying on stretchers with capsarii clustered around them. He asked for Coventina, and a medicus pointed vaguely in the direction of the cubicles. He poked his head into each in turn, finally finding her stitching up a legionnaire with a long slash on his leg. She signaled for him to wait, finished up bandaging the leg, then washed her hands in a solution of water and vinegar. Her dress was stained with blood, and she had a bloody smear across her forehead. He had never seen her look this exhausted.

She kissed him lightly on the cheek. "We hear the fighting has stopped," she said.

"Yes, and I think Marcus is trying to arrange a truce to avoid more bloodshed," said Demaratus.

"A course I heartily endorse," she said, finding a stool and taking a seat. "The face of war among my people is nothing like this."

"How is Cassius?" he asked.

She shook her head. "He is alive, but just. He lost a lot of blood. The doctor has sewn him up, and there is nothing much else to do except watch him and pray to your gods. If he is still alive by morning, he has a chance. Sabina is with him. The poor girl has seen too much this day."

"How are you?" he asked.

"Well enough, my love. I am tired of pain and death, but that is what war is about, isn't it?"

"It is," he said. "Can I get you anything?"

"Peace would be good," she said, rising and putting her arms around him. "I need to tend to others, my love. Cassius is just down the corridor. You should say something to Sabina." She kissed him and called for a new patient.

Demaratus found the cubicle where Cassius lay unconscious,

Sabina seated next to him, her hand on his arm. "Are you well?" he asked gently.

She gave him a weak smile, tears welling in her eyes. "He is so hurt, Demaratus," she said softly, her lower lip quivering.

"But he is Cassius, Sabina. He is a force of life. Stay with him and give him your strength," he said, patting her shoulder.

She nodded mutely and turned back to the wounded cavalryman.

Demaratus left, sobered.

XLI

Marcus wrapped his cloak tightly around him. Dawn had yet to make its appearance, and it was cold this time of year in Baetica. The Victrix's legate had responded to his note, proposing that they meet on the ground of yesterday's fighting. Both had agreed to come alone, prompting Flavius to grumble. But if this was going to be a negotiation, neither commander wanted an audience.

Maximus appeared shortly, also wrapped in a cloak. He walked halfway into the field and waited for Marcus to join him.

They nodded to one another. "You wanted to talk, Marcus. What is on your mind?"

"Let me lay out the way I see things, Maximus," said Marcus. "Both of our legions fought well yesterday. Your withdrawal was not a retreat, but a sensible realignment. I estimate that we have both taken casualties, but not enough to prevent another day of battle. But time is your enemy, Maximus. We are refilling our ranks. They are not real legionnaires, but you must have noted that our auxiliaries fought well yesterday."

"We too are refilling our ranks, Marcus."

"From where? And time is still your enemy. We have unlimited supplies and potential fighters. You are on your own and far from your base. You must know by now that we have intercepted your supply column."

"Our supplies got through," said Maximus curtly.

"But slowly, and that problem is likely to get worse," noted Marcus.

"You have a point here?" retorted Maximus.

"I suggest we come to an agreement that will avoid further bloodshed," said Marcus.

"What would that agreement look like?" asked Maximus.

"The VI Legion Victrix, the Ist Ausetanorum, and your remaining cavalry will withdraw to Valentia. The VII Legion will guarantee you unmolested passage. We will see to your badly wounded and pledge their safety. The VII Legion will abandon its base in Legio and remain in Corduba. We will pledge not to move north of Valentia, and you will pledge not to move south of that city. We will, in essence, divide the province of Hispania," said Marcus.

Maximus was silent, considering the offer. "I will have to get approval from my superiors," he said at last.

"No," said Marcus. "We two have the only legions in Hispania. I doubt you can expect any help. The Gallic Empire will be preoccupied with defending southern Gaul from an attack by Roma. On the northern border, the Franks and the Alamanni are certain to take advantage of the turmoil generated by the breakaway to raid or invade."

"And I do not expect much in the way of help from the

Empire," continued Marcus. "Between preventing the Goths from crossing the Danubius and preparing to reclaim Gaul from the breakaway empire, it will be too busy to spare anything for us. It will take months for you to hear from your superiors. That would result in our legions facing one another for a very long time, disrupting commerce, and paralyzing Baetica. That is not acceptable. It is also not in your interest."

"And why is that?" asked Maximus.

"Because we will rally Baetica to our side. Day by day, we will strengthen and you will weaken," said Marcus.

"We can rally our supporters in Hispania, Marcus. Two can play that game," said Maximus.

"Can you really?" challenged Marcus. "How successful were you in recruiting soldiers from Casearagusta? Tarraco? Barcino? Even Valentia? Hispania has seen the face of civil war before, Maximus. It stood with Pompey against Caesar, and it paid a terrible price for that choice. They want nothing to do with war, and they would rather not choose sides. They may cheer you on, throw roses in your path, but do they flock to your standard?"

Maximus was silent.

"I, too, have superiors, Maximus, but I have not consulted them. I am, after all, the supreme military authority in Hispania, just as you are the military authority of the Gallic Empire. We will make this decision here and now, or we will fight. The choice is yours," said Marcus.

The VI Legion legate looked back at the Victrix's marching camp, which was just beginning to come awake. Small fires to cook the morning's breakfast crackled. The sky was lighter in the east, but the morning was still bitter cold.

"You will treat my wounded?" he asked, turning back to Marcus.

"We will. And those who wish to rejoin the VI Legion will be guaranteed safe passage to Valentia," said Marcus.

"We will need an extra day to organize ourselves," said Maximus.

"You have it," said Marcus.

"Then we have an agreement, although my superiors may not accept it. It may be that we meet again," said Maximus.

"That is true for me as well, Maximus. But that will not be today or tomorrow," said Marcus.

The legate of the VI Legion nodded and turned back to camp.

Marcus turned to find Flavius striding up to meet him. "What's it to be, sir?" asked the optio.

"Peace, for now. They are withdrawing to Valentia and pledge to remain north of that city. We need to see to their wounded. Alert the doctor," said Marcus.

"If we had fought today, we would have won," said Flavius.

"Won what, optio? There certainly would be more dead and wounded, but a victory here would not end the civil war," said Marcus, who was suddenly very tired. "We are small players distant from the center of power."

"What do you think Carthago Nova will think of this?" asked Flavius.

Marcus shrugged. "If they want to fight, they can march on Valentia, but that seems unlikely. The Gallic Empire will have the east from Valentia north and the gold mines in the west. We agreed to abandon Legio and base ourselves in Corduba. Compromises are always painful, but that is their nature."

"I don't think the men will mourn for Legio. And they will certainly be fine with not fighting today, sir," said Flavius.

"Spread the news to the camp and send someone to fetch the doctor," said Marcus. He wanted nothing more than to sleep, but there was still a lot of work to be done.

* * *

Sabina had nodded off during the night, but she awoke when Cassius stirred. His breathing seemed stronger and a little color had come back to his face. She stood up and stretched. She was hungry, but reluctant to leave the cavalryman's side. Eventually, Rachel came to the rescue, bringing a cup of watered wine, a small loaf of bread, and a wedge of cheese.

"How is he?" she asked.

"I am not sure, Rachel. He seems to be breathing better, but he is still unconscious," said Sabina.

"Why don't you go to the garden for a little while and get some food into you," said Rachel. "I will sit with him."

Sabina didn't want to leave Cassius, but Rachel argued that she needed to eat and drink if she was going to nurse Cassius. "He may be in this state for a long time, Sabina. You need to keep your strength up." Sitting on a bench in the garden, Sabina wolfed down the bread and cheese, and drained the watered wine in a single gulp. When she finished, she slipped out of the valetudinarium, breathed in the morning air, and said a quick prayer to Aurora, who was spreading her rosy cloak in the east.

By the time she got back to Cassius she was feeling much better. Rachel left to tend other wounded soldiers, and Sabina settled herself next to the cot. She nodded off again, only to be awakened by a question.

"How is Rosa?" asked Cassius in a whisper.

"She is fine, Cassius. She misses our rides," said Sabina, a tear rolling down one cheek. "You must get better so we can ride together again."

He gave her a weak smile and closed his eyes again. His breathing seemed stronger now. She put her hand behind his head, tipped it up to give him a sip of water, then laid his head back down on the pillow.

"Oh, Cassius, you have to get better. Please," she said, slipping her hand into his.

XLII

A week later, Corduba threw a party. It was not a triumph—only the Roman Senate could designate a triumph—but it was the city's version of one. Crowds of people, looking happy and relieved, drank prodigious amounts of wine and cheered the VII Legion as it paraded through the city's center on its way to the forum. Marcus led on his very fat horse. He had had to explain to the organizers that a chariot was out. Again, only the Senate could approve its use. Many of the wounded marched, and some who were not wounded wrapped bandages around their arms—the girls greatly favored those who'd been injured over unmarked legionnaires. Cassius wanted to ride, but the doctor—and his entire ala—told him that they would physically block him from mounting a horse if he even tried to do so. However, it was Sabina who kept him grounded. She crossed her arms and firmly explained that it was out of the question, and please get back into bed. And he did.

Marcus handed out awards—Cassius won his second Civic Crown and a Hasta Pura for conspicuous valor. Phalerae were handed out by the basketful, and decurions gave speeches. And, celebration and ceremony concluded, people returned home.

* * *

"So, my conquering hero, what now?" asked Aelia, as she and Marcus sat together in the garden. She sipped wine, but Marcus drank only water, trying to clear his head after the day's festivities.

"Well, I have divided the Roman Empire without asking anyone's permission, so I really don't know. I may be hailed. I may be executed," he said.

"You saved half the province for Roma, and the wealthiest part at that. How could the Emperor or the Senate possibly object?" she asked.

"I drew a line from Valentia to Olisipo and gave it to the Gallic empire, Aelia," he said. "I have also unilaterally moved the legion's base from Legio to Corduba, and pretty much handed Hispania's gold mines to Postumus. A commander of a single legion really doesn't have that kind of power."

"My, you have been busy, haven't you, my love," said Aelia. "You realize, Marcus, that Rachel and I had this all planned out."

Marcus put down his cup. "Really?"

"We agreed that we did not want to live in Legio, while the men we loved were residents of that cold and dreary place. Now here you are in Corduba. You don't think that happened by accident, do you?" she asked.

He smiled. "Impressive, Aelia."

"Never underestimate the power of women," she said, leaning forward and kissing him. He returned the kiss, and then sighed.

She sat back and looked at him. "What troubles you, Marcus?"

He was silent for a long moment. "I am tired, Aelia," he sadly acknowledged. "I have spent most my life thinking of ways to kill people. I am weary of it. And yet it is all I really know how to do."

She put her arms around him. "We are not the same people we were when we first met, my love. You tire of war, I tire of warring with my brother, and so much feels unsettled for us both."

He nodded. "I no longer want to be the chooser of the slain, Aelia. I do not want to send people out to die anymore, and yet I feel I have no choice."

"We have each other, Marcus," she said. "We must make do with that. And we can be happy if we let ourselves be. I suggest we make the effort."

He kissed her. "No argument."

"Good," she said, "because you would lose."

* * *

"What now?" asked Coventina. She and Demaratus were seated on the steps of the huge temple to the emperors.

He shrugged. "I myself am not clear, Coventina. I assume the VII Legion's permanent base is now Corduba, which has its advantages, except for one."

"And that is?" she asked.

"You," he said. "We are far from your mountains and your people, and I saw how important they were to you when I visited you there. So, I think I will turn your question around and ask, 'What about you?'"

Coventina sat back, looking out over the forum. "I will miss my mountains, Demaratus, but I grew fond of city life during my time in Tarraco. I will not miss being cold, I will not miss fetching water, I will not miss bathing in cold creeks. I am quite smitten with your baths. And the good doctor has asked me to be his principal assistant, which appeals to me. Plus, I am not just speaking for myself."

Demaratus gave her a puzzled look. "I don't understand, who else are you speaking for?

She gave him a considered look.

"Oh," he said. "Really?"

"Yes, my Greek, my sailor, my signifer, my love. You are going to be a father."

"My," he said. And again, "Really? That's wonderful," he said, quickly recovering.

She kissed him. "We will see. But it appears we both have a new home."

* * *

Flavius searched through the crowd, looking for Rachel. He found her sitting on a bench just off the forum. Her expression caused him to hesitate. It was dark, brooding, unhappy. He had never seen her this way.

"Rachel?" he said, tentatively.

She didn't respond. She appeared to look through him. "Flavius," she said, after too long. Her tone was flat and emotionless.

"Rachel, are you well?" he asked. She didn't respond at first, which sent a shiver through him.

"Well? I am alive and unwounded," she said, "unlike those young men I have been caring for. I overheard one of the officers say he was disappointed that the fighting was over, because he was certain that the Gaul legion would have been destroyed if they had fought another day." She looked up at him. "Do you agree?" Her voice was soft, but her eyes signaled a challenge.

Flavius hesitated. In some ways, he was frustrated that Marcus had negotiated a truce. But he also knew that how he answered Rachel's question would profoundly affect his future. He looked at the ground, gathering his thoughts. He was tempted to lie— he knew what Rachel wanted to hear—but a lie is a fragile thing to build a life on. He looked up and said, "Yes."

She nodded. "Sabina is 13-years-old, Flavius. For the rest of her life, she will remember holding a young man as he died. I have those memories as well. I hate war and you live for it," she said. "I have seen what war does, Flavius. I don't know if I can live with someone whose mission in life is to inflict pain and death."

He was quiet for a bit. "I do not live for war, Rachel, it is my job. It is all I know. It has lifted me and my family out of poverty and it has given me a comfortable life. I know nothing else. But I have thought about what Marcus did and have come to see he was right. Would I have done it? I would like think I would, but I can't lie to you. But I do know that if I never fought another battle, that would be fine with me."

She sighed. "Maybe that will have to do."

"Rachel," said Flavius, "I love you. I have for a long time."

She looked up at him, surprised.

"Did you not know that?" he asked.

"I was not reacting to what you said, Flavius, but that you said it," she said. "You are not always so forthcoming."

"When it is important I can speak from my heart," he said, "and I want to be with you."

"Then we will try, Flavius." she said. "Come and sit by me."

* * *

"Didn't you want to go to the celebration?" Cassius asked Sabina. He was lying on his cot in the valetudinarium, a bandage around his waist and another wrapping his leg.

She shook her head. "No. Somehow, I cannot celebrate what we have just gone through, Cassius. War is not like I imagined it."

He nodded. "No. It is an institution whose disappearance I would not mourn. One of the reasons I love your uncle so much is that he does what he can to avoid it."

"And yet he is so good at it," she said.

"He is an interesting man, Sabina," he said.

"And when you are better, what will you do, Cassius?" she asked.

He looked a little startled. "Well, I first have to reorganize my ala, and see if we have enough mounts, and then...."

"No, my cavalryman, that is not what you are going to do," she said.

"It isn't?" he asked, looking confused.

"No, the first thing you are going to do is to take me and Rosa riding in the countryside, where we will find a nice shady place near the river and have a picnic. That is what you are going to do when you get better," she said firmly.

He smiled. "I would like that above all things, Sabina Aquillius."

Place Names

Cities and Towns
(ancient/modern)

Asturica Augusta / Astorga
Antikeria / Antequera
Baetica / Andalusia
Barcino / Barcelona
Brigantium / La Coruña
Caesaraugusta / Zaragoza
Capera
Carthago Nova / Cartagena
Clunia
Colonia Claudia Ara Agrippinensium / Cologne
Corduba / Cordoba
Emerita Augusta / Mérida
Elmantica / Salamanca
Emporiae / Ampurias
Enora / *Évora*
Gades / Cádiz
Gaul / France
Hispalis / Sevilla
Ignatius Portus

Italica
Legio / Leon
Lucentrium / Alicante
Lucus Augusti / Lugo
Malaka / Málaga
Mauretania / Morocco
Mediolanum / Milan
Metellinum / Medellín
Norba Caesarina / Cáceres
Narbo Martius / Narbonne
Olisipo / Lisbon
Pax Julia / Beja
Ronda / Ronda
Saguntum / Sagunto
Salamantia / Salamanca
Tarraco / Tarragona
Valentia / Valencia

**Rivers and Seas
(ancient/modern)**
Anas River / Guadiana River
Baetis River / Guadalquivir River
Oceanus Atlanticus / Atlantic Ocean

Structure of the Roman Army

A ROMAN LEGION

A Roman legion was designed to be a tactically flexible fighting force. To enhance that flexibility, it was divided into discrete units. In that way, a legion resembled a modern infantry division, which is divided into brigades, battalions, regiments, companies, and squads. The legion's units could act independently of one another, so that they could reinforce a unit that was in trouble, exploit a weakness in the enemy's line, or block an attempt to outflank the legion. Mobility was the essence of a legion's tactics and made it virtually invincible for almost 700 years. Modern armies owe much of their organizational structure to the Roman legion.

A legion was constructed as follows:

Contubernium: An eight-man squad, the smallest unit in a legion.

Century: Made up of 10 contuberniums. A century is normally 80 men, commanded by a centurion. (For more, see below).

Cohort (regular): Composed of six centuries, approximately 480 men.

First Cohort: Composed of five centuries, but each century is composed of 160 men. A First Cohort would consist of approximately 800 men.

Legion: Made up of 10 cohorts. When headquarters units are included, plus specialists, a legion would consist of approximately 5,400 men.

Legate: Legion commander.

Tribune: Senior legion staff officer (normally three per legion).

Prefect (Praefectus castrorum): third in command.

A ROMAN CENTURY

The century was the smallest tactical unit in a legion. That is, it was the smallest unit capable of fighting on its own. It was closest to a modern infantry company, although smaller. In the case of a century from the first cohort, however, it was somewhat larger than a modern infantry company. A century had four officers:

Centurion: Commander

Optio: Second-in-command

Signifer: Holds century standard during battle and keeps the unit's books

Tesserarius: Junior officer. Also sets sentry duty and oversees camp construction

Centurions
(in order of seniority)

First Cohort	Regular Cohort
Primus Pilus	Pilus Prior
Princeps	Pilus Posterior
Princeps Posterior	Princeps Prior
Hastatus	Princeps Posterior
Hastatus Posterior	Hastatus
	Hastatus Posterior

The five centurions of the First Cohort make up the Primi Ordines, a group of the most senior centurions.

The commander of an auxiliary legion is called a "Praefectus."

Glossary and Notes

Acetum. Sour wine, the standard drink of soldiers.

Ala. Auxiliary cavalry unit, roughly the size of an infantry cohort.

Atrium. Living room.

Capsarii. Soldiers who rendered first aid.

Century. Basic administrative and military unit of a legion.

Cohort. Basic tactical unit of the legion.

Centurion. Commander of a century.

Colina. Kitchen.

Cornu. Roman war horn.

Contubernium. Smallest unit in a century.

Cubiculum. Bedroom.

Dolabra. Infantry entrenching tool, a sort of pick-axe.

Decurion. Magistrate of a town or city.

Domus. House.

Garum. Fish sauce.

Gladius. Short stabbing sword of the Roman infantry.

Greaves. Armor to protect a centurion's shins.

Hastile. A steel-headed staff carried by optios.

Latifundia. Landowner.

Legate. Commands a legion.

Lemures. Hostile ghosts.

Medicus. Medical aides (plural: *medici*).

Medicus Ordinarius. Centurion of medical workers.

Optio. Second-in-command of a century.

Paenula. Cloak with a hood.

Paludamentum. Formal cloak worn by officers.

Phalarae. Medallions worn on an officer's harness.

Pilum. Heavy spear of the Roman army (pl. pila).

Praetorians. Emperor's personal legion, the only legion
    allowed in Rome.

Prefect. Third-in-command of a legion.

Principia. Army headquarters.

Pugio. Short dagger.

Quaestor. Magistrate elected for one year.

Quingeniaery. Cavalry unit composed of 16 turmae of
    30 men each, usually 480- 500 men.

Sagum. Cloak used by soldiers, fastened at the right shoulder.

Scutum. Shield of a legionnaire, a 4' x 2' 6" rectangle,
    curved to deflect blows.

Signifer. Officer who carries century standard; also oversees
    a unit's books and soldiers' pay.

Signum. Century's standard.

Spatha. Long sword used by Roman cavalry.

Stipendium. Soldier's pay, paid 3x/year (pl. *stipendia*).

Taberna. Tavern.

Tablinum. Library.

Tesserarius. Junior officer in a century, oversees assigning guard duty.

Testudo. "The Tortoise," infantry siege maneuver forming a
wall and roof of shields.

Tribune. Senior staff officer in a legion.

Triclinum. Dining room.

Turmae. Basic cavalry unit, normally 30 men

Valetudinarium. Hospital.

Bibliography

Adkins, Lesley and Roy A. Adkins. *Handbook to Life in Ancient Rome*, Oxford University Press, 1994.

Appian: Wars of the Romans in Iberia. Translated by J.S. Richardson, Aris & Phillips Classical Texts, 2000.

Byrne, Eugene Hugh. "Medicine in the Roman Army," *The Classical Journal*, Volume 5, No. 6, pp. 267-272, April 1910.

Campbell, Brian. *War and Society in Imperial Rome: 31 BC- AD 284*, Routledge, 2002.

Goldsworthy, Adrian. *The Complete Roman Army*, Thames & Hudson, 2003.

Grant, Michael. *The Army of the Caesars*, Charles Scribner's Sons, 1974.

Griess, Thomas E. *Ancient and Medieval Warfare: The West Point Military History Series*, Avery Publishing Group, Inc., 1984.

Keppie, Lawrence. *The Making of the Roman Army: From Republic to Empire*, University of Oklahoma Press, 1984.

Le Glay, Marcel, Jean-Louis Voisin and Yann Le Bohec. *A History of Rome*, Blackwell, 2001.

Luttwak, Edward N. *The Grand Strategy of the Roman Empire: From the First Century AD to the Third*, Johns Hopkins University Press, 1979.

MacMullen, Ramsay. *Roman Social Relations*, Yale University Press. 1974.

Milne, John Stewart. *Surgical Instruments in Greek and Roman Times*, Augustus M. Kelly, Pubs., New York, 1970.

"The Roman Army Medical Service," Malton Museum, maltonmuseum.co.uk, 2007.

Richardson, John S. *The Romans in Spain*, Wiley-Blackwell, 1998.

Southern, Pat. *The Roman Empire: From Severus to Constantine*, Routledge, 2001.

Acknowledgments

As with all the books in *The Middle Empire Series*, I would like to thank those who devoted their time and talents to bringing *Corduba* to print. Roz Spafford, my longtime teaching partner, made invaluable editorial suggestions. Her discerning attention to structure made this a better book. While this is a work of fiction, I aimed at historically accuracy to the fullest extent possible. I am indebted to my brother and sister-in-law, Danny and Wendy Hallinan, who brought their wide-ranging knowledge of Roman history to ensure that events that touched on political events during the period were depicted accurately. My friend Jack Radey, a military historian, was an indispensable consultant as I mapped the battlefield maneuvers of the VII Hispania and VI Victrix. Many thanks, too, to Betsy Wooten and Alice Kelly for the careful copy editing and to Ann Higgins for this fifth wonderful cover design. As always, I am grateful to Caroline Jennings for the essential work of preparing the manuscript for print. This book would not have been written without the encouragement of my wife, Anne Bernstein, who also did the final edit, and the excellent care by my doctors, Alexander Dimitri Colevas, Beth Beadle, and Floyd Christopher Holsinger, who kept me alive even longer than it took to write the last two books. Thank you all.

Conn M. Hallinan was a longtime columnist for *Foreign Policy in Focus*, "A Think Tank Without Walls," and an independent journalist. He held a Ph.D. in Anthropology from the University of California, Berkeley. For 23 years he oversaw the journalism program at the University of California, Santa Cruz, where he won the UCSC Alumni Association's Distinguished Teaching Award, as well as UCSC's Innovations in Teaching Award and its Excellence in Teaching Award. He also served as Provost of Kresge College at UCSC, retiring in 2004. He was a winner of a Project Censored "Real News Award" and lived in Berkeley, California. The Middle Empire Series are his first works of fiction.